WE LOVE YOU,
CHARLIE FREEMAN

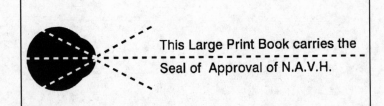

This Large Print Book carries the Seal of Approval of N.A.V.H.

WE LOVE YOU, CHARLIE FREEMAN

KAITLYN GREENIDGE

THORNDIKE PRESS

A part of Gale, Cengage Learning

GALE
CENGAGE Learning·

Farmington Hills, Mich • San Francisco • New York • Waterville, Maine
Meriden, Conn • Mason, Ohio • Chicago

GALE
CENGAGE Learning

LIBRARY OF CONGRESS CATALOGING-IN-PUBLICATION DATA

Names: Greenidge, Kaitlyn, author.
Title: We love you, Charlie Freeman / by Kaitlyn Greenidge.
Description: Waterville, Maine : Thorndike Press, 2016. | Series: Thorndike Press large print African-American
Identifiers: LCCN 2016020139| ISBN 9781410492081 (hardcover) | ISBN 1410492087 (hardcover)
Subjects: LCSH: Families—Massachusetts—Fiction. | Sign language—Fiction. | Large type books.
Classification: LCC PS3607.R455 W4 2016b | DDC 813/.6—dc23
LC record available at https://lccn.loc.gov/2016020139

Published in 2016 by arrangement with Algonquin Books of Chapel Hill, a division of Workman Publishing Co.

Printed in Mexico
1 2 3 4 5 6 7 20 19 18 17 16

*For Ariel
and Samuel
and Ariel*

"This car doesn't feel like ours," I said.

"Well, it is now," my father replied. "So get used to it."

Outside of the car it was dark and hot and early morning August in Dorchester. Through the crack of the window, I could smell every part of the city — every slab of asphalt, every rotting plank of wood siding, every crumbling stucco wall, every scarred and skinny tree — I could smell all of it beginning to sweat.

I sat back in my seat. I knew I was right. Our old car was a used silver Chevy sedan, a dubious gift from my uncle Lyle, a mechanic. The Chevy's backseats were balding, the foam cushions peeling with faded stickers from some long discarded coloring book. The Chevy's body slumped over its axis, slung way too low to the ground, so that when you opened the car's doors, their bottoms scraped the curb.

The new car was a 1991 silver Volvo station wagon, next year's model. The Toneybee Institute paid for it. It had a curt, upturned nose that looked smug and out of place beside the lazing sedans and subservient hatchbacks parked on our block. Being inside the Volvo felt like we were in public. None of us could bring ourselves to speak. We were all too humbled by the leather interiors.

My mother, in the driver's seat, adjusted her rearview mirror. My younger sister, Callie, kept playing with the automatic windows until my mother told her to stop. Up in the front seat, my father tugged on his fingers one by one, trying to crack his knuckles, but the cartilage wouldn't break. I shifted my legs, and the leather skin of the seat stuck to the backs of my thighs, made a slow, painful smack as I leaned forward.

"They know we're no good with animals, right?" I moved again and the leather creaked beneath me. "I mean, you told them that?"

"What are you talking about?" My mother rolled down her window, began to fuss with the driver's side mirror. "We're great with animals."

"We are not. We're terrible with pets."

"Well, that's fine because we won't have a

pet." My mother had been saying this for weeks. "Charlie isn't a pet."

"He's a research monkey," my father added.

"He's a chimpanzee." This was Callie.

"He's more than a pet," my mother corrected. "He's going to be like a brother to you."

My father said, "That's going a bit far, Laurel."

"What I'm trying to say," she began, "is that we just have to treat him like one of us. Like he's part of our family. We just have to make him feel like he's one of our own and he'll do fine."

"But all our pets die."

"Charlotte." My mother was scanning the street now.

"It's true. That rabbit you bought me when I was five and Callie was born."

"He was depressed." My father turned in his seat. "It was because we kept him under the kitchen counter." My father had a notebook open in his lap, the pages turned to the start of a geometry lesson plan, but he hadn't written anything yet. Over his shoulder, I could see where he'd drawn a grove of interlocking pineapples in the sheet's margins.

"In our defense," my mother said, "we had

to keep him there. We just didn't have the space."

She tugged at her side mirror again. She frowned, made an appreciative "ah," and rolled her window back up. She touched a button on the dashboard, and the mirror gave a delicate little shudder and began to angle itself toward her.

She glanced over at my father, grinned.

"Very nice," he said.

I stuck my head in the space between them. "That rabbit died because he ate his own fur. He choked on it. He died because he choked on *himself.*"

"Is that true?" Callie strained against her seat belt, trying to catch what we were saying.

"No." My mother swatted at me. "Charlotte, get back there, get back in your seat. Put your seat belt on. You're upsetting your sister."

We didn't even have seat belts in the old car. I ran mine across my chest, clicked the buckle closed.

I waited.

Then I said, "Dad's fish."

My mother shot me a warning glance in the rearview mirror.

"Dad was in charge of the fish and it still died."

No one answered me.

After a while I said, "And it didn't even die. It just kind of *flaked* away."

"I think I'm going to be sick," Callie moaned.

"He had mange." My father turned again in his seat, trying to catch Callie's eye. "I've told you this before. He already had it when we brought him home from the pet store."

But I persisted. "Mom had to take that fish out of the tank and put him in a paper bag and bury him at the park because he was so messed up he would have polluted our toilets. We made a fish too sick for a *toilet.*"

"I'm going to be sick," Callie declared.

"Charlotte, no talking." My mother leaned forward and switched on the radio and a too deep voice intoned, "W-I-L-D Boston." That station was at the top of the list of things that my mother forbade us. "Nothing but booty music," she'd say, a dismissal that made me and Callie squirm in embarrassment. Now, though, she turned the volume up until the sound buzzed over us, drowning out our words.

My last piece of evidence I signed to Callie underneath the stutter of a drum machine. *The mice,* I explained with my hands. *We had mice and they died of heart attacks because they mated too much. They fucked* — and here I spelled it out because I didn't know the sign for that yet — *they f-u-c-k-e-d to death.*

How did they do that? Callie signed back.

I shook my head and turned my face to the window.

We drove past the clapboard double-deckers of our block, the high stoops overlaid with deciduous piles of supermarket circulars and candy bar wrappers and petrified, heat-stiffened leaves. We passed the restaurants my mother hated and banned: the Chinese food spot and the fried chicken spot and the Greek pizza parlor with its burnt-faced pies and the Hilltop Corner Spa, a grocery that sold milk only in cans and reeked of ancient fry oil and greasy mop water. We passed the check cashing spot on the corner.

By the time we got to the turnpike, we were the only car on the road. Dawn was over, the sun was high, and we were hot. It did not occur to any of us to turn on the air-conditioning; it had never worked in our old car. The Chevy's vents just shuttered and coughed and panted out something like secondhand smoke. When my father thought to flick the switch in the Volvo, we were all pleasantly surprised by the steady breeze that floated around us, cool and fresh, not a hint of nicotine.

We were going west, past empty fields and aluminum-sided barns and an alfalfa farm with a sweet scent that filled the car as we approached, then spoiled into the stink of manure as soon as we passed.

My mother, at the wheel, only scanned the road ahead, ignored the green.

Three months before, she and my father had sat us down and informed me and Callie that we were lucky. That we were about to embark on a great adventure. That we might even make scientific history. We had been chosen, over many other families, families with children who weren't half as smart as we were, who didn't even know how to sign. We, the Freemans, had been chosen to take part in an experiment and we were going to teach sign language to a chimpanzee.

"It's all to see what he can sign back to us," my mother said. Her voice was not her own. It was usually measured, weighted. But now it swooped high and went giddy, a little breathless, as she explained, "It's to see what he might say."

"They're going to start calling him Charlie," she said.

"They gave him my *name*?" I was disgusted.

"Only part of your name." My mother was excited. "It's so that he feels comfortable, you know, 'Charlie' fits with Callie and Charlotte."

"You gave him my name," I repeated.

"It's more like a junior situation," my father said, and my mother and Callie laughed.

I did not laugh. And Callie stopped laughing altogether, began to cry, when they told us we would have to move, leave Boston and the block, move to a place that neither of us had heard of. "You'll love it," my mother told her, her voice back to measured again.

Beside me, now, in the car, Callie huddled over the strap of her seat belt, the band barely saving her from a wholesale collapse into her own lap. She'd propped a piece of construction paper against the back of a book that she held against her knees, the better to sketch a welcome card for Charlie. My mother asked both of us to make cards but I refused. "What's the point of giving a card to somebody who can't read?" I'd asked. But Callie took to the assignment happily, steadily producing a greeting card a day for Charlie over the last month.

For this latest iteration, Callie drew a

portrait of our family. First she sketched her own face, then our mother's. Our father liked to say that Callie and our mother had the same face, heart-shaped, so Callie drew herself and our mother as two loopy valentines. Even though she tried her hardest to be neat, both their heads came out lopsided. Above the crooked lobes of each heart she drew their hair: short spiraling Ss, for their matching Jheri curls.

The hairstyles were new. Another thing my mother insisted on changing before the move. At Danny's His and Hers on Massachusetts Avenue, the hairdresser actually gasped at her request for a cut, to which she replied, defensively, "There won't be anybody who knows how to do black hair where I'm going. This is the easiest solution."

My mother had good hair, a term she would never use herself because, she said, it was so hurtful she couldn't possibly believe in it. But my mother's hair was undeniably long and thick, a mass of loose curls that Callie and I did not inherit and that she was determined to cut off before we began our new life.

She tried to talk both of us into joining her, but only Callie took the bait. My mother got her with the promise of hair made so easy and simple, you could run your fingers through it. When it was all over, Callie was left with an outgrowth of stiff, sodden curls that clung in limp clusters to her forehead and the nape of her neck and made the back of her head smell like burning and sugar.

Next on the card, Callie drew our father's face — round, with two long *J*s flying off the sides. These were the arms of his glasses. She drew his mouth wide and open: he was the only family member who she gave a smile with teeth. And then she drew me. I was a perfect oval with an upside-down *U* for a scowl. She drew my hair extensions, long thin ropes of braids that Callie charted at ninety-degree angles from my head. She drew the crude outlines of a T-shirt. Then she stopped for a minute, her pencil hesitating. She slyly glanced over at me — she knew I was watching — and then she made two quick marks across the penciled expanse — signifiers for my breasts, recently grown and far too large. A pair of bumpy *U*s drawn right side up, to match the upside down one she had for my mouth.

"Take them off."

Callie replied, under her breath and in a singsong, "Breasts are a natural part of the human body, Charlotte. Breasts are part of human nature." Another of our mother's mantras, one she had been saying, obviously for my benefit, for the past year and a half. I was fourteen, Callie was nine, and what was a joke to her was an awkward misfortune for me.

Callie put her pencil down, the better to sign to me with her hands: *Breasts are a part of human development.* Stealthily, I reached over and pinched the fat of her thigh until she took up her eraser again and scrubbed the page clean.

When she'd finished, she reached into the backpack at her feet and pulled out a pack of colored pencils. With thick, grainy streaks of brown she began to color in our family's skin. She did so in the order of whom she loved the most: our mother, whom she believed to be the smartest person in the world; our father, whom she knew to be the kindest; and, finally, me.

She stopped the nub of her pencil, wavering.

What is it? I signed.

Charlie should be in the picture. She frowned. *He's part of us, but I don't even know what he looks like.*

She leaned over the sheet again and cupped one hand close to the paper so that I couldn't see. When she was finished, she sat up and pulled her hand away. Above each family member's head was now a trail of three circles, each individual string of thought bubbles leading up to a single swollen cloud with Charlie in its middle. She made the cloud too oblong, she messed it up, so she had to draw Charlie lying down on his stomach. She drew ears that stuck out, a wide, closed-mouth grin; thick monkey lips pressed together, a low-hanging gut, four paws. She gave him a curling tail. Above all of this, in her best longhand, Callie wrote: *We Love You, Charlie Freeman.*

Too generous, too sweet, so openhearted and earnest it stung. I curled my lip, turned away, watched the trees rush by instead.

We were still the only car on the road and my mother was driving fast. Me and Callie had only been this far from the city once before, the previous summer, when our parents sent us to a black, deaf overnight camp in the backwoods of Maryland. They said it was to improve our signing, but I think it was to make sure we would find friends. In Dorchester, our constant signing, our bookish ways and bans from fast-food restaurants and booty music, assured that me and Callie were unpopular on the block. At the camp, the hope had been that among others who knew our language, at

18

least, we would find a home. But it didn't work out that way.

That past summer, Callie and I braided plastic gimp bracelets that only went around each other's wrists. We made yarn God's Eyes that were never exchanged with anybody else, that followed us home to gaze sullenly from the kitchen window over the sink. It was quickly discovered that we could hear and did not have deaf parents. The other campers were black like us, but they were truly deaf and suspicious of our reasons for being there. Except for a few spates of teasing, they left the two of us alone.

At that camp I'd learned a host of new signs — for *boobs,* for *shut up,* and for *suck it.* But the most dangerous thing that camp had taught me was the awful lesson of country living: out there, in the open, in the quiet, all the emptiness pressed itself up against you, pawed at the very center of your heart, convinced you to make friends with loneliness.

I leaned my head against the window. Through the glass, I heard a steady whine, wind sliding over the car. I secreted my fingers into my lap and began to finger-spell — all the dirty phrases I'd learned the summer before, all the rough words that had been thrown my way, spelled out on the

19

tops of my thighs, protection from that low whistle of wind moving all around us.

I fell asleep to the blur of a thousand trees. When I woke up, the radio was still on, but only every third word came through. The rest was static.

"Turn it to something else," I called, but up front, my mother shook her head.

"There is nothing else."

Everything outside the car was a belligerent green. Just below my window a thin streak of stone skimmed along, the same height as the highway posts. As we drove, the gray crept up through the undergrowth until it revealed itself to be a thick, granite wall the height of our car. Then in one abrupt swoop it towered over us, the very top edged with a trail of glittering sunlight — the reflection of hundreds of shards of glass, scattered razor side up in the cement.

"Is this it?" my father asked.

My mother switched off the radio. "This is it."

The wall broke apart for two iron gates, opened just wide enough for a car to pass through. A brass plaque was bolted into the stone: THE TONEYBEE INSTITUTE FOR APE RESEARCH, ESTABLISHED 1929. Below that, in smaller script: VISITORS BY APPOINTMENT ONLY. Just beyond all this, we could see the start of a long gravel driveway and a narrow kiosk with white plastic siding swirled to look like wood grain. A security post, but it was empty.

My mother rolled down her window and honked the horn twice. We could hear the sound echo off the trees around us.

"Warm welcome," my father said.

"The guard, what's his name again? He must be up at the institute." My mother leaned over the steering wheel and carefully nosed the car through the gates, trying not to scrape the Volvo.

The Toneybee Institute's main drive ran between two tidy rows of white elms, behind which, on both sides, was the murk of a darker, fatter forest. The drive was long but sputtered out abruptly, right at the base of the institute's steps.

The whole brick front of the building reared up at us out of all that green. "Oh, it's a mansion," Callie said, but it didn't seem that way to me. It seemed like some cardboard false front a bunch of schoolchildren put together out of refrigerator boxes and painted up to look like their idea of grand.

The main building was brick and squat, flanked by two towers, with wings beyond. Stuck all across the front of the building was a stone orchestra made up of cement angels with asphalt violins and trumpets, chubby, stony mouths frozen wide in song. My mother had told us that before the Toneybee was a research institute, it had been a music conservatory. Huge curling flourishes hung over the windowsills and building corners. There were flood lamps tucked up underneath the armpits of the building's stony cherubim. Crowded underneath the decorations was a bank of brass doors with a shallow flight of steps.

My mother parked right beside the steps, careful to make sure the Volvo lined up with them perfectly.

Callie was the first one out of the car. She bounded up the stairs, straight to the brass doors with their yellowing Plexiglas panes. She cupped her hands against the windows, trying to see past the film until my mother caught up with her and pulled on her shoulder.

After a few minutes, through the cloudy glass we could see a heavy form coming toward us. The whole brass doorframe buzzed, and then the form behind the glass grew larger and darker. It leaned on the handle and held the door open. It was the guard, a squat man with the whitest, thinnest skin I had ever seen. So thin that you

22

could see the purple and red veins of his balding skull. He had a regular white dress shirt on, with two gold epaulets Velcroed to the shoulders and a clear plastic badge clipped above his heart, with a ragged paper insert with the laser-printed epitaph SECURITY.

As we shuffled through the door, he held out his hand. "Lester Potter." He tapped the badge on the front of his shirt. Then, "Dr. Paulsen will be down in a minute."

When we were all through the door, he strode to a small desk in the lobby, sat down, and opened his newspaper, at which point we apparently became invisible to him.

It was hard to make out the size of the lobby. Everything was covered in dark wood and velvet, which gave the room a gravitas it maybe didn't deserve. The whole back wall was a grimy pink marble slab with roman numerals and Latin epigrams carved into its face. It was too murky to see anything more specific than that. The Toneybee kept the lights banked low: weak wattage bulbs made weaker by all the green glass lampshades. On either side of the room were heavy leather double doors, studded with brass. All that marble gave off a cold, dank sweat that hung in the air and clung to our skin and chilled us. Lester, in his chair, had buttoned a cardigan over his makeshift uniform. A modern standing metal lamp, the kind with many arms, the kind you would find in a teenager's bedroom, stood beside his desk.

Callie wore a pair of jelly sandals, and the thick, plastic soles sank deep into the heavy carpet, leaving bite marks in the pile. I brushed my hand against one of the heavy oak walls, felt the grain of wood scratch against my neon fingernail polish, and shivered.

It was clear that none of us belonged there. And Lester Potter did not belong there, either — his makeshift uniform even shabbier and suspect, as he propped his elbows on his little desk and strained to read the newsprint in the glare of the lamp. None of us belonged there and we were all nervously ignoring the fact.

My father walked the length of the room, Callie trailing after him. He wandered around, pushing on some of the doors. Lester Potter lowered his newspaper to watch but said nothing. My father settled in the center of the room, where a statue of a man stood, stocky and messy haired, BEETHOVEN carved into the base. My father glanced at Lester Potter and then, with a studied casualness, leaned against the statue, crossing his ankles. Callie reached for his hand.

Lester Potter still watched my father. He was leaning over his desk now as if he was waiting for something to happen. But he said nothing. My mother opened her purse and began searching its contents for an imaginary stick of gum. My cheeks burned and I focused on the brightest thing in the room — the white crown of Lester Potter's head, the veins of his scalp glowing through the gloom.

It felt like a full ten minutes before we heard the shush shush shush of rubber soles on carpet.

"Hello, hello," a woman's voice stuttered. "I'm sorry to be late."

My mother was already smiling eagerly. "Dr. Paulsen."

Dr. Marietta Paulsen was the Toneybee Institute's research director. It was she who had conceived of the whole experiment, had handpicked us to lead it. She came at us with a nervous skip.

I'd already decided, months ago, when I'd first heard her name, that I would not allow myself to like Dr. Paulsen. I saw now that she was much older than my mother, but she wore her hair like a little girl's, cut close to her chin, fine bangs held back with two rose tortoiseshell barrettes. She had tiny pale eyes, set close together at the center of her face. They flickered back and forth in a way that made me feel both sorry for her and uneasy for myself. She was very tall. I noted, with a rush of satisfaction, that she had a wide, flat, obvious backside. She probably ties that cardigan around her waist to try and hide it, I told myself. She wore a gray wool skirt and an ivory-colored blouse, thick black stockings and bright green clogs and on her hands, a pair of blue latex gloves.

"I hope the drive was all right. Laurel, Charles, you've been here before, but still, it's easy to get lost." As she spoke, Dr. Paulsen peeled off her gloves, balled them up, and stuffed them into her blouse's breast pocket, a rubber boutonniere.

She hesitated for a moment as if she was deciding something. Then she reached out and grasped my mother's shoulders, pulled her into an awkward half embrace. "It's so good to see you, Laurel," she said into the top of my mother's hair. "I can't tell you how excited everyone here is. We really can't wait to get started."

My mother, pressed under the crook of Dr. Paulsen's arm, tried not to look startled. She lightly patted Dr. Paulsen's back.

"We're all excited, too."

Dr. Paulsen let my mother go and turned to the rest of us. She rounded her shoulders forward and lowered her chin so that she could meet my father's eye. "Good to see you again, Charles." She shook his hand briskly. For Callie, who held my father's hand, Dr. Paulsen put her hands on her knees and squatted, looked full into Callie's face. "Lovely to meet you."

She stood up and turned to me.

"And you, too, Charlotte." Her eyes flicked briefly over my T-shirt, the one I had worn despite my mother telling me it was too tight. To Dr. Paulsen's credit, she only frowned her disapproval for an instant before she met my eyes and smiled. She held out her hand.

When she parted her lips to grin, behind her white, white teeth, I caught a glimpse of her tongue. It was the yellowiest, craggiest, driest tongue I'd ever seen. It surely did not belong in that mouth, in her, and I shot a look to my mother, who widened her eyes, who gave one quick shake of her head that told me to ignore it. I turned to Dr. Paulsen and smiled very widely back at her.

Dr. Paulsen turned to Lester Potter, nodded a thanks to him, and then led us through the double leather doors to the

27

hallway beyond. The hallway smelled like furniture polish and rotting brocade and underneath that something else, something warm and dark and rude. Wild animals.

"This is the west wing." Dr. Paulsen walked ahead of us. "Your apartment's here, on the second floor."

"Where are the chimps?" Callie asked.

"They live in the east wing," Dr. Paulsen said. "But we'll skip that for now. It would be too overwhelming to visit today."

All along the hallways were offices and labs and conference rooms, and Dr. Paulsen made a show of stepping into each one. The rooms had high, arched ceilings and gilt windowpanes that clashed with the wheelie chairs and gray-faced conference tables. One large room was a working lab with banks of counters and sinks and refrigerators, the labs' sinks piled high with dirty glass vials. The animal smell was strongest there, battling with the reek of warm bleach and floor wax.

Every room we entered, Dr. Paulsen pointed to each of us and said, "Laurel and Charles and Callie and Charlotte," to whoever was inside. Mostly women in shorts and tank tops, despite the clammy air-conditioning. No one wore a lab coat like Dr. Paulsen's. While Dr. Paulsen introduced us, I could feel them looking curiously at me and Callie. But before any of them could step forward to introduce themselves, Dr. Paulsen ushered us out of the room again. "Too many names to learn today." We kept walking.

"There are twenty researchers working at the institute," Dr. Paulsen explained. "They all live off campus. We have eighteen chimpanzees in total. Plus the ground staff, the cleaning crew, myself, a small administrative staff and security."

"Oh, we've already met security," my father said.

"Yes. Lester," Dr. Paulsen said sheepishly. She slowed her pace until she walked beside my father. "There's only one of him, so we can't have him always at the gate — he can't be two places at once. We really should probably have more security, you know, those animal rights protesters. It can get nasty. But we're privately funded, thanks to our founder, Miss Toneybee-Leroy. We're very low profile. She's made sure of that. We're kind of off the radar. Or at least we have been."

We kept walking, Callie threatening to break into an honest run until my mother caught her hand and gave it a shake. They walked ahead of us, Dr. Paulsen studying them. Without breaking stride, she drew a piece of chalk from her pocket, flicked her tongue over its stub, and then slipped it back. I was the only one who saw her do it.

At the end of the hallway was a plain wooden staircase. "This is the private entrance to your apartment," Dr. Paulsen told us. "We'll get you settled in."

But beside the stairs was a large oil portrait banked with lights, the brightest we'd seen in the institute so far. The plaque on the portrait read miss JULIA TONEYBEE-LEROY, FOUNDER, 1929.

It was hard to tell from the painting if Julia Toneybee-Leroy was meant to be beautiful. She was a thin-boned woman with a fleshy jaw. She wore a green evening gown with long sleeves and a neckline cut too low, and she was sitting in an armchair. A thick curl of dull gold hair was painted against her neck. Her eyes were too frank. It was the gaze of a zealot. I didn't know that word then, but even if I had, I wouldn't have known enough, the first time seeing her, to use it for Miss Julia Toneybee-Leroy. I only knew that something inside of me flipped over when I saw that picture.

In the painting, beside her, on a table, held up by a stick through the skull, were the bright, white bones of a squat skeleton.

"Why are there baby bones in that picture?" Callie asked.

Dr. Paulsen blushed a painful red. "Those bones are the remains of the first-ever chimp to live at the Toneybee Institute."

"Oh," Callie said. She did not sound convinced.

"Her name was Daisy," Dr. Paulsen offered.

Callie was still gazing up at the picture, trying to give it the benefit of the doubt. "How many chimps die here, like that?"

"Oh, it's not like that, Callie," Dr. Paulsen rushed to explain. "Daisy died a long time ago, from a cold. There was nothing they could do. She wasn't used to the winters. But we're properly heated now and we take good care of everyone here."

"Well, is she still alive?" Callie nodded at the woman in the painting.

"Julia Toneybee-Leroy? Yes, very much so."

"That doesn't seem very fair," Callie muttered, and my mother reached out and rubbed her arm, a comfort and a warning. "It's okay, Callie."

Dr. Paulsen hurried us up the flight of stairs and away from the troubling picture. We arrived in a short, overly lit hall. This one had only one door, again of plain wood, with a buzzer set in the wall. Dr. Paulsen unlocked the door and we filed behind her into the front room. Our boxes had already been delivered and they were piled in towers all around us, but the furniture belonged to the Toneybee. We'd sold all of ours back in Dorchester. "They're giving us brand-new furniture," my mother had crowed. "Can you imagine?"

The couch in the front room was just as saggy and broken down as the one we'd had in Boston. There were also a few wooden end tables that looked rich: dark wood carved with heavy curlicues. But when I stood beside one, I saw that the flourishes were nicked and the tops of the tables were scarred and printed with an infinity of fading water rings. I leaned against the table and it tottered slightly back and forth. One back leg was shorter than the others.

Callie ran ahead of us, deeper into the apartment, throwing doors open as she went. I was slower, making a show of being unimpressed. I trailed my fingers over the freshly painted walls, pressed on the glass in the windowpanes. Behind me, I could hear my mother and Dr. Paulsen. Dr. Paulsen murmured something very low and my mother's answer back was quick and light and clattering, her new voice here, overly bright.

They'd decided something. My mother called to me and my father, "Dr. Paulsen thinks it's best we all meet Charlie now."

Charlie lived behind a door in the living room. He had a large, oval-shaped space with low ceilings and no windows and no furniture. Instead, there were bundles of pastel-colored blankets heaped up on the scarred wooden floor. Even from where I stood, I could tell the blankets were the scratchy kind, cheap wool. The room was full of plants — house ferns and weak African violets and nodding painted ladies. "They're here to simulate the natural world," Dr. Paulsen told us, but I thought it was an empty gesture. Charlie had never known any forests and yet Dr. Paulsen assumed some essential part of him pined for them.

Charlie sat beside a fern. A man knelt beside him. "That's Max, my assistant," Dr. Paulsen said.

Max was wearing jeans and a red T-shirt, his lab coat balled up on the floor. He was pale, with messy red hair. He was trying to grow a beard, probably just graduated from college a couple years earlier.

In front of us now, Charlie had gotten hold of Max's glasses and was methodically pressing his tongue against each lens. Max tried to coax the glasses away, but every time he got close, Charlie only bent forward and licked him, too, all the while looking Max in his small brown eyes. Max broke some leaves off the fern, ran them around Charlie's ears and under his chin, distracting him.

"They're playing," Dr. Paulsen explained.

But it seemed more like a very gentle disagreement. Charlie shook his head at the leaves but stayed doggedly focused on tonguing Max's glasses.

"Max," Dr. Paulsen called, and he squinted and waved. He picked up Charlie and brought him to us.

As he came closer, Charlie let the glasses hang loose in his hands, and he craned his neck toward Dr. Paulsen. Now he looked like a baby. Taped around his waist was a disposable diaper. A few of his stray hairs were caught in the tape's glue, and he kept dipping his fingers under the rough plastic hem, trying to worry them loose.

My father went to him first. He gently rubbed the top of Charlie's head, not wanting to scare him. Charlie flinched and my father moved away. Next came Callie, who smiled and smiled, trying to get Charlie to bare his teeth back, but he wouldn't do it.

Then it was my turn.

I reached out my hand to touch him. I thought he would be bristly and sharp, like a cat, but his hair was fine, so soft it was almost unbearable. I could feel, at its downy ends, the heat spreading up from his skin beneath. I pulled my hand away quickly. The scent of him stayed on my fingers, old and sharp, like a bottle of witch hazel.

Charlie yawned. His breath was rancid, like dried, spoiled milk. Later, when he got used to us, he would run his lips up and down our hands so that all of our skin, too, smelled like Charlie's mouth and the hefty, mournful stench of wild animal.

My mother was the last to hold him. She was crying and she said through her tears, her hands shaking as she reached out to touch him, "Isn't he beautiful?"

I wanted to say something snide. I wanted to say what I had been telling her since she told us about this experiment: that this was crazy, that she was crazy, that it would never work. I wanted to sign *bullshit*. But I looked into my mother's face, wet and wide open with joy, and I couldn't help myself.

"Yes," I told her, "he's beautiful."

Dr. Paulsen stayed for dinner, but none of us even pretended to eat. We were all watching my mother and Charlie. She sat at the head of the table, Charlie on her lap, a baby bottle in her hand, trying to get him to drink. She kept her face bent close to his, her chin butting the end of the bottle.

Charlie spit the nipple out once, twice. Each time he rejected it, Dr. Paulsen's hands rose up as if she wanted to push it back in his mouth herself. My mother only saw Charlie. She refused to be discouraged. The fifth time, he took it. With a loud, rude swallow he began to eat. He drank until the little plastic bag inside crumpled down on itself. He loved the bottle so much he wouldn't give it up until my mother rolled a piece of lettuce and held it to his mouth. He parted his lips long enough for her to pull his empty away.

Dr. Paulsen studied them, her hand close to her mouth in a fist, faint yellow streaks at the corners of her lips. She dropped her hand and I saw the chalk fall back into her pocket. She wiped her fingers on the hem of her sweater.

She turned to my father. "You're ready to begin teaching at Courtland County High?"

"Yes," he said. "Especially because Charlotte's going there, too. She and I will help each other — you know, find our seat in the lunchroom and make friends and all that.

Maybe we can even share a locker."

But Dr. Paulsen didn't laugh. She was watching my mother and Charlie again. We all were. "And how do you think you'll like teaching at Charlotte's school?" she repeated.

My mother looked up. "It's getting late for him to be awake, isn't it?"

"I suppose you're right." Dr. Paulsen hugged each of us good-bye. She patted Charlie quickly on the head. At the front door she stopped, turned. "He likes another drink before bed. Make sure to sign it to him, tell him what you're doing."

She took a step backward, still watching Charlie. But he had set her aside, was concentrating on twining his fingers through my mother's hair.

When Dr. Paulsen was gone, my mother told us it was time for bed.

Our first luxury at the Toneybee: Callie and I got separate rooms. Hers was at one end of the hall and mine was at the other.

I made it halfway to my room before Callie ran up behind me.

"I can't find my pajamas," she said, breathlessly.

"So?"

"So, can you help me find them?"

"I have to put mine on first."

"That's okay. I'll come with you."

In her room, we were shy with each other. Callie tried to hide herself while she changed. When we were both finished, I began to leave, but she caught my hand.

"Well, what is it?"

"Shouldn't we say good night to them?" Callie asked.

"I don't want to," I said, and regretted it.

"Why?"

"They should have stayed with us, not Charlie."

"We're too old for that."

"That doesn't matter. It's our first night here."

"They asked us to say good night." Callie still held my hand. She shuffled her feet back and forth over the marble floor and we both listened for a bit to the unfamiliar sound.

"I feel bad not saying good night to them," Callie said finally.

I sighed. "Fine. We'll do it. Come on."

When we got to our parents' room, they were already in bed. In the soft glow from the lamp on the nightstand my father sat propped up on a bank of the Toneybee's pillows, his glasses off, a book open on his lap. My mother was already curled up beside him. It was only when we got to the edge of the bed that we saw Charlie lying in the space between them.

My mother said, "This is a onetime thing."

Callie leaned forward to kiss them good night. She bent toward my mother but just as her lips brushed her cheek, Charlie lifted one thin finger and swatted it hard across Callie's face. She jerked back, surprised.

"It's okay. You scared him, that's all," my mother explained.

Callie nodded, tried to smile. It was special to be touched by Charlie, even if it was a blow. "Good night," she called to Charlie, who kept his finger crooked above his head, a warning.

I took Callie's hand and we turned and started down the hallway back to her room. We were halfway there when we heard it. First it sounded like something in a cartoon — "hoo hoo hoo" — too silly to be real. Then a wheeze. Then a wail, so low, so long, so hollow, that it sounded like the most sorrowful sound in the world. It was a very old sound, something that had welled up from a deep and hidden place to whip and sting the world. The sound suddenly broke, left a jagged stillness that was worse than the crying. I held my breath. It was a relief when it started up again.

Callie and I hurried back to our parents' room.

When we got there, all the lights were on. In the glare of the overhead lamp I saw Charlie cling first to my mother's nightgown and then to the sheets of the bed. He arched his whole body and then flattened himself over and over again.

My mother knelt beside him on the bed, trying to get her hands on the small of his back, on his arms, anywhere, but he wouldn't be still. With his mouth that wide open, I could see all the way down his throat, maybe almost to his heart, to something red and shaking.

My mother was saying over and over again, "Please, sweetheart, please love, please." My father was out of bed, standing behind her, hands hovering above her. "All right now, all right now," he murmured.

But Charlie kept crying. He would not be comforted by any words they said.

Nymphadora of Spring City, 1929

My mother was a Star of the Morning. My father was a Saturnite. I was first an Infant Auxiliary Star, and then I was a Girl Star, then a Young Lady Star, and three years ago, right before Mumma and Pop drank a jigger of cyanide each, I became, in my own right, a full-blown Star of the Morning, Fifth House, Second Quadrant Division, North Eastern Lodge of the colored hamlet of Spring City in the town of Courtland County, Massachusetts.

After my parents committed suicide I declared, if only to myself, that I was no longer a Star of the Morning. But even now, three years on, I can't stop wearing my pin. During the day while I'm teaching class, it's hidden under my shirt collar, pinned right up close to the front of my throat. At night, after I've dressed my hair and put it in its cap, after I've rubbed my face first with cold cream and then a worn, oily piece of cham-

41

ois, I do what Mumma showed me. I stand in front of the mirror, my skin all greasy and soft, and I take off the pin while staring at my reflection. A Star of the Morning is never allowed to look directly at her pin. My pin is a small brass knot filed down to look like a burst of light, with a rusty garnet in the middle. When I was an Infant Star, I would stand in the mirror beside Mumma, watching our reflections' fingers at work unfastening our pins and I was filled with love. I thought it was the most beautiful thing in the world. Mumma told me it was better than a diamond.

Stars of the Morning always take off their pins before they sleep, and always before their evening prayers, so as not to make a false idol out of it. Now when I take off my pin, I place it on my nightstand, and then, if I was to follow what Mumma taught me, I am supposed to reflect on my moral failings during the day and recite the Lord's Prayer because Stars of the Morning are good Christian Negro women. But no one, if they could read my thoughts, would call me a Christian anymore, and besides, I don't believe in prayer, so during this bit of the routine I try to just sit quiet on my bed. But after years of ritual, I can't help myself. Even when I'm dumb, the blood in my ears pounds out the rhythm of "Our Father, who art in heaven." To drown out these pious cadences, in my head I sometimes chant the obscene version I learned as a girl: "Our Father, who farts in heaven, whorish be his name."

I am a thirty-six-year-old unmarried, orphaned Negro schoolteacher, in charge of a room full of impressionable young colored minds and every night, I sing a dirty nursery rhyme to help me go to sleep. It is enough to laugh, if I did not always feel like weeping.

The time for prayer over, ready for bed, the last thing I do before I lie down and blow out the light is to stand before the mirror again and pinch the pin between my fingers and very carefully stick it to the lace collar of my nightgown. I've slept with the pin for as long as I can remember. At the base of my neck, just below the collarbone, is a livid red line from its sharpest end drawing on me.

My best memory is of Initiation. I was seven years old. We stood in front of the church basement door, on a lawn so bright you could see the green even in dusk. My mother was the most powerful Star in Spring City so I was the head of the line,

43

even though I didn't want to be. I was terrified. An older girl had once told me that to become an Infant Star, they set your hair on fire. Her friend said the big women Stars made you shake a dead lady's hand, the hand of the very first Star who ever lived. "The big women Stars keep it in a special box," she said, "and when you shake it the bones crunch and the dust gets on your fingers. The dead lady's dust is what makes you a Star."

I had asked Mumma about all of these rumors and she told me they were nonsense and those girls were just jealous. Their mothers were loose women and the girls had proven themselves unruly and so they could never become an Infant Star like me. But I remained uneasy, and when I pressed Mumma, she still wouldn't tell me exactly what happened at Initiation. All my life I thought we had no secrets between us. The year before, when our tabby Dina birthed a litter, she told me frank and true how cats and people were made. She told me how the universe came to be, and where our earth stood in it, and that God did not live in the sun but in the breath and air and dust around and within us. "The sun is just a very bright ball," she told me. Which was more than the other mothers told their children. But she wouldn't tell me about becoming a Star, as many times as I asked her.

For Initiation, I wore a white lace dress and patent leather shoes Mumma ordered special from Boston. Nine little girls pressed against my back, all breathing heavy. We had to fast for a day and a night before Initiation. According to the bylaws of the Stars of the Morning, Infant Stars are supposed to consume only milk and honey, and they have to chant "I am a vessel for the light of our Lord" before they drink it. But no one in Spring City could afford honey, so we drank our milk with raw brown sugar instead. I breathed the rotten sweetness of it on the other children's spit and in their girlish sweat.

I squeezed my eyes shut very tight and kept them that way until I heard the basement door of the church rumble open. I heard the girls behind me breathe quicker, talk faster. I felt something brush against my hand. The dead woman, I thought, but the hand that took mine was fat and warm and it led me very carefully down the steps and into the church basement. Once I was there, it smelled the same as it always had, like earth and the moths that ate the choir robes and the greening tin of the church

45

collection plate. I almost opened my eyes. But a voice said, "Keep your lights closed, Infant Star." Right beneath my chin I felt a point of warmth and I knew that it was someone holding a candle close to my face. This comforted me, somehow, to know the light was near. I heard the other girls stumble down the stairs one by one. Most gasped. A few of the very young ones started to cry. Then I heard the basement door rumble shut. I opened my eyes. And I laughed.

I laughed because even though the room smelled just the same, when I opened my eyes I saw it had become the most beautiful place I have ever been in my life, before or since. It wasn't dark. The earth walls were covered in white paper. What seemed like a thousand candles were lit all around us, in tiny glass and tin lanterns. Strings of white hydrangea were threaded across the top of the room. Clouds hung down from the ceiling and for a moment I thought, Mumma's brought down the very sky to greet me. But then I saw that it was just tulle, from Miss Vera's dress shop, doubled up on itself to seem like heaven.

We jumbled ourselves all up until we formed a new line. I was now in the middle. Mumma strode out before us in a long white robe trimmed with yellow. She held a gold-bound Bible in her hands. She opened a page at random, and one by one we had to hover a finger over the Bible, let it fall down, and then read from whichever passage we chose. The passage gave us our secret name, the name only other Stars knew us by.

The poor girl before me chose Herod, and she cried and cried because she was going to have to go by the name of a known baby killer. I thought for certain Mumma would let Herod pick again, but she only looked on sternly as another Star patted the little girl's back and told her some quickly made-up nonsense about this being a splendid opportunity to restore honor to the name. I was relieved, then, when I picked Nymphadora. My real name is Ellen, but Nymphadora is so much better. I bet you didn't know there was a Nymphadora in the Bible. There is. Colossians 4:15. Later I found out our Bible was a mistranslation — it should have read "Nympha," and Nympha should have been a man. It was by some lucky magic that I got so fine a name as Nymphadora of the Spring City Stars.

Nymphadora sounded beautiful and elegant and pretty and peak. I liked that the Nymphadora in our Bible ran a church in her own home. I was proud of the name, but when I turned and threw a smile at Mumma she did not return it.

When we were all newly named, Mumma inspected the ten of us and still did not speak. She raised her hand and Miss Vera and another Star rolled out a tea table stacked with food. Real food: bowls of potatoes and biscuits and a lank turkey with its bony ankles wrapped in paper to keep its marrow warm. Our deflated stomachs, milk-lined and sugary, leapt in revolt. But Mumma wouldn't let us eat. Instead, she stood in front of the table.

"Girls," she said, "you are almost Infant Stars. Do you know what makes a Star shine?"

No one answered. We were all watching the spread behind her, too hungry to speak.

"Girls," she said, "I have asked you a question. A tenet of being an Infant Star is to speak when you are spoken to. So we will begin again. What makes a Star shine?"

The newly named Herod sniffed loudly, wiped the snot from her face. "The light of heaven?" she offered, cautiously. It was a good guess, as we'd had to drone this phrase incessantly for the past few days as we fasted.

"No," Mumma said. "No. Not the light of

heaven. What makes a Star of the Morning shine, what makes an Infant Star shine among all the other pieces of dust and dirt and rock that are our Lord's creations, is self-control. Denial. Denial builds up inside little Infant Stars like you, makes your moral fiber strong like flint, so that when the world tests you, when the world rubs up against you all vicious and sharp and everything within you, everything is telling you to give in, all you desire is to give in, do you know what happens? You don't give in. You don't become soft. You ignore your desires. The world's trials stir up a light in you so strong, so pure, so true, no man on earth can put it out. Denial of your desires is what makes an Infant Star shine."

Mumma leaned up against the table and crossed her arms over her chest. She lifted her chin up to the paper clouds and began to declaim.

And even though she was my mother and even though I worshipped her, I wanted to groan because I was a smart little Star and I could read between the lines and see, despite that turkey's paper socks, promising meat kept warm, we weren't going to be eating anything anytime soon, and when we finally did, it would most certainly be cold.

"The very first Star denied herself everything so that she could be a beacon of light for others. Her name was Mary Whitman and she was a slave."

Herod gasped at this. We were Negroes, it was true, but we were all Northern Negroes, born of at least two generations of freed men. Those with slavery closer to them than that kept it hidden. The first Emancipation Day was nearly forty years past. Slaves were the Israelites in the Bible, they were the figures drawn in quick blurry clouds of black ink in the illustrated editions of *Uncle Tom's Cabin* we read in school. Though we understood that some of us were once them, and that we had to bake cakes every church bazaar for those down who were still pretty much them, it never occurred to us as children that slaves could live in Spring City, Massachusetts, any more than camels could.

"Yes," Mumma said. "She was a slave and she ran away and came here to the North. But in order to run, she had to deny herself everything. She had to deny herself love. She had a mother and father and husband and little babies and she had to leave them behind. She had to deny herself love. And she ran and she ran and when she came here, when she came to the North, she was so full of light from her trials that she became a Star. And she began this sister-hood, to teach other Negro women how to shine like her. Because in order for the Negro race to survive and thrive, we need a hundred stars, a thousand stars, full of light to show others the way."

Mumma rested against the table and I heard the wood groan and just a whiff, just the tiniest hint, of melted butter filled the air.

"Not everyone can be a Star," she contin-ued. "Not everyone can be so strong as to deny themselves to make sure the Negro race survives. But we believe you Infant Stars have the potential to become Stars of the Morning."

And here, Mumma gestured to Miss Dora, who brought her a wooden-backed chair, which Mumma sat down on, arranged her skirts, made herself comfortable, and I cannot remember the rest of the speech from that night, because my attention was taken up with keeping my lips pressed tight together and sucking hard on my own tongue to keep from standing up, pushing my own mother aside, and lapping up the mounds of potatoes stacked behind her.

Later, when we were leaving Initiation, my stomach full, Mumma said, "I wish you hadn't picked Nymphadora for your name.

51

It's just not right."

"I like it." I could still taste a bit the turnip greens' juice on my lips.

"Yes," she said. "I suppose it's pretty." She sighed. "I was hoping you'd have a more sober name. Like Joshua or David."

Mumma's star name was Job. She was so, so, proud of that name, of its rectitude and serendipity. Choosing that name confirmed to her that she was born to be a Star. And if she was meant to be a Star, then me, made in her image, must be destined to be one too.

She straightened and peered ahead of us into the dark. We were walking along the short stretch of Main Street. All around us was night and Mumma and I kept our eyes out for the blazing lantern that hung from the sign of our store.

Mumma took my hand in the dark. "It wasn't you that picked Nymphadora," she said. "It was Providence." And then I knew that this was grave, because Mumma didn't like to get religious unless the situation absolutely warranted it. She accepted it as the will of the universe that my Star name should be so scandalous. She decided, "There's a reason for it. Only time will tell us what it is."

■ ■ ■ ■

I think my name, its rowdiness, I think it all was leading to Dr. Gardner and what he asked me to do, and what I agreed to do, and I know it would kill her all over again if she knew. Sometimes I can't help exercising the perverse logic that maybe Dr. Gardner's friendship is part of the Providence Mumma believed in so heartily. As soon as I think it, I feel the cynicism so fiercely, like a sharp pain in my eyetooth. And then I make the pain keener when I remember that, in the end, even Mumma herself had given up on Providence.

She and Pop left me behind. I was not even in the house with them when they killed themselves. Mumma sent me out on what I know now to be a fool's errand: she told me the undertaker needed some tincture immediately and sent me to his house far from the center of town, knowing it would take me nearly an hour to walk there and back. While I was arguing with Mr. Dawes over the tincture — he insisted he had not ordered it and I insisted he must have, because Mumma and Pop never made mistakes — they drank their secret drink.

Mr. Dawes called me a batty old girl, and

while I drew myself up in my patent leather boots and huffed away from him and did my best to make a dramatic exit from his lane, Mumma and Pop sat in their seats by the fire and they seized and shook and raged in their chairs. By the time I came home and found an envelope tacked to our front door with my name on it, written in Mumma's hand, it was done.

I took the envelope, already knowing something was wrong, and opened the door with one hand while slitting its top with the other. I called their names as I unfolded the note, not even really reading it, walking to the parlor where I found the two of them. Their death jitters had thrown them from their seats. Pop was curled around the feet of his armchair and Mumma was laid out, five-pointed, in the middle of the throw rug.

I smelled their death and then I read the letter. There was no more money. That was the long and short of it, though it took Mumma ten pages to say so. They were on the verge of bankruptcy. They'd been skimming from their own till for years, and when that no longer was enough, they'd begun to take from the Stars' and Saturnites' treasuries. The money had all been for me. For my good dresses and elocution lessons and the Negro teachers' college out of state, all to make me a presentable bride for a man who never came. And then they feared they had taken too much and they would be discovered. It was money that made them lose their faith. They said in the note that all of this was for my own good. They didn't want to burden me with their disgrace. They told me to tell everyone they'd suffered strokes, simultaneously, and died together in each other's arms. They thought this was a chance for me to make a fresh start. They still thought maybe their investment had not been in vain, that maybe I could be married — this is how I knew their grief had made them delusional.

I put down the note and I looked at them again, my father curled in on himself like a baby, my mother wide open to God. Without thinking, I took an oil lantern from the mantel and I went to the back of the pharmacy, to Pop's office, and I smashed that lantern down, as hard as I could, into the green leather ledgers Pop used for accounts. I smashed and smashed until the books went up in flames and I stood and watched until my eyes watered and I gagged on the smoke and then I fled. I ran into the street and raised the alarm and people came with buckets but it was too late. I stood in the street and all the other Stars, the very ones my mother couldn't face, came and stood around me. They rubbed at the soot on my cuffs and collar, they rubbed the soot on my face, and they shook their heads and said what Stars always say when one of us dies: "A good light gone."

I watched the house burn and felt the Stars' hands rub my back and pat my arms and all I could think of was the math. My parents poured two cups of poison, not three. They left me behind.

Have you ever heard of colored people killing themselves? And over money, too. As if a colored person has never been broke before. We do not commit suicide. That kind of nonsense is for white people. We endure. We are the masters of endurance. We get stronger and stronger until we shine like Stars. But Mumma and Pop ultimately did not believe this. And when I found out that they didn't believe, that the tenets of the Stars were hollow words to them, I turned cold and raging inside. I turned mean.

The other Stars watched me closely after my parents died. They were waiting for me to crack, but I never did. They watched as I went to the school every day and then returned to the room I let from a retired Star named Sermon on the Mount. They knew there was something wrong, but I would not break for them.

Still, the loneliness began growing inside me, until it was a large gaping maw that, I swear, pulsed in my chest right before bed, in the morning, and in the cold, as regular as any wound. I missed my one true friend, my mother. She and I were close in a way I don't think many other mothers and daughters were. I slept beside her every night of my childhood: so near to her back, I could probably sketch the constellation of moles and freckles on her skin there. When I was a very little girl, every morning I would wake before her and arrange myself so that when she woke, we were eye-to-eye.

I miss her, with a never-ending ache that I did not think was possible, that crowds out any other feeling and certainly all my reason, and any good sense.

Dr. Gardner began coming to Spring City at the beginning of April. He just started showing up in the evenings. At first, he didn't come near us. He hung around the shops on the border, where Spring City meets Courtland County. The whites in Courtland County consider Spring City their Negro Quarter, but on the border are the in-between places that all of us have to use: the rail depot with the dusty cafe; the cobbler and the notary; the general store.

Everyone in Spring City knew who Dr. Gardner was because there'd been rumors about him all through town for at least a year. We knew he worked up in the monkey house. He came to Courtland County the year before, when little Julia Toneybee-Leroy, the neighborhood heiress to a rubber fortune, returned from her Congolese safari with a dead monkey and ten more live ones on the way.

Very soon, Julia Toneybee-Leroy let it be known that she wanted to convert her mother's estate into some kind of all ape zoo, with Dr. Gardner as the head. The place used to be a music conservatory, the best to be found between Boston and New York, everyone said. The first summer after my parents killed themselves, I went there for an outdoor concert, stood on the section of lawn reserved for colored patrons of the arts, and heard a Bach concerto so sweet and sad it drew the ache of my parents' demise from my chest and forced me to weep in public. I didn't even cry at their funeral. I had felt all the eyes of the Stars on me, eager to see my grief. To cry in front of them would have been unbearable, an admission of defeat, a humiliation, so I bit the inside of my cheeks to keep my eyes dry.

I was my mother's daughter to the very end, till the moment they put her in her grave. But the music of that conservatory broke me down to tears and I didn't care who saw it.

When Julia Toneybee-Leroy fired all the music teachers and sent home the students, she installed the animals in their place. We never did see the monkeys move in: just heard the ten of them making a racket in the specially equipped freight car she had run up the tracks and past Spring City on the way to the newly named Toneybee Institute for Great Ape Research. Last fall, she brought in Dr. Gardner.

Julia Toneybee-Leroy said it was all for magnificent revelations in science, shortly forthcoming, but everyone in white Courtland County and black Spring City alike thought she was just using the monkeys as a cover to have an affair with Dr. Gardner. He was supposed to be an evolutionary genius and the next Charles Darwin, if some were to be believed.

After a few weeks of lurking around Spring City's border, Dr. Gardner got bolder and crossed over. He walked up and down our streets leisurely, waving every so often at the people he passed. He did this despite the children who would stop stock still when he saluted them, and just stare, despite the strained smiles of the women and the reluctant hellos of the men. He made a supreme effort to disregard the very obvious fact that we did not want him here. He walked around and surveyed the houses for a few days more, and then he started bringing his sketch pad. I caught him once or twice, standing near the wooden fence around my schoolyard, leaning his pad against a post and watching intently as the boys and girls cried "Red Rover."

When Dr. Gardner slouched around our streets he made everyone in town uncomfortable, the women most of all. They asked Mr. Dawes, the undertaker, to talk to him about it. To see what was what. But Mr. Dawes said he didn't want to get caught up in it. He said he had too much to do to worry about a skinny white man drawing cartoons and we should all have too much to do, too.

So the Stars of the Morning of Spring City got together and asked me to address Dr. Gardner. They asked me because with Mumma and Pop dead, I am alone. I don't have any kin, not even a mangy husband or brother to protest, to say, "Why are you picking on Nymphadora?" They took advantage of the fact that I am a thirty-six-year-old orphan.

One Tuesday night after a Star meeting, Nadine Morton took me aside. We were folding up tablecloths and as we held an expanse of white lace between us, as we brought the corners together to make them kiss, she said, "Just find out what he wants. And once he tells you, suggest that perhaps he can find it elsewhere."

Nadine really was the one who should have approached him. She and I both knew that. She was hired up at the Toneybee Institute shortly after Julia Toneybee returned, though nobody knew what exactly Nadine did up there. She claimed she was not allowed to say. Nadine had trained as a nurse with the Red Cross in the Great War, she'd worked with an all-colored battalion, but when she came back home to Spring City she'd had to take in washing because the only hospital around was twenty miles away and didn't hire colored nurses. Up at the Toneybee, with her mysterious duties, Nadine presumably worked with Dr. Gardner, or saw him more often than I ever would. But it gave her a special kind of satisfaction for her to order me to do it. She was showing her power, now that Mumma was dead and she was the biggest Star of the Morning in Spring City.

I took a moment before I answered, let Nadine squirm. "All right, Sister Saul," I said. Saul was Nadine's Star name and she hated it. This is why I did not rise to the same position as my mother. I am too ornery. I have no social graces.

After that, the next time I saw Dr. Gardner walk past my school room, I went to the door and I called after him, "Hello, hello, hello," to get his attention. Maybe the three hellos were too much.

He turned, very surprised. "Hello?" he called back, just like that, a question. And then he raised his hat to me. When he spoke, I heard his accent. I already knew, from town gossip, that he was English, but his accent was still a surprise. Still, the way he stared at all of us, the way he gazed at our faces before sketching us down, I thought he couldn't have seen many colored people wherever he came from.

I invited him into the schoolroom and offered him a seat at one of the pupil's little desks and I sat down at another. He was so tiny, so unassuming, and then again, he was not American and so probably unfamiliar with how to correct the Negro impertinence of giving him the seat of a child.

Looking at him, at his bony knees pressed up against the underside of the wood desk, at his oversized hands with the nails bit down to the faintly bloody bed, he didn't seem like anyone's secret lover. That rumor about him and Julia Toneybee-Leroy had to be wrong. How could an heiress fall in love with this wisp, with his thinning hair and dirty shirt collar. Did we honestly believe she would import a population of apes as a noisy cover to allow her to conjugate with Dr. Gardner in peace? Dr. Gardner could never inspire something that florid. I could not imagine him conjugating. He was younger than me, I thought. He couldn't have been more than thirty. He looked even more virginal than I did.

But when he sat down, I sniffed the chimps on him, first thing. It was the most distinguishable thing about him. Here was this flute of a man in a jacket too big for him, with damp cuffs, wandering around, smelling of something so powerful it could not possibly have come from inside him. It had to be a borrowed scent.

As a Star of the Morning, I have been trained in the art of polite conversation, but I'd pretty much given that up. So I did not bother to coyly draw Dr. Gardner out. I wasn't afraid of him, either. I said sweetly, "Dr. Gardner, you are annoying my students."

"Oh. I didn't mean to." He drummed his fingers across the desktop and then glanced at me shrewdly. "How, exactly, am I doing that?"

"You follow them through the streets and hang around the school yard, taking their likenesses without their permission."

He blushed. "They're just sketches. For my own education."

"It makes them uneasy."

"I don't want to do that." He slumped in his chair like a scolded child. This was not what I expected, and made me, for just a minute, want to lord it over him. So I pressed. I said again, my voice sweet, "You make the girls self-conscious and you make the boys feel funny."

"That is not my intention. Please, tell them to pretend I'm not here."

"But it's very obvious when you are here, Dr. Gardner."

"Oh." He began to nervously peel the skin on his left thumb as if it were an onion.

"Well." He peeled some more, and the flesh reddened. "Well, what if I ask them to pose for me instead? If it makes them that uncomfortable. What if I arranged a formal drawing session, with your help?"

"Why would you want to do that?"

Dr. Gardner stopped peeling at his thumb.

"I am an anthropologist." He smiled widely. "That means I study people."

"I know what it means." I tried very hard to keep my voice light, but I was not successful because he blushed again.

"I'm sorry to presume that you didn't."

I sat back a little, surprised that a white person would understand my tone, surprised they would feel it enough to want to apologize. "Well, go on."

"I am an anthropologist and I enjoy studying all people. The people of Spring City are excellent specimens."

I kept my face blank.

"By 'specimens,' " Dr. Gardner continued, "I mean they are good examples —"

"I know what 'specimen' means as well," I said, a little darkly.

"If you are familiar with the science of anthropology, you can see why I would want to draw your students."

"Yes. And I can see why I shouldn't allow it. I don't want them ending up somewhere in some study, examples of Negro buffoonery, like you scientists like to do. I won't have them studied, if that's what you want to call it."

As I spoke, I flushed hot at the frankness of my words, but then, I told myself, it wouldn't matter. I expected Dr. Gardner to pretend not to know what I meant. I assumed he would do was what most white people would do in his position: save themselves the embarrassment and plead ignorance, force me to articulate. But instead, Dr. Gardner shook his head, almost impatiently.

"No. Not like that. Nothing like that at all. I understand your suspicion, but let me make it clear. I don't have any prejudice toward the Negro people. In fact," — here his voice rose, nasal and shockingly high, to near breaking — "I love the Negro people. I love them so much that I've devoted myself to making a study of them. Of you. Of your life and ways."

I sat back in my narrow little chair. "You are aware that's already been done?"

"Yes, by many very stupid men." He got me to laugh at this, so he pressed on. "They don't have the appreciation and respect that I do. They study you with some sort of secret agenda, with malice."

"You've never heard of Dr. Du Bois? He studies us with something other than malice. You've never seen his work for the Paris Exhibition?"

"Of course, of course. I'm a great admirer. I haven't seen the Paris studies, though. I've only read about them."

"You should see them." And then I did something I had not done in a long time, not since my parents died. I voluntarily told someone something about myself. I said, "I was in his original prints."

Dr. Gardner was very excited by this. "You were?"

"Yes. When I was a girl."

"Dr. Du Bois took your picture?" And he was so interested, so guileless in that moment, I nodded, very shyly and I told him about how all of Paris saw my picture as an Infant Star, although I didn't know it then.

Just after our Initiation, a man with a camera, one of those great black boxes, billowing with heavy dark curtains, that's how long ago it was, he came to Spring City. The man was the exact same color as the weak tea my mother served him in our parlor. He even sounded like a teapot when he spoke: the air whistled in between his front teeth on every third or fourth word. This was in 1898, when I was five. We knew that he was from the Berkshires, too; that he'd grown up just a few towns away. He told us it was his mission to take photographs of all distinguished Negro people across America — the first true record of our race in the brand new century to come. With Mumma's permission, he had all the

67

little Stars line up in our white dresses and he took our photograph in the field beside the church. And then he picked the three brightest Stars for a "study" — that's what he called it.

"You should learn to use that word," I told Dr. Gardner. "It makes everything sound official."

He laughed at that and said he might.

The weak-tea-colored man sat each one of us Infant Stars in a velvet chair and he took a close portrait, a three-quarter length, and then a full. And then he packed up his camera and was gone, off to the rest of the world.

The pictures returned to us three years later, in a red leather album. The front said in gold letters THE PARIS EXHIBITION, 1900. There were pictures from Georgia, from North Carolina, from all over the South. From Chicago and the Plains: all the notable Negroes of America, divided up and cataloged by region. We were in the Northern section. All of us Stars, and me myself, haloed in my solo portrait, we were all there as a grand representation of the glory and the flower of the Negro race. I wasn't named, but underneath my image Dr. Du Bois had placed the label "A stellar example of Northern Negro Lineage."

"I was a beautiful girl," I told Dr. Gardner, unembarrassed, and he had the good manners to not look shocked. When I was an Infant Star, there was no comparison. I really was beautiful enough to be included on a list of Negro Greats. It hasn't carried over into adulthood. My full cheeks have grown heavy and my eyes that were large and inviting as a girl now are just goggled and popped, their whites all bleary and yellow. My young skin was shiny and smooth but as soon as I entered adolescence it began to spot, and when my parents died, all the light went out of it completely. Now I've got a conspicuously dying front tooth, a distinct shade of gray, impossible to hide. I am not beautiful and I am sarcastic and I believe I am better than most in this town and that is why I am a thirty-six-year-old orphan with no husband and why no man in Spring City has ever even held my hand. The fact that my star name is Nymphadora has become a kind of perverse joke. The other women say it now with a lilt that betrays their amusement and it pricks my skin every time they do.

Of course, Mumma was very proud of my inclusion in Dr. Du Bois's work, but Pop was horrified. He never liked to brag. He was just as powerful in the Saturnites as

Mumma was in the Stars. The Saturnites are the Stars' brother organization. But you would never know how powerful Pop was to talk to him, and he only wielded his influence occasionally. When he saw the album page, at my image printed all alone and burnished with drawn-on curlicues he said, "Nothing good can come of this."

And he was right. All the other Stars, and even a few Saturnites, were furious and accused Mumma of favoritism, of telling Dr. Du Bois to give me a special place. But Mumma said the Stars were just jealous, that Dr. Du Bois recognized good breeding when he saw it. I guess you could say that picture was the start of my parents' downfall. Mumma, poor Mumma, was convinced I would grow into an even greater beauty and in anticipation of my imminent flowering, she began to buy me finer clothes and nicer hats and even a piano. And the waste of this is even more shocking because the girl in that photograph no longer exists. I am not a beauty anymore and certainly not a testament to the Negro race.

But as a child, I was just excited that a bunch of Parisians had seen my photograph. We were reading *A Tale of Two Cities* in school, and so I imagined some descendant of the unfortunate Dauphin, some secret

French prince, seeing my photograph in the Paris Exhibition and falling in love with me and searching throughout Massachusetts for me and finding me and marrying me and making me a Northern Negro princess.

"It was the greatest regret of my childhood that that didn't happen," I said.

And for a third time, Dr. Gardner surprised me. He genuinely laughed, not in disbelief like most white people would, but in appreciation of the joke.

Since my parents killed themselves, I don't count myself astonished by many things or many people. Dr. Gardner was my first surprise in a long time, and because of that, I felt a flash of affection for him.

Dr. Gardner sensed it and seized on it, pressed me further. "Let me sketch the children. Shouldn't they have a dream like that? My drawings won't end up in front of any Parisians, but they will make your students feel, for a moment, wholly unique and special and *looked at.*"

And he really did read me well because those were the exact words that would get me to say yes. I told him he could do it if he would agree to stop lurking around with his notebook, and he pretended to be offended by this, but he smiled, too, showed me the little gray pebbles of his teeth and I decided he was relatively harmless.

He sketched my students first in a group and then as they played, and really, they weren't as uneasy as I'd pretended they were. And I told Nadine Morton to humor him, and he would leave after that, so she persuaded the other Stars to let their children participate.

But the problem was that he kept coming back. Dr. Gardner was never satisfied with one sketch. He returned week after week, interrupting my class and, worst of all, recess. That was my one free hour of the day, when I took an old *Police Gazette* to the back of the classroom and read stories of murder in peace while discreetly sipping sherry out of a porcelain teacup.

It was odd. After my parents killed themselves, I developed a passion for crime stories, the bloodier the better. Pop used to keep a copy of the *Police Gazette* curled and hidden behind the till in our general store. Mumma hated it, called it vulgar, but it was the forbidden talisman of my childhood, glimpsed only occasionally, before it was snatched from my hands. Now that they were dead, I realized there was no one to stop me from reading the *Police Gazette* if I so chose.

If I am being honest, I like the girls in the

Police Gazette the best. Murder is interest-ing, but I save my copies so that I can study the girls again and again. The ones with the curls piled on their heads and the fat thighs crossed or tossed across the backs of divans. The ones with the cinched-in waists. The cover girls I like the best, not the girls on the inside pages. I like the way they hold their arms curved over their heads, and their backs arch. It makes their large bosoms rise up, this is certain, but I like it, too, because they are so vulnerable, so open. The very beating hearts of themselves are wide open to the world if the world would have them, if the world would only be clever enough to sift below the heavy, fleshy white rolls of décolletages.

Sometimes, if I've drunk too much sherry, if the day outside is cold and gray, I set down my teacup and fold up the paper and throw my own arms back like that, dangle them over the back of my little wooden school desk chair and toss my feet up on the scarred desktop, cross my own scant thighs. As I totter on my narrow seat and try to keep my balance, I know I am not nearly so reckless, so open, so brave as those women in the *Police Gazette.* I reckon I resemble more a hoary, staid starfish, show-ing my prickled and shellacked underside to the world, waiting to be poked so that I can curl all my arms back in defense and hide my tender underside again. I chalk it up to another luxury only white women have: to be that open and vulnerable to the world. If Mumma could see me, she'd slap me hot and fast for ever comparing myself, my good and beautiful and dutiful and clean Negro self, to white flesh. And she would be right and she would be wrong. Because I do not wish my own skin was white. What I envy is not their skin but their insouciance. I envy the freedom to sin with only a little bit of consequence, to commit one selfish act and not have it mean the downfall of my entire people. Where indecency and mischief do not mean annihilation. I envy that their capacity for love is already assumed, not set aside or presumed missing, like it is for us Negro women. That's what I wish that I had from those pictures.

My one small personal pleasure, though, my contemplation of the beautiful and courageous hussies of the *Police Gazette,* was ruined once Dr. Gardner showed up because the children were always coming in to complain, when they should be outside, hallooing and leaving me in peace. And the other Stars, of course, were furious with me and implied that I had misled them, because the drawings hadn't stopped and their children were annoyed.

Fed up, I went outside myself one afternoon and found Dr. Gardner again, crouched close to a game of jacks with that obnoxious sketch pad. I explained to him that I thought we had an agreement and he would leave after his pictures were done.

"But I can't," he bleated. "I haven't sketched nearly enough." He didn't bother to stand up or stop watching the game as we talked. He squatted in the dirt, his eyes intent on the dull flash of gunmetal in the dust.

I stood over him. "Sketch what you can today and then I am going to have to ask you to leave."

Of course, he did not have to do what I told him. He was a white man in the black part of town. The law was on his side and he could return as often as he liked. But that wouldn't have suited him. He wanted to be *liked,* you see. That was his weakness. He wanted us, all of us Negroes, to like and maybe even to love him. It's why the children grew uneasy around him. Dr. Gardner was too eager, too solicitous. When they barged into my quiet school room to complain, each and every one of them, "Miss Ellen, why can't that crazy white man just yell at us or leave us alone?"

"Please, Miss Jericho." Dr. Gardner was still in the dirt at my feet. "Please. Just let me draw the children a few more times."

"I can't allow it."

And here he turned cunning. Because he really did make a study of people, and I think, from our first conversation, he knew my weakness. "I'll leave if you let me draw you instead," he said.

Nobody ever thinks a plain old woman can be vain, but I agonize over my appearance. I spend hours in the mirror before class, my pin safely hidden away, attending to the wisps of hair that still stand up in graying licks, despite the hot comb. I wash and cream my face three times a day. I do this despite the fact my skin's been dull for years. Whatever extra money I have after paying my boardinghouse fee and paying the barbershop for its old *Police Gazette*s, I spend on very small bottles of sharp scent which I have the courage to wear no place, except on the occasion of going to bed early on a Friday evening.

So when Dr. Gardner said, "Let me draw you instead," I am ashamed to say I only slightly hesitated.

"I suppose I'll do it," I said. "If you really agree to leave my pupils alone."

"I swear I will." He stood up now, dusted his knees. "Come to my rooms tomorrow afternoon." When I hesitated he shook his head slightly. "The landlady will let you in."

"Then I definitely can't come. She'll spread it around the whole town and I'll lose my position."

"Then come when she's not at home, through the back way. By the road closest to the woods. We'll make sure no one sees you, I promise."

A Star shines because of self-denial. I thought of those women in the *Police Gazette*. I thought of my seven-year-old self, flower of the Northern Negro Race. I thought of the sweet surrender of knowingly making a mistake, and knowing, hoping, things would be fine despite it all. No Negro I'd ever heard of or met had ever done that. I thought of those cinched waists on newsprint, tossed into the fire when I was through with them, twisting up into annihilation.

"Yes," I said.

LAUREL

Laurel told her daughters that they were special. This was why the Toneybee Institute wanted them. "You know how many families applied to do this?" she said in the months leading up to the move. "So many. But ours was the only one with kids who already knew how to sign. I was the only one with girls that smart."

They knew how to sign because Laurel was special, too. She had grown up as the only black girl in the state of Maine. Or, if not technically the only one, then at least the only one in a one-hundred-mile radius. She always said it that way, too, a "one-hundred-mile radius," so that Callie and Charlotte imagined a large bull's-eye, its red rings hovering over the state's border-lines. The small dark circle at the rings' center was Laurel.

Laurel's father, Theodore Quincy, was a former serviceman. Her mother Nancy was a seamstress. Together they bought a Christmas tree farm in Farragut, Maine, because they liked its solitude.

They never explained to Laurel what awful noises of the world had driven them to choose the muteness of assimilation. Each morning, Nancy Quincy stood at her stove and stirred a pan of oatmeal. Theodore Quincy sat behind her at the kitchen table staring out through the window, cutting down every tree he saw with his eyes.

Theodore and Nancy had not counted on it being so hard, so very, very hard, to be the only black family in a one-hundred-mile radius. But it was too late to give up, once the place was bought and Laurel was born. To admit defeat would have broken what little heart they had left. Nancy and Theodore willed themselves to believe that this life was best for Laurel. At least she wasn't a hooligan. At least she wasn't running the streets of Boston. She had air and trees and an overpowering sky tamping down to meet her. That had to count for something.

"None of the white people ever said anything outright mean to us," Laurel lied to her daughters. By which she meant that she allowed herself to remember only once or twice when someone called her "nigger." She would never say that word out loud to her girls. "It wasn't like that," she explained. "It was just the opposite. They were always so polite. They were so polite it nearly killed me."

For Laurel, growing up in Farragut felt like the whole world was holding its breath around her. As she moved from her home to the road leading to school and back again, she entered a kind of airless delirium. Her favorite sound in the world was that of the soles of her own penny loafers scuffing on gravel as she walked to school. It was realer than the scrape of her mother's tin spoon in the pan of oatmeal at the stove or the click in the back of her father's throat as he lit imaginary fires behind his eyes and dreamed of burning pines. Whenever Laurel shuffled her loafers over the gravel, she shut her eyes and opened her mouth, tried to swallow that noise and keep it safe in the well of her neck. When the indifference of town overwhelmed her, she'd hum and hum until she brought back up the sound of her own shoes on gravel.

Once she reached town, the atmosphere was even tighter, like a lung suspended in motion. At school, the teachers spoke in loud, bright voices to try to draw her out but never named the thing that made her different.

On the playground, children screeched and ran and skipped, and Laurel sat beneath a pine tree and watched them. She rubbed a patch of sap between her fingers, and every time the stickiness pulled at the skin there, she closed her eyes in gratitude for the pain. Each stinging smack told her brain and her skin and her blood, "I am here, I exist, I am here."

It was in this climate of reticence — never being asked more than what was polite, never being spoken to first in public, always being courteously omitted, the eschewal of ever naming things outright — that Laurel grew to hate the failures of the spoken word.

By the time she was ten years old, she had had enough. She stopped speaking. She still talked at home, but out in the streets of Farragut, she wrote everything down on a notepad with a golf pencil she nicked from the bank. She wrote notes to the grocer; to her teachers; to the few classmates who directed conversation her way. She wrote notes to the wind and the trees and the stars — her companions — and she tore up the paper as soon as she was finished writing and dropped fistfuls of it around the farm, to ensure their delivery.

For a half year, she was solved. Her teachers gladly accepted her notes, relieved to have a bona fide reason to ignore her. They palmed the sheets of paper and trained their eyes to forget her for the rest of the day. Laurel moved silently through the school's hallways and the stream of calls and shouts and giggles ebbed and flowed around her. She felt proud, contained within herself, a smooth, perfect rock at the bottom of a river. Not a part of the current, it was sure, but not because she wasn't good enough to be counted as water but because she was made up of a different element entirely — she was silent and strong and adamantine stone. When she was mute, Laurel was finally happy. She'd bucked the spoken word.

It was Nancy who ruined it for her, who found a semester's worth of discarded notes in the bottom of a battered schoolbag, who marched Laurel to class and said to the teacher, her voice shaking to stay calm, "Why didn't you ask her to speak?" and the teacher, perplexed, "Because we thought this was better," and Nancy again, her voice nearly hoarse with the effort to stay cordial, to not show her anger, "Please treat her like everyone else. Teach her like everyone else. She needs to speak like everybody else. Please ask her to speak."

Nancy hustled Laurel out of the classroom

and into the cab of their pickup truck. Before she even put the key in the ignition, Nancy reached for Laurel's golf pencil and silently, efficiently, broke it down into splinters. She gathered all the pieces in her fist, rolled down her window and tossed them on to the curb.

"We've got enough problems out here," she told Laurel as she brushed the lead dust off her palms. "You don't want to make being peculiar one of them."

Being the only black family for a one-hundred-mile radius had one benefit. Laurel and her parents were famous. For nearly a decade running, the Quincys' tree farm was the only entry for the entire state of Maine in *The Colored Motorist's Guide to America*. They were, officially, the northernmost Negroes in the United States. Day-trippers from Boston, defiant honeymooners, bored servicemen on leave from the Navy Yard in Portsmouth, New Hampshire — they all came to the Quincy tree farm to gawk and take pictures. *The Colored Motorist's Guide* told them where they could and could not sleep, in what towns the citizens would shoot them if they stayed there after dark, and here, in a book that listed what was possible and what was not, was the impossible printed plain on a page: Negroes in Maine.

The summer Laurel was eleven, the Hallelujah School for the Colored Deaf found the tree farm. They came at the end of the season, in a white rusting school bus, with their name printed on the side in bright blue paint. The bus pulled up alongside the farmhouse's front gate and idled as about a dozen boys and girls pressed their faces to the windows and stared at Laurel where she played. She ignored them.

She was bored of tourists. They were black, but they spoke to her parents with a condescension Laurel felt in her bones, though she didn't have a word for it yet. "It's a living, I guess," they said, while drinking her parents' lemonade. And the kids who came with them, who hung over the sides of doors chewing gum and staring at the jagged ends of Laurel's hot-comb pressed hair, spoke too quickly, in a high pitch and with a force Laurel found bewildering. It was giddiness that made them talk like that, something Laurel had never heard before and so could not understand. Here was an even harder truth to live with: she couldn't trust any words, even when the people speaking them looked like her.

So Laurel pretended not to hear the bus's engine.

The bus door folded open and a woman

84

came down the stairs. She took the liberty of opening the Quincys' front gate herself, and she walked up to where Laurel sat in the grass drawing in her notebook. She was probably only about nineteen or twenty, but she seemed like an adult to Laurel. The woman wore a flowered skirt pressed into sharp pleats, but when she held out her hand Laurel could see faint stains on the armpits of her blouse.

The woman said: "You're the Quincys? You live here?"

Nancy came from the house and into the yard and shook the woman's hand. The woman said that her name was Mary Ann Grannum and she was a teacher at a colored school for the deaf in South Carolina. They paid for their classes by touring the country every summer in an acting troupe. Nancy asked, "How do the students give their lines?" and Mary Ann smiled. "We're special."

They came from a place that had been forgotten by time, a school founded to teach signing to the colored deaf, started right after the Civil War by well-meaning Yankees and quickly taken over by the colored citizens themselves. Over the years, when other deaf schools banished sign language, declared it backward and a threat to the wholesome spoken word, subscribed to the theory that sign language would encourage the deaf to marry only each other and create a perpetuating race of non-hearers, and swaddled the hands of their most defiant students in thick cotton mittens, the students at the Hallelujah School paid no heed to any of that and kept signing. They became a rarity: black children who could speak with their hands.

The Hallelujah School for the Colored Deaf's all-sign-language productions were famous in their home state, Mary Ann explained, and that summer was their first tour of the North. It ended in Portsmouth, New Hampshire, where there were still black faces in the audience. They were certain they wouldn't see anyone any farther. But then they read the entry in their *Colored Motorist's Guide* and so they'd decided to see the impossible before they headed back south.

Nancy led Mary Ann and her students around the farm, Laurel following from a few feet back, trying not to seem too interested. There were ten performers in the troupe, most younger than her, seven or eight years old, but there were a couple adolescents: a girl and a boy, both magnificent versions of fourteen who walked with such assurance, that Laurel, sulking behind them, was ashamed of her own steps.

Laurel had thought the deaf would be soundless, but these people weren't. Some made a careening sound as they walked. Mary Ann, the teacher, breathed in soft, heavy sighs through her mouth. Laurel liked the sound. The visitors had a queer scent, too, like a damp swath of canvas that had dried in grass.

The tour ended in the kitchen, in the mudroom where Mary Ann told her students, in spoken words, to stand in a line, and Nancy poured glasses of milk for each of them. The two teenagers, the boy and the girl, were the last to enter the kitchen, and as soon as they came through the door they got excited. They raised their hands eagerly, opened their eyes wide, and the boy made a high gasp. At the sound, Mary Ann turned, made a quick scan of the room, and gestured at the two of them. They lowered their hands, chastened.

Nancy frowned. "Is there something wrong?"

Mary Ann said, "It's nothing."

Nancy stopped pouring the milk.

"It's your washing machine."

"What about it?" The machine was an old hand-crank one, a heavy drum in the corner by the door, a wringer bolted to the top and a line of rust creeping up around its belly.

"We haven't washed our clothes since we left South Carolina," Mary Ann explained. The Laundromats along the way wouldn't let them. Or rather, they could put their clothes in the washer, but they were watched the whole time and more than once accused of breaking a machine. They had an iron in the back of the van for keeping their costumes neat, and so they used this, pressing their sweaty shirts and blouses into straight lines. That's why they smelled like burnt cloth.

Nancy said, "You're welcome to use it," but Mary Ann shook her head.

"We don't accept charity."

"Please, it wouldn't be that."

But Mary Ann was adamant. She kept saying, "We are not a charity. We don't take handouts." From her voice, it was impossible to tell the emotion. Only her frown told Laurel that she was angry.

Finally, Nancy asked her, "What if you give us something for it? What if you stay here for the night, eat dinner, wash the clothes, and you put on your show for us. My husband would like to meet you, I'm sure."

So Mary Ann and her students rigged up

a sheet between the two pine trees in the front yard. Laurel and her parents sat before it on their wooden kitchen chairs. Mary Ann placed a storm lantern behind the sheet, right at the center. Five of the Hallelujah players came out in front of the sheet, and five stayed behind it. They all held up their arms and then the play began. It was the story of Hagar, though Laurel didn't know it. The Quincys were not religious.

The teenaged girl, the very pretty one, played Hagar, and Mary Ann and the teenaged boy played Sarah and Abraham. Mary Ann curled her back into a crone's hunch. The boy wore a fake white beard. Another boy, younger, stood to the right and narrated the action with spoken words.

Young, beautiful Hagar, wrapped in white cloth, knelt on the ground.

Abraham, in a blue-and-white bathrobe, stood beside her. He reached into the folds of his coat and pulled out a baby doll, its porcelain skin splashed with brown paint. He said, "Ishmael," and behind him, his shadow spelled the name: the smallest finger held up straight, then a fist, then motions so fast that Laurel could not follow them, though she tried very hard.

Hagar took the doll from Abraham and held it in her arms and rocked it. She kissed the porcelain crown of its head while behind the sheet all five shadows held their arms up as high as they could. They touched their pointer fingers to their thumbs, spread the remaining fingers wide, circled their hands slowly over their heads. The narrator, standing in front of the sheet declared, "They had made a family."

Next, Sarah came forward. She crossed one crooked leg over the other and ominously circled Hagar and her baby. The narrator said: "Hagar fled from Sarah's face," and Hagar stood up, as if to run. Behind the sheet, the shadows stopped moving their hands. They twisted their legs up into trunks, their arms into branches, hung their heads, the better to be Hagar's wilderness.

Alone, in front of the white curtain, Hagar held her baby in her arms and first ran right, then ran left. She ran forward and stared out into the night, over Laurel's head. She beheld the black sky above her for one long, terrible moment and then she shut her eyes and dropped to her knees and called out, "Lord." Behind her, one of the trees unfurled into the shadow of a girl. The shadow threw out her arm, threw her thumb and forefinger into an L and in one long pull brought the letter from her heart to her hip.

A small boy in a white shirt and white

pants came from behind the sheet and went to Hagar where she knelt with her eyes closed. He was meant to be an angel. He took Hagar by the elbow and raised her up. He held up the baby and called, "I will make multitudes of him." The boy's voice was deep, as if he were already a man. He shouted: "God opened her eyes" — and Hagar obeyed. Then the boy said: "And she saw a well of water."

But by then, Laurel was hardly paying attention to the actors in front of the sheet. Instead, she watched the shadows behind it. Their hands made the words — made Hagar and her banishment, Hagar and the terrible wilderness — real. When the angel got to the last word of his speech, *water,* his shadow on the other side of the sheet stood against the bright white expanse and tapped three fingers to its chin.

Mary Ann and her charges wouldn't stay in the house. They slept in their bus. All night long Laurel watched from her bedroom window, afraid that it would drive away and take its secret with it in the night. The next morning, she was up early. She followed Mary Ann around as she and her students took down the sheet from the pine tree's branches.

She forced herself to speak. "How did you

learn to move your hands like that?" she asked. And Mary Ann said, "It's sign language."

A package came in the mail a month after they left. The emblem of the Hallelujah Colored School for the Deaf was printed on the envelope and it was addressed only to Laurel. Inside, a book. It was very old: a dictionary that had been printed in the previous century and had been held by many hands since.

All the Maine winters and springs and summers that followed, Laurel sat with a hand mirror in her lap and signed her ABCs to her reflection, until her fingers learned the rhythms. Her favorite sign was the letter *p*. It reminded her of sitting in the school yard under the pine tree, rubbing sap between two fingers, the stickiness of resin summoning her back into this world.

She was no longer adrift in Farragut, Maine. She had discovered a universe where silence wasn't cold and stony but warm and golden, where there was no need for speech. Signing was full. Signing made words important. It was beyond condescension or awkwardness or fear or loneliness. It wasn't avoidance or dismissal. It was, as far as Laurel was concerned, the perfect language.

It was lucky for Laurel that by the time

she graduated from high school, sign language was beginning its revival. She finally had others to sign to. She enrolled in a teachers' college to become a sign language interpreter.

College was the first time she tried to sign to another black person, her roommate, Dorothy Marshall. Dorothy watched Laurel's hands for a bit and then she laughed at Laurel for a long time before telling her she signed like a white girl. Laurel's eyes watered at the insult, but she decided, in the end, to be practical about it. No matter, she told herself, no matter. It was not as if she didn't understand division. Borders existed everywhere. It was silly to expect there would never be any. Growing up, Laurel decided, was learning to grudgingly respect the borders and even come to call them beautiful.

In honor of her lost Hallelujah Players, Laurel resolved to use black sign language whenever she could. "It was the seventies," she explained. But in truth, it wasn't as flippant as that. She fell in love with the black dialect's beauty: she loved the theatricality, the delicacy, the force of it. She came to believe that it was her charge to show this beauty to the rest of the world. When she left school, she made a pact with herself to always sign black. But when she applied for jobs at deaf schools, her potential employers shifted uncomfortably in their seats when they saw her sign and politely suggested she apply for assistant positions, not lead teachers.

She should have started signing white again, at least get a shot at the better jobs, but Laurel was stubborn. She truly believed that she could win people over to see her side of things. They only had to see black sign language, she was certain, to understand that it was special. She took the assistant positions, and when her daughters were born, she taught them to sign with the accent. But because she wouldn't sign standard, she was never promoted. She spent nearly fifteen years as a teacher's assistant.

So when Laurel first read the job announcement pinned to the bulletin board in her teachers' lounge at the deaf school where she worked, she took down the piece of curling fax paper and stuffed it in her purse so that none of her co-workers could apply. In the weeks that followed, she skipped work and drove for hours to the Toneybee Institute and schemed and charmed her way through the interviews.

Laurel never doubted that she loved Charlie. She loved him before she even met him. But it wasn't love that made her insist upon the innocence and beauty of Charlie and the experiment. It was her complete and utter exhaustion at being underestimated.

When she got to the Toneybee, for the first time in a long time, with the scientists and the lab assistants at least, Laurel signed white. But at night, when they were gone and it was just her, just her and Charlie, she signed with the drawl.

CHARLOTTE

That first night, Charlie gripped the front of my mother's nightgown and made those terrible noises and she clutched him back even tighter. She waved her one free arm at us. "Charles, girls, not now, go."

My father scrambled off the bed. He took Callie and me by our shoulders and hustled us out of the room. When we were safely over the threshold he halted, then turned and gently shut the door behind us, careful not to slam.

We huddled together in the hallway, none of us wanting to move. From the other side of the door, my mother's voice was pleading now. That was the scariest part. My mother did not beg for anything from anybody, but here was her voice now, warbling, "Please, love, please, love, please."

Suddenly Charlie stopped. There was no noise at all, not even a groan of defeat.

After a moment, my father began walking

us to our rooms.

Callie took his hand. "There's nothing wrong with Charlie, right? Like, he's not sick or something?"

"Probably not."

"Will he do this every night?"

My father said he didn't know.

When I was alone in my bedroom, I couldn't lie down. I opened the window, stuck my hands out into the deep night air, and wagged them at the dead countryside. If I squinted, I could see the woods through the dark.

I listened for any sound. I would have preferred the sounds of Dorchester — a creaking floor, the dirty sigh of a city bus's exhaust pipe, the scattered footfall of a neighbor stumbling home, an ambulance's siren, the heavy husk of Callie breathing — I'd rather have any of that than this nothingness.

I leaned farther out the window and looked up. All summer long, as we got ready for the move, my father told me about the constellations I would see when we lived in the countryside.

"I see stars in Boston all the time," I countered.

"Nah," he said. "You're just seeing satellites."

Now, I wanted to see the shapes in the stars: the bear, the scorpion, the crab, and the lion. But when I looked above me, all the stars were tangled. They didn't make any forms or symbols — they were meaningless and mute. But the earth and the trees and the water below me were not. All in a rush, the night broke and I heard waves from some water, somewhere, burping up against a shore. I heard the rancid woods creaking. And then suddenly, the rise of a bass cry, some animal caught up in its own dreams.

I slammed my window shut, not caring anymore about the heat. I turned on the overhead light and then I lay in bed, absolutely still, until I heard a click click click, and the room sputtered into darkness. I sat up in bed with a start, even more terrified, and the lights sprang back on. The Toneybee had our bedroom lights on a motion sensor, a way to save money. I lay back down, tried to calm my breathing but the lights went out before I quieted. I held my hands up above my head and frantically signed nonsense into the air until the light clicked back on. I did this over and over again, waited for the timer to run out, then furiously called the lights back. My arms tired. I had exhausted myself. I could fall

asleep to the snapping sound of the Toneybee Institute's economy.

Nobody wanted Charlie. Not at first. He
came into this world unasked for, a problem
to be solved.

He was the result of an unplanned preg-
nancy in the lab. His mother was a loud,
nosy, gap-toothed teenaged chimp named
Denise. She was supposed to be on the Pill.
All the girl chimps at the lab were — it was
standard policy. But Charlie's will to exist
was stronger than progestogen, and so Denise managed, somehow, to conceive him
despite the grubby patch of hormones stuck
to her hairy side. None of the researchers
even suspected Denise was pregnant. They
noticed she was irritable sometimes, and
that her middle was swollen, but they
chalked that up to a rough adolescence.
Charlie's father was a mystery: there were
two or three older chimps sniffing around
Denise for a bit, pushing at her shoulders
and backing her into corners before the
researchers could shoo them away. Dr.
Paulsen and her assistants never got close
to figuring out who exactly was the culprit.
Charlie was a fatherless child.

No one at the Toneybee noticed Denise
was pregnant until the day Charlie was

born. It was on a summer morning, and some of the chimps were allowed into the yard for outdoor observation. Denise usually spent her time outside good-naturedly bullying her friends, but this particular day, she abruptly left off swatting at a younger girl chimp, turned on her heel, and staggered over to a shaded corner in the pen — the farthest one from the observation deck. Once, twice, she rocked back and forth on her heels, and then clumsily squatted down into the dirt. She sat like that, low on her haunches, for the rest of the afternoon, only moving to stay in the shade, following it, inch by inch, as it drifted across the yard. Dr. Paulsen and her team watched her all day, tracking her inertia. She bared her teeth and screamed at anyone or anything that came near. Even the other chimps left her alone. Confused and brave Denise was determined to give birth alone.

Late in the day, just past dusk, as abruptly as she sat down, Denise reached between her legs and pulled up something damp and dark and strange and tucked over. She rested the thing beside her in the dust. She stayed close to it for a little while, occasionally prodding it with one knobby finger. But when it was dark, when all the other chimps had been coaxed back inside and she was all alone in the yard, Denise put her palms on the ground and pushed herself up. She staggered back, then forth. She was still very weak, the hair on her thighs and ankles matted down with dried wet and blood and dirt. She swayed once more. Then she grunted, turned her head, and strode away, leaving Charlie down in the dirt, never once glancing back.

It wasn't Denise's fault that she left Charlie behind. She wasn't callous by nature. It was only that she had been hand-reared. She was raised by humans, so never knew her mother's touch. She didn't know what to do with a baby.

After that first night of crying, my mother told Callie and me this story in a hushed and hurried tone, as if she was betraying some trust with Charlie. When she finished, she stood up, her face chastened and sad, and left us to go back to him. As soon as she was gone, I turned to Callie and pressed the fat tip of my tongue against the inside of my cheek until a round little bulb popped out there.

What's that? Callie signed.

"Knocked up," I told her. "It means dumb kids get pregnant." Another dirty sign learned at summer camp and put to good use. We began to laugh but when my mother came back in the room, Charlie on her hip, neither one of us could bring ourselves to tease him to his face. He seemed too fragile for that. There was something about the set of his shoulders, if he didn't know you were watching he would kind of slump them forward, already wary of the world, preparing himself for defeat.

It was true what my mother said about him. He was beautiful. Large, deep-set eyes, well-formed teeth, perfectly circular nostrils. But his chin was weak and recessive, and his eyes, as well formed as they were, as soft and full as his lashes grew, his eyes never lit on anything for long. He was too nervous to look anything in the eye.

Our first afternoon with Charlie, we sat with him in front of a standing mirror. My mother propped it up longways against one of Charlie's bare walls. She and Callie and Charlie rolled a red ball back and forth among the three of them until my mother rolled the ball away from Charlie, toward the reflection. He followed. She picked up the ball and tapped it against the glass. She put her own finger to the mirror, then touched the center of her chest and signed *Mother.* Then she handed the ball to Callie, who tapped it on the floor in front of her,

102

then to her own reflection, and signed *Callie*. Callie rolled the ball to Charlie again. My mother touched Charlie's chest very gently with the rubber ball, then touched it to his reflection in the mirror. The first few times they did this, she signed his name, too, *Charlie*. On the final round, though, and I don't know why she did, she didn't sign *Charlie*. She signed *chimp* instead.

As soon as she was finished, Charlie looked down at the ball in his own lap, then up at the reflection of the chimp with the red ball in his lap. He didn't make a sound, just stared for a few moments at the face in the mirror. His eyes flitted for a second to Callie, to my mother, both of whom were nodding, holding out their hands for him to roll the ball back. Charlie glanced again at his reflection and then he drew his little bullet head deep into his neck, hunched his shoulders, raised his fists — and my mother, on instinct, lunged quicker, lunged faster, held him back before he could beat up his own shrieking reflection.

It was worse than his scream that first night. That one was unbearable because it was so sad. This one was angry. He tore and scratched at my mother's arms. His lips drew back so that we could see his yellowing teeth and black gums. If he'd wanted to, he could have bitten my mother, gashed her good. But he didn't. Instead, his eyes still fixed on his reflection, he raised his hands to his own face and scratched at the skin there until he drew red. He calmed down when he saw that, stopped thrashing in my mother's arms, sucked some of her shirt's cloth in between his lips, gathered what he could of her between his teeth and held it there, trying to calm himself.

My mother rocked him back and forth and Callie was crying and I was standing up, I was at the door, I was calling for my father, for help.

Max came first, then Dr. Paulsen, dry tongue clacking, green-gloved hands plucking at the fake pocket square at the front of her blazer, ready to wipe Charlie's spit and tears off my mother's face.

At dinner that night, my mother insisted she was fine. She squared her shoulders when my father pointed to the damp spot on the front of her shirt. She tried to recount the story as if it was a joke — "He just didn't recognize himself, poor thing" — but her voice shook as she spoke.

"Were you scared?" my father asked Callie. "It's okay to be scared."

Callie wouldn't answer. "What's going to happen to Charlie?" she asked.

He was not with us at dinner. He had been taken to some unknown part of the institute. "They gave him a sedative," my mother said carefully.

"Having to spend a night on sleeping pills with Dr. Paulsen is punishment enough for what he did."

My mother shot me a look.

"This is Charlie adjusting to us and his surroundings," she began to say, but my father shook his head.

"Enough."

"I'm telling you Charles," she started again, "it was the mirror that did it. We'll take the mirrors out and he'll be fine. He must have thought it was another chimp in there, playing with us."

But that's not what happened. I'd watched in the mirror, the light in Charlie's eyes change. I didn't tell my mother. She would have said I was projecting, that it was impossible. But after that I became even warier of him. Callie and I stayed away from my mother and Charlie during the day, and Max and Dr. Paulsen came back to their posts in Charlie's bedroom. My mother doubled down on her efforts to love him. She carried him on her hip or in her arms, and when he grew too heavy for her, she put him down but always held his hand in hers. "He only has to get used to us," she said. "Then he'll be better."

NYMPHADORA OF SPRING CITY, 1929

Dr. Gardner officially lived at the Toneybee Institute with the apes and his army of assistants and the heiress Julia Toneybee-Leroy. But he'd taken rooms near the border of Spring City for his anthropological study. They were just a block or two from the train tracks that made up the border of Spring City and white Courtland County, in a tall, rickety wood-frame house whose back let out on a creek and a scruff of woods.

To get to Dr. Gardner's rooms, I had to walk first outside of town, then circle back into the woods and through the underbrush, and then, heaving from all that effort, sweating with anxiety, crouch in the rooming house garden while he made sure his landlady was out, and that no one from Spring City, and no white person from Courtland County, was around.

When he was certain it was safe, he came

down near the little bit of woods and stuck his hand through the branches to take my own sweaty one and led me very politely up to his room, as if I were coming in from the street like a proper visitor. But once I was inside, he turned and locked the door.

I started at that. He said, "I can leave it open."

"I would prefer it if you did." I pulled my bag closer to my chest. Why I even brought a handbag on this errand, I did not know. It was empty anyway.

"It's just, if my landlady returns, she could walk in at any moment and interrupt and then you'd be discovered."

He was cunning, that Dr. Gardner. I saw his point. I let him keep the bolt across the door.

"What will we do if she comes?"

"You'll jump out the window." He smiled with those stony teeth, but I did not, so he closed his mouth. "No," he said. "I'll tell her I'm indisposed, that will get her away very quickly, and then I'll go down first and keep her occupied and you can leave through the back door. I can just talk to her about the weather and she'll listen as if I'm reciting great news. She says she loves my accent, that it's very distinguished."

His room was actually quite large, nearly

the whole length of the house. There wasn't a bed, only a low couch and an easel, and near the window, but not in front of it — he was that careful — he'd taken the trouble to set up a tray with a saucepan of steaming water. "I couldn't get a teapot," he said sheepishly. He had a dish filled with pale-colored cookies that looked far too expensive for him.

"Those aren't from Spring City." I was fishing for information, but I didn't have to press hard because he told me straightaway that Julia Toneybee-Leroy — "Julia," he called her, not Miss Toneybee-Leroy — had them shipped to the institute from London and allowed him to take as many boxes from her pantry as he liked.

I took one cookie, then a second, then a third. Dr. Gardner didn't eat or drink anything. Instead, he began talking to me about musculature.

Did I know that an adult male chimpanzee had the strength of five grown men?

No, I did not.

Did I know that chimps had distinct calls, as far as he could tell, detailing their love of nature and their love for their companions, danger and fear and apprehension, and even a cry so keen and piercing that Dr. Gardner and his staff had only been able to describe it as "homesickness," and though this explanation delighted Miss Julia Toneybee-Leroy, it embarrassed him because it was so unscientific.

He meant this as a joke, of course, so I laughed. "What are you doing up there with those apes, anyway?"

"Julia thinks they can talk."

I laughed again. "I may not be a fine evolutionary mind like you, Dr. Gardner, but I know talking apes are impossible."

"Don't be so certain." He pulled at the cuffs of his sleeves until they were down closer to his wrists.

"They can't really talk."

"But Julia thinks they can. That's why she hired me. To prove her right."

"I don't believe it." I was annoyed that he was trying to trick me.

"You don't have to. It doesn't change the fact that I was hired, and have a staff and nurses and a cook, all to prove that chimpanzees can learn to speak a human language."

"But you're supposed to be a genius."

He flashed all those yellowing teeth again. "Who told you that?"

"It's all anyone over there in Courtland County says about you."

"Think of that. I'm a genius."

"But even if you are not," I said, impatient, "aren't you worried people are going to think you're a fool when they learn what you're studying? You have to have had better career prospects than proving a rich girl's fantasies correct."

"How do you know I don't believe they can talk?"

"You're smiling too much when you talk about it. And I'm not an idiot."

"Well." He sat back in his chair and closed his eyes halfway. "The truth is, she pays me a lot of money." Even though he blushed slightly and his tone made it sound like another joke, I could tell that he was proud.

"But aren't you worried about your scientific reputation?"

"I'm young," Dr. Gardner said, his eyes still half closed.

He sounded so smug and satisfied, so full of promise that I wanted to reach out and pinch those blushing eyelids till they opened stark and wide.

"Besides," he said, "My real work, my real name, won't be made here. I'm very lucky she asked me to do it. What I wish to study, what will make me famous, I am able to investigate at the same time I do this work for Julia. Courtland County and Spring City are so perfectly aligned with my study. And the apes. They just make my study so much better. A controlled population, you see."

I understood him in a flash. I thought of all those sketches of my students, running and jumping and playing with mouths wide and the sweet in my mouth turned to ash.

"Is that why you're so intent on sketching us, then? You're going to compare us to your chimpanzees?"

"No." Dr. Gardner sat up straight now. He sang, sincere. "I've told you before. I love the Negro people with all my heart. Since I was young, I've been fascinated by your vitality and culture and —"

"I feel sick." I put my fourth cookie back on the plate.

"Please," Dr. Gardner said, "let me be direct. You have to believe me. I wish nothing but good for American Negroes and I believe my studies can right great wrongs done by science. I can provide a service to you. I can speak to your greatness, just like your Dr. Du Bois. I just need to find the right collaborator."

I eyed the dead bolt on the door, and Dr. Gardner followed my gaze. He said, sadly, "Please eat another cookie." When I didn't move, he leaned across the table and began pouring me a cup of tea.

"Do you know, some scientists still think

our musculature is different from yours? They say Caucasian skulls and bones are different. But they're not. Not at all. There has been no unbiased biological study done of the American Negro, by one trained to study human beings. At least, I don't think there has. And as I've told you, the citizens of Spring City are excellent specimens."

"We are people, Dr. Gardner, not specimens. If you're going to profess to love us so much, you should learn to use the correct term."

He sat back. I was certain he would start with his nervous twitches again after this reprimand, but his thumbs and shirt cuffs rested in peace, unmolested.

"I call everyone a specimen. It's not meant to be an insult. Julia Toneybee-Leroy is a specimen, just as my assistants are specimens, just as the oldest chimp in the colony is a specimen, just as I am a specimen and you are, too."

He leaned forward here, in his seat. "What I propose to you, Miss Jericho, is that you work with me to create a proper monument to the American Negro race. A very good study. Like what you were asked to do for Dr. Du Bois. I think we understand each other well. We already laugh together. This tells me we can work together."

"It tells you I'm being polite."

"See?" He was excited now. "See? You wouldn't make that joke with any other white person. We're already comfortable together! I think I can trust you to work with me, to realize something great."

Mumma had always warned against being fresh, of course, of even joking slightly with white people. "They can't tell when we are fooling," she'd scolded. "They take everything we say so serious." But here, with Dr. Gardner, I was beginning to think that maybe Mumma was wrong.

"So you want to sketch my portrait?"

"Of a kind." And here he did not hesitate anymore. He took a deep breath. "In the past, the science of racial prejudice and ignorance thrived because of biased and inaccurate readings of specimens. What is necessary is an unbiased, clear-eyed measurement of the American Negro's frame. I hope, with you, I can start this process."

"Well, where do you want me to sit?"

"I would rather you disrobe and lie on the floor," he said, quick as a flash.

At this, I stood up and walked toward the door.

"Please, please, don't misunderstand. One of the many ways my people have done your people injustice is because we insist that you are built for exploitation. That your behinds and stomachs and backs and brains are somehow destined for it. I need, I absolutely need, a specimen —"

I put my hand on the dead bolt.

"Fine, fine, a *person* like yourself to prove this wrong. When I have drawn your body as it actually is, I shall also divulge your history. That you're a chaste and respectable and intelligent woman. That you're a schoolteacher and a wit. That none of these things are written on your body. Or rather, they are there, if people care to see —" Here, he got excited, caught up in some internal argument.

I still pulled at the door. He saw, and he made his final push.

Dr. Gardner told me that he would use the sketches to advance the cause of my people, of Negroes everywhere, but as he spoke, all I could think was, My people killed my parents. And I realized if I was being honest, I haven't cared about the cause of my people since Pop and Mumma died. I don't care about their future.

To be fair, Mumma and Pop poured the cups themselves; they were the ones who drank. But it was my people, with their grasping and jealousy and desperation for morsels of an always-better life that drove my parents to do it. And now it does not matter that I am a grown-up Star. I realized, as he babbled on and on about the majesty of sable hues, that it does not matter if I lie on my stomach and show Dr. Gardner my ass, even though he claims it's all for science. None of that matters at all, because Mumma and Pop are dead. The sun is just a ball of light and nothing really matters anymore, so Dr. Gardner can do what he likes and my people can burn in hell.

To be a Star of the Morning means you put your faith in the potential of things to come. You believe in a bright shining future for the Negro Race. You believe in promise. You speak only in terms of faith. There is no past when you are a Star of the Morning, only the infinite future of goodness and justice and fairness and light, sweeping out before you.

I thought of this future goodness, this future greatness. And I thought of the women in the *Police Gazette,* unburdened by history or expectations, only quivering, present flesh suspended in a lithograph. All that freedom. "You will be seen," he promised. To be seen was better, I felt it in my bones: it was better than self-denial, better than shining like a Star.

There was a screen in the far corner of his

room. It was dark green silk and printed with tumorous flowers. I walked behind the screen and counted the flowers as I unbuttoned my dress and stepped out of my skirt, imagining, as I bumped up against them, that they could rub off the old silk and on to my skin, covering me, at least a bit. I have spent hours standing on my bed frame, studying myself in the dresser mirror in my rented room. I have come to the conclusion that despite my face, my flesh is good, and wished many times that someone else could confirm it. Drawers off, last of all. I pinched my hips and my middle and then I thought, You are in it now, Nymphadora. You cannot turn back, and I walked from behind the screen and over to where Dr. Gardner stood. I looked him in the eye the whole time and to his credit, he held my gaze.

"Just . . . lie down there," he said, "and make yourself comfortable." I looked to where he pointed, but I didn't get down. Dr. Gardner kept his eyes on my face. "It *is* awkward, isn't it?"

I nodded.

"It should be like this . . ." And he got down on his knees and then slid onto his stomach and grinned up at me like an idiot, until I laughed again, because he really did seem ridiculous and I felt what I thought was that freedom. It was a joke between us, a good grand joke, and he was smart enough to get it.

I got down on the floor.

He sat on the floor as well and took up his sketch pad and began to talk about England. It turned out he was not the son of some Baronet or industrial captain, like I had imagined. In England, he was poor. He told me, "Any Englishman can tell by some slips in my accent, but here in America it just sounds refined." Dr. Gardner was smart and studied hard and won a scholarship to a public school, but he was poor, and he apparently had never forgotten it.

As I lay on his floor, the front of me pressed into the rough planks, the back of me up in the air, he told me he spent every afternoon of his childhood in nearly the same position: on his stomach, lying on his bedroom floor, reading a set of children's encyclopedias. They were castoffs from the family his mother cleaned for. That other, richer family had long since outgrown them.

He read each volume through at least five times before he was sent off to school. He liked them all, but he was drawn to "A," because in its frontispiece was an engraving of the Great Chain of Being. He would study it again and again. The Great Chain of Being was drawn as a kind of staircase, each organism on earth assigned its proper step. "I would lick my finger," Dr. Gardner told me, "and trace what I thought were the bones of the world."

He followed earth to air, flesh to spirit, from mineral to plant to animal to man to the angels. "In the subset reserved for people, the spindly feet of the staircase went from Negroes, to white women, to white boys, and then men: each accompanied by a small cameo representing their perfect form, their progression of being precisely illustrated from lowest to highest."

Here, he glanced up from his sketch pad. "Stay still please, Miss Jericho. Would you like a cushion to rest your head on?"

I said I would. He got up from his seat and tossed me a very thin pillow. I placed it under my head. It smelled like horse sweat, but I appreciated the gesture. I adjusted myself again, and he was quiet for a bit.

"Why did you like the Great Chain of Being so much?"

"I didn't *like* it. It made me nervous. All those steps, one, two, three. I used to have a three-legged cat and I would wonder where he fit on the chain, if he was inferior or superior. In my heart, I knew he was as good as an angel, but according to the chain

119

he was below my ma and dad. And that didn't seem right."

"That's very observant of you." I couldn't keep the sarcasm from my voice, but this seemed to delight Dr. Gardner further. It seemed he liked to be teased.

He stopped talking for a bit, leaned over the edge of the pad of paper to look closer at me. I wanted to blush; in fact, I believe my behind did blush because the skin on it suddenly felt very warm, but Dr. Gardner was good enough not to say anything about it.

Instead he said, "I worked hard and when I left my place in primary, my teachers recommended me as a scholarship student to a good secondary school and when I got there, I was relieved that no one mentioned the Great Chain of Being. When someone finally did, it was my teacher, Mr. Townes. And he only mentioned it to say it wasn't proven by science. He said it was more of a metaphor. It took me a long time to under-stand what he meant. At the time, I thought he was agreeing with me, that the ideas that lead to the creation of the chain weren't real, that they were false beliefs. But I learned that he actually meant the opposite. He meant that the chain, to him, was more real than any science."

Mr. Townes taught Dr. Gardner and his fellow students the fashionable evolutionary theories of neoteny. Little Dr. Gardner learned that white men alone retained the intelligence and imagination endowed to children's brains well into adulthood; that women and coloreds bloomed too quickly into a stupefying maturation, a runny adolescence and old age that spoiled their intelligence and clouded their sense of reason.

"That seemed wrong, too," Dr. Gardner explained. "But everyone went along with it. You were supposed to be able to tell maturity by measuring earlobes, if you can believe it."

"Earlobes?" I turned my head on the pillow.

"Yes," he said. "We were separated off into pairs and we had to measure our own earlobes and our friends'. Except nobody wanted to pair with me because they knew I was a charity case. Mr. Townes ended up pairing me with a boy named Jessop, who protested, saying, 'Why are we measuring his ears, anyway?' Meaning me. Jessop said, 'He's low class. He's going to have women's earlobes or, worse, a black's.'

"And Mr. Townes told us, very gravely, 'Gardner's all right, Jessop. He's not *that* kind of low class. He's as evolved as you and me.' "

I heard the pencil stop scricking for a moment, then the heavy, dull rub of the eraser across the page. "Ah, hell," Dr. Gardner exclaimed suddenly. "I've ruined it."

I took the opportunity to get out of my pose. I sat up and wrapped my arms around myself. "What's wrong?"

"I can't capture the angles correctly. From where I am. I can't get the curve right at all. It's coming out all wrong. I keep ruining it." He looked down at the paper, frustrated.

"Don't get so upset," I said. "What angle do you need to make it better?"

He kept looking at the paper angrily. "I don't want to impose."

"You are already imposing."

The tip of his pencil wavered over the paper.

"Could I sit a little closer?" he said. "Just . . . to see the lines better."

I felt my whole skin prick with apprehension. "I suppose."

He inched a little closer to me. He crossed his legs and settled the sketch on his lap and generally seemed much happier. I trundled back over to my spot on the floor, glanced down at the planks for a moment trying to remember exactly where my knees and elbows had been. Then I sighed, told myself it didn't matter, and lay myself down, my cheek back on that horsey pillow.

"So, you liked Mr. Townes?" I said, after a bit, trying to get used to him being so close, urging him back to his story. "He defended you?"

"No." The pen went scrick scrick scrick busily over the paper. "I hated Mr. Townes. I suppose he thought he was giving me the utmost compliment, telling that idiot Jessop that I was really one of them. But right then and there, I wished for the shortest earlobes imaginable, shorter than a lady's, shorter than a black's if that was possible, if it meant I could get that smug smile off that dumb prat's face. I didn't ever want to be considered good enough to be one of whatever he was.

"I know it sounds silly now. But it was the first flash of feeling I ever had. I knew in my heart that Mr. Townes was wrong, just like the Great Chain of Being was wrong, but since all of what he said was printed in a book I thought it must be true. I was convinced my heart was wrong and this made me uncertain. Ashamed, actually. So it was a kind of freedom to find out that it wasn't my heart that was wrong. Knowledge could be untrue."

One more long, satisfied scrick and Dr. Gardner stopped for a moment, entirely pleased with himself and the results.

"You can sit up now, Miss Jericho."

I sat on my knees and crossed my hands demurely in my lap, but it didn't matter because Dr. Gardner wasn't studying me anymore. He was looking at the drawing, and I could tell by the set of his mouth he was quite pleased with it.

"May I see?"

He looked up then. "No," he said. "I'm sorry Miss Jericho, but I can't allow it. Self-consciousness would spoil these drawings. Just absolutely ruin them. I can't have that." Then he began to busy himself with putting his pencils away.

I got up then and moved back behind the silk screen with flowers.

I pulled on my slip and the sack dress Nadine Morton had given me secondhand, then the bloomers that reached to my knee, gray with so many washings, and all that cloth was cold on my skin and then I felt something sick and sad come over me.

Nymphadora, I said to myself, through tears, you are a selfish little Star. You've known this since you were a child, sitting in that church cellar, sucking on your tongue and dreaming of greens dressed with bacon fat instead of abnegation. As much as you wished to please your mother with self-denial, as much as you begrudge her and Pop for lacking it, you know you don't have it in you, either. It's not part of your constitution. Any light you had in you that made you a Star, was because you were simply reflecting Mumma's shine. Nymphadora Jericho, you are petty and weak, and with every fiber of your being, in every piece of your overexposed flesh, in every rotten bit of your heart, you've just knocked out whatever light was put in you.

I had lain naked on my stomach and only listened to his stories, and made up louche and sarcastic replies. One of the most important things Mumma drilled into me was never to let a white person think that they knew you. In Spring City, Mumma and Pop and all the other Stars and Saturnites were planets, possessing deep and mysterious seas, complicated deserts, forests of knowledge and pain. But step across the border into Courtland County and they were little more than rocks, pebbles really, to the white people that lived there. Small and insignificant, without the weight or density to command even the smallest orbit. Mumma told me that this underestimation was an advantage. It meant you could do things white people would never even know about. Your invisibility was your power.

I give it up, I almost said out loud to myself. I realized, through my shame that I *wanted* to be seen by Dr. Gardner. I wanted it very much, and that made my disgrace worse. Giddily, I began to argue against my shame. I told myself that I was in his sketchbook now. I was no longer invisible to Dr. Gardner or to any of the white people who would see his studies. Mumma was wrong. I was seen, and, I thought, I knew I flattered myself, but I thought it anyway, that I would finally be known for my true self, my self that wasn't pure but still was equal to any Star of the Morning, any married woman, any white person, anyone who believed themselves better than me. And still, a part of me was enough my mother's daughter to know I was being a fool. And for that particular kind of foolishness, I could never be forgiven. Who cares? Who cares? I thought.

I knelt and showed my ass for Dr. Gardner, and I knew I would do it again. But I was planning to do worse than that. An ass is just an ass. I was less ashamed of the drawings of my behind than the fact that I wanted to tell Dr. Gardner my true history. I longed that he should know every fault and failing, know when I cried and when I raged and when I just sat dumb. I wanted Dr. Gardner to know my very worst self.

When I came out from behind the screen, I saw he had slid himself back into his seat at the tea table. He noticed my expression and immediately made his own soft to match it. He patted the handle of the pan of water.

"It's lukewarm by now. But have one more cup of tea with me?"

And even though I knew he only said it to be kind or, rather, to make sure there was no awkwardness between us, to take away any whiff of a whorish transaction, I accepted the offer. See, I told myself, as I drank, we are equals. Almost.

"So you must understand," Dr. Gardner said suddenly, as if we had been talking the whole time, "I know what it means to be misclassified. For the very *system* of classification to be so utterly wrong and backward and unfair. That day in class, when Mr. Townes defended my earlobes and said they were as good as any others, I knew he was full of it, the school was full of it, and it led me to question so much more.

"Sometimes it feels like I am always in revolt against my own kind. I am always in revolution against what people who look like

127

me think. It used to make me sad and very lonely. But there's a joy that comes in constant revolt. It becomes a comfort. And I am glad to betray my own kind when their motives are so false. Why are you crying? Did I upset you?"

But I couldn't answer. I could only double over, feel my clothes warming to my skin, and the tears on my face. Dr. Gardner pushed the plate of cookies under my nose. It was all he could think to do and to make him less embarrassed I took one and managed a bite. He reached out a rough and well-chewed hand to pat my shoulder, but I only felt it distantly. I was overcome with the taste of snot and salt and refined sugar in my mouth.

CHARLOTTE

We tried hard to make the Toneybee ours. Callie and I left the apartment every morning, skirting past the portrait of Julia Toneybee-Leroy, giving a joking salute to Daisy's bones. Downstairs, we scribbled halfhearted graffiti in obscure places, tucked wads of chewing gum under windowsills, made a point of running up and down every hallway as loudly as possible, if only to impress on the still bulk of the institute that we were there.

But that was impossible. There was just too much space. The downstairs rooms were already set aside for official business; the apartment belonged to our mother and Charlie. The front hall was Lester Potter's domain — he sat in its shabby gloom, only leaving to keep sweaty lookout in the overheated guard box. Every two hours, from 9 a.m. to 5 p.m., we heard the faint whine of the golf cart he used to patrol the grounds, as he made his truncated orbit from the front hall to the front gate and back again.

The very top floor of the Toneybee Institute was a warren of old rehearsal rooms. Callie and I found the back staircase that led up there. We tried to be quiet the first few mornings, but very quickly gave that up once we figured out nobody cared about the attic.

The doors to the rehearsal rooms were haphazardly shut off, a few pieces of plywood nailed across them. We forced the flimsy planks off and rummaged through the spoils we found behind them: dead and dying instruments; reams of old musical scores; brocade and lace left in piles to rot. Each room had the vinegary odor of old resin, sticky brown on the ragged split ends of limp violin bows. We forced ourselves to stay up there until the backs of our necks were slick with sweat. We found five brass pipes — the mute ends of some dead organ, the metal beginning to spot with age — scattered across the floor of one of the rooms. We screamed into the ends of them until our throats were hoarse. We found a whole orchestra's percussion section. Callie pried metal slabs off the xylophones and threw them against the wall while I heaved a balding timpani onto its side. When I got it turned over, I tore a slit in the drum skin with the foot of a music stand. I convinced Callie to wiggle through it and lie in the bowl and then I pulled the slit closed and beat on the skin with a nearby mallet until she fell out of the drum's belly, laughing, bruises on her forearms.

When we were bored and bruised enough, we'd come back downstairs in time for lunch in the staff cafeteria. Dr. Paulsen joined us. Her yellow tongue flicking back and forth, she told us all of Charlie's sorrows. Max, beside her, looked pained but didn't interrupt.

For the first year of his life, Charlie was raised by the Toneybee researchers. They tried to teach him sign language. He showed an interest in the beginning. He watched curiously whenever someone began to move their hands. Every two weeks, a different lab assistant fed and bathed and dressed him. "But so many people caring for him," Dr. Paulsen said, "it got too confusing." Some put his socks on the wrong feet. Most forgot that he hated bananas and tried to feed them to him. Often, they grew bored when he simpered and cried out to be petted through the night.

"He didn't like anyone," Max said.

"Max is being modest," Dr. Paulsen countered. "Charlie only likes him. He'd do anything for Max. Max can get him to wear overalls, to sign *doll*. Max even trims his ear hair. He learned the first initial of Max's name, didn't he?"

Max nodded. "When he was smaller, he'd lie on my lap and press the letter *M* into my arms. He was sweet. He used to just grin and grin, he was so happy."

"But he has a temper," Dr. Paulsen said. Charlie was prone to shrieking bursts of annoyance. "We could never figure out what would set him off. When he's very, very mad, he won't sign to us at all. He balls his hands up into fists and tries to sit on them."

"You should understand," Dr. Paulsen continued, "Charlie is used to a lot of attention, but he doesn't know love. He's learned a very cruel lesson. And now he thinks that it doesn't matter how often he kisses someone's neck or how lovingly he grooms you, or how well he performs or how sweetly he nestles into you. He thinks — and why wouldn't he when he's never seen otherwise — he thinks that everyone, every last person, will always leave him."

The table was quiet as we took this in. Callie swallowed.

"But," Dr. Paulsen said excitedly. "That's why you girls are so important." She glanced at Max. "We've been working for so long at the Toneybee Institute, for nearly seventy years, to understand how much a chimp can communicate. And we can't do our work if one of our own is lonely or in pain."

"Why can't you keep raising him?" I asked.

Dr. Paulsen's eyes shone. "We need a family like yours." Her tongue darted across her lips. "To make him feel loved.

"Imagine," Dr. Paulsen continued, "a chimp who truly felt like he was part of a human family. Who could tease you and love you like a brother — that would be a very interesting chimp indeed. And with a real live family, Charlie can prove not only that chimps can learn sign language, and understand the signs for *blue* and *book* and *ball,* but he can understand something else, too. He can know love," she finished, the words so earnest they stung.

She likes families, I signed under the table, into Callie's arm, *because she doesn't have one.*

Lunch in the cafeteria became unbearable. Our mother sometimes joined us, but more often she ate with Charlie in the apartment. Our father preferred to read or prepare for classes, rarely eating lunch at all. But Callie and I were popular in the cafeteria. We felt

133

the eyes of the research assistants and the secretaries on us as we moved with our trays, as we sat at our table, as we ate our food. Dr. Paulsen sometimes came to sit with us, but every day Max and a different assistant joined us for lunch. They asked us the same questions over and over again: What were our favorite subjects in school? Did we like to read? What were our favorite books?

Nothing would stop the flood of small talk. Whatever answers we gave, Max and the other assistant would glance at each other as if we had said something important but it was unclear what profound thing we were saying to them. Callie told them once her favorite book was *The Phantom Tollbooth,* and Max and the assistant with him, a chubby woman named Ronnie, had nodded gravely at this answer. Every question they asked, though, seemed like a buildup to something they would really prefer to know. It was as if they were avoiding a larger question and they always lost their nerves before they would get to it. Back home in Dorchester, we had been proudly obscure and I was beginning to miss it.

"It's like they want something from us," I told my mother.

"What do you mean?"

We were at dinner, the one time when we all came back together. Charlie sat at the head of the table. Before she served herself, my mother painstakingly divided the largest cut of meat into bite-sized pieces for him. When she turned her attention to her own plate, every bite of food she raised to her mouth went through Charlie's fingers first, ground down and kneaded and knuckled and sniffed, thoroughly investigated before Charlie would allow it to pass between her lips.

Charlie raised a handful of smashed macaroni up to my mother's mouth and I looked away.

"It's like they're watching us for something," I said. "Like they want us to say something different."

"They're curious about you because you are in the experiment. This is new for them. They're just excited."

"But what do they *want* from us?"

My mother sighed. *I don't know, Charlotte,* she signed. Then she said, "We should talk to Dr. Paulsen about it, you and I."

"How could that possibly help?"

My mother said, "I'll talk to her."

Charlie struck the table with his spoon, and my mother turned to him.

Max said he would take us to the Toneybee's lake. My father had been asking him about it, and so he offered to walk us all there — me, Callie, my father, and Charlie.

I stood in my bedroom, pulling at the straps of the previous summer's bathing suit.

Callie sat on the floor, watching me.

"You never swim anymore, anyway," she said.

"I might."

I hadn't unpacked all my clothes yet and I knelt on the floor, searching through a duffel bag for a T-shirt long enough to reach my knees.

"You won't."

I stood up. *Leave,* I signed.

Callie began shifting through the rest of my moving boxes as if she would discover something new there, as if she didn't know all of my belongings already. It didn't matter to her what she wore — bright green overalls and a two-piece bathing suit, with Minnie Mouse's head on the chest, her little girl stomach pouting over the waistband. She strummed her fingers across her paunch in an upbeat rhythm, unashamed, stopping every so often to reach into her overalls and hitch her bathing suit bottom over the fat on her hips.

"You're too old for Minnie Mouse," I told her.

"I don't care," she said, but she crossed her arms over the face on her chest.

She took a prism paperweight out of a box, held it up to her left eye, and pointed it at my bedroom window. She made sure to flash the light from the glass in my face, tracking me around the room, annoying me until Max and Charlie joined us.

Charlie wanted to touch everything: my books, the clothes in the duffel bag, the ragged cardboard flaps on the moving boxes. He stretched his hand out at the flash from the prism in Callie's hand. Callie shook the light at him until he opened his mouth wide and a dry, husking sound came out.

"What's that?" I asked, alarmed he would start crying.

Max said proudly, "He's laughing."

I had a bunch of old cutouts from *National Geographic* pinned to the wall — maps of the world. While I sifted through a pile of oversized sweatshirts, Max walked Charlie to each map. He took him past the Americas, Antarctica, Asia. He stopped in front of each and signed its title to Charlie.

"He can't understand countries," Callie told him.

"I know," Max replied. "But it's good for him to understand that there's a word for everything."

When Max got to *Africa,* he opened his palm wide, spread his fingers over an imaginary hump, and then clamped them shut into a fist.

Callie gasped. I began laughing.

"What is it?" Max said.

"Max," I sputtered.

"What is it?"

"What was that?"

"What do you mean?" He started to make the sign again. "It's *Africa.*"

"No!" Callie shrieked, eyes sliding from me to Max, unsure whether to laugh or to be afraid. "Don't do that!"

"Who told you that's Africa?" I said.

"The last ASL tutor here."

Callie decided to laugh.

"It's not?" Max hesitated. "She was wrong?"

"No, it's not," I said primly.

"Africa is this." Callie curled her fist into the sign for the letter *A,* circled her face, and touched her thumb to her nose, flattening the tip.

138

"Aw, Callie," Max stuttered, and he began to turn red. "Don't do that. Please don't do that."

"Why?" She kept her hand to her face.

"Because it's racist." He looked up at both of us now.

I laughed harder. "It is not."

"It is. Look, you're touching your own nose for Africa. You're pointing to your own nose and you're making it flat . . ." Here he hiccoughed, glanced once again to the ground, then up and rushed through the rest, forcing himself to meet my eye. "And some people, a long time ago, used to believe that all Africans had, you know, a flat nose and that it was inferior."

Callie pressed her thumb down hard and wheezed out, "A flat nose is inferior."

"Oh, Jesus," Max groaned. "That's not what I meant."

"Well, your sign is wrong," I crowed, triumphant. "This" — I copied his first gesture, making the hump — "means something dirty."

"What are you talking about?"

"It doesn't mean 'Africa,' " I said. "It means . . ." I lost my will for a moment. But then I looked at Max, his eyes wide and skeptical, and I gained it back again. "It means 'tits,' " I said, and had the satisfaction of seeing him finally look away.

Callie gasped. "Charlotte!"

Max was even redder now, but he was not going to admit defeat. Instead he said, carefully, to the floor, "Who told you that?"

"They showed us at camp last summer." No one had actually shown me. A couple of older boys had pointed at my swelling T-shirt and made the sign and I figured it out from there.

Max shook his head. "Well. I guess we both have a lot to learn."

"How do you not know that?" Callie began to laugh again.

Max turned his face to Charlie. He was going to overlook us.

"It's not his fault," I told Callie, loud enough so he could hear. "Don't be mean. Max only knows white-people sign language."

Max stiffened but didn't respond. He wouldn't play with us. He was just going to let my insult hang out in the air, till the juice dripped out if it, till it dried out and curled in and broke up into dust.

"Girls," my father called from the hallway, "Max, are we ready to go?"

Max rubbed Charlie's back. "We're ready," he answered, and stalked out of the room.

Callie stood up to follow. Before she left the room, she turned and gave me a cool once over.

"Your bathing suit is stretching funny." She signed *Africa* at my chest, across the boobs.

Callie and I followed my father, Max, and Charlie down our back wooden staircase, into the big baroque hallway. We went through a last set of heavy double doors and then we were outside. Across a balding lawn, there was a short run with barbed-wire fencing strung along its sides. The fencing scrambled down to a pond with a small island in the middle and a motorboat lying belly up in some weeds on the shore. There was a deep gauge in the soil, hardened into stiff mud, from dragging the boat back and forth.

"The chimps like to swim?" my father asked.

"No, they hate water," Max explained. "It's terrible getting them into the boat, but they love it once they're across and on the island."

I walked over to the boat. The shoreline was just patches of brittle grass, blistered with dirt. The water shined bright from far away, but up close it was a dull brown. And the current was off. It didn't ebb back and forth like a normal pond — it churned in little circles.

I pointed. "Why's it doing that?"

"That's the pump," Max said. "It's a man-made pond. Miss Toneybee-Leroy had it put in a long time ago, back in the fifties I think."

I spread out my towel. Even on the driest piece of grass, the mud bled fast through the terry cloth, stained the front of my T-shirt brown.

Callie ignored the mud. She surged into the water until it came up to her knees. My father followed. Max stood beside my towel for a little while, watching them. Charlie clung to his neck, a wary look on his face. Callie suddenly turned in the water, rushed toward my father, and with one heavy push swooped a wave of water at him, laughing. Charlie flinched.

"He's nervous," I said.

Max glanced down at him. "We could walk him around a bit to distract him."

"All right."

Charlie wouldn't let Max stand him on the ground, so he rode on his hip instead. We started walking toward the woods.

"You know, Charlotte," Max began. "I really am sorry."

"For what?"

"Just . . . everything. The way we've started, I guess."

"You shouldn't be sorry. I'm the jerk."

We were on a lesser used footpath, the trees and bushes overgrown, and Max held back some branches so that I could pass.

"See?" I said. "You can't even deny it. So don't say you're sorry."

He laughed.

"I don't think you're a jerk."

"You're just being polite."

Charlie began to fidget, reaching for the leaves we passed. "Do you like it here?" Max began again.

"You always ask us that."

"Everyone here just wants you and Callie to feel comfortable."

"Well, I'm comfortable."

"I've known you long enough to know that's a lie."

"You wouldn't want to hear the truth."

"Yes, I would."

"It would make Dr. Paulsen cry."

Max smiled and I smiled back.

"She *would* cry," I continued. "She'd choke on the chalk in her pocket."

Max laughed again. "Nothing gets past you."

Despite myself, I flushed at the compliment.

"I think I can handle it, though."

"Fine." I stopped on the path. "You want to know what I think? I've never seen so many white people in one place in my life." I scanned his face for his reaction. I wanted him to wince, but he didn't. Instead he nodded.

"I suppose that's strange."

"It is." I waited some more.

"Well, we're all happy you're here, you know."

"You all just stare at us. At me and Callie. It's weird sometimes. And everyone asks too many questions."

Again, he nodded. I had confirmed something for him.

"I hope you don't think I'm one of the ones who ask too many questions."

"You're the worst of all."

He laughed and turned to walk back to the pond.

I followed. As I walked behind them, Charlie shifted on Max's hip. Dr. Paulsen had warned us not to hold his gaze for long, that he would take this as a threat, so I only met his eyes for only a moment and then focused on watching Max's back, the shift of his shirt as he carried Charlie up the hill. But Charlie kept angling his head to catch my eye, and when he did, he would grin when I turned away, taking pleasure in his dominance.

Max murmured something low to Charlie, something that sounded like "calm down." Then he called to me, "You don't have to play with him if you don't want to."

But I was stubborn. Charlie sought my gaze and every time, despite my annoyance, I submitted, I lowered my eyes and then looked back up at him. I didn't like the patterns of this game, but I wouldn't break them. I kept going, to Charlie's squirming delight — a grudging act of kindness, not given willingly, not given happily, certainly not given with love, only defiance. *You don't know me,* I signed to the space between Max's shoulders. *I can be good. I can be better.*

CHARLOTTE

I wasn't sure if I could still smell it. Through the cloud of diesel and old chewing gum and cracked leather seats in the very back of the school bus, I thought I could still faintly smell Charlie's urine on the cuffs of my sweater. It was under a layer of synthetic lilies, courtesy of the half bottle of detergent my mother poured over the shirt, but still, I thought it was there. I leaned my head against the bus window, scanned the road up ahead for signs that we were getting closer to Courtland County High School.

The night before, I'd carefully chosen my new school clothes — a polka-dot blouse and stretch stirrup pants and a white hair scrunchie — and laid them out on my bed. I had scrutinized every part of the outfit, weighing one against the other, hoping they might equal up to something that could be read as good. My mother, Charlie always with her, came to inspect the final choice and as she pressed her hands against the seat of the pants, testing to see if they were too sheer, Charlie unhooked his leg from her side and a stream of piss dribbled from the corner of his diaper and down over my outfit.

"Oh, Charlotte, oh honey, I'm sorry."

My mother was full of contrition, but Charlie didn't care. He only watched her calmly as she knelt and gathered up my clothes and doused them with the detergent and then perfume and then finally sprayed them all down with air freshener. In the morning, I sniffed the damp sleeves and breathed in the ruin and I would have worn something else, but there was my mother, asking hopefully, "How is it?" and I pulled the shirt over my head.

"It's not bad. I can still wear it."

She sighed, relieved.

I was the only student on the bus so I was not able to tell if the stink was real or part of my imagination. I was not sure yet if it was going to spoil the only good thing about moving to the Toneybee Institute. Here, in Courtland County, I had the benefit of being unknown. Back home in Dorchester, I had been with the same kids since kindergarten and they all remembered me as the know-it-all who got uppity and insulted everyone in a secret language she spoke with her hands. At the start of eighth grade, some of the other girls spread a rumor that my signing was not to be trusted. They said it wasn't much different from what Jamal German did when he looked you in the eyes and rubbed on himself in public. After that, every time I lifted my hands to sign, the girls all turned away. They squealed to each other, "Ooh, she nasty." They didn't even bother to say it to me.

In Courtland County, I would be new. And I thought, for sure, that I would be the only black girl. I decided this would be an advantage. These kids had probably never even seen a black person before. There would be no other real black people to compare me to, only the ones on TV. And every television sitcom I had ever watched had told me that black kids were infinitely cooler than their white counterparts and that white kids knew this. I'd never had white classmates, but I took these plots as an article of faith. Back home, I only learned what was cool by listening to others' conversations. Here, I reasoned, those scraps of intelligence could be worked into a social genius. They wouldn't know I was a mess. My clothes would seem up to date in the Berkshires, not horribly out of fashion. My hollow brass door-knocker earrings strained my earlobes and knocked against my neck as the bus jerked. But I had to believe that out here, in this wilderness of whiteness, everything I wore would stand in stark relief, become urbane sophistication, the trump card of biologically ordained, racially innate coolness.

But Charlie's accident. I sat in the very back of the bus. I had claimed the seat of rebellion, but at each stop made, no one sat next to me. A few boys would start toward it, ready to claim the last seat for themselves, but when they saw me sitting there they stopped halfway down the row, slid into the first free bench, their eyes skidding over me. They couldn't possibly catch it from that far away. I kept my forehead pressed to the glass of the window, the grease from my braids making a gauzy halo on the pane.

The leather of my bus seat creaked. A girl eased in beside me. She was grasping a stack of books to the front of her faded purple fleece jacket. Tortoiseshell glasses were perched on top of her head like a crown and she had a silver canteen in her hand. When she unscrewed it, I smelled fresh coffee. I was instantly impressed. Back in Dorchester, nobody was that adult. Even the bad kids, the ones who dragged on cigarettes before class, even those kids only drank hot chocolate.

The girl dumped her books on the expanse of seat between us. She gave me a guarded smile. "You're new."

"Yeah,"

"I'm Melissa. You live in Spring City," she declared.

"No," I said, confused. "I live here, in Courtland County."

"Where?"

I didn't want to say the Toneybee Institute. I vaguely pointed to my left, toward the highway underbrush dashing beside us. "Back there."

"It's okay if you're from Spring City. I volunteered there this summer at the food bank. I'd much rather be from there than boring Courtland County."

"I'm from Boston," I said.

"But didn't you just say you live in Courtland County?"

"Yeah, I do. Now."

Melissa studied me over the lip of her canteen. She took in the earrings, the scrunchie, the front of my shirt. She swallowed her coffee. "Okay," she said.

She thought I was lying and what was worse, for some mysterious reason, she had decided she should humor me.

She sat her canteen down between us and opened a book. I turned toward the window and pretended to write her off.

Boys were always easier to figure out. Whenever I spoke, their eyes opened wide, as if I had pulled down the collar of my T-shirt and my nipples sprouted mouths that spit my words out for me.

The boys looked at you like they knew something about you, but you knew they didn't, not really. They only thought they did, and though their stares were unsettling, there was nothing to actually be afraid of in them. What they thought they knew about you wasn't real, was some story they made up behind their eyes, easily guessed at, predictable, and ordinary, as mysterious and complex as the plot of a Road Runner cartoon.

It was always the girls who were different. Melissa's expression was the same as the girls' in Dorchester. Their heavy-lidded eyes would light first on their friends' faces, then on the better-looking boys', then quickly to the front of my chest. Their mouths would harden, register something mysterious in the upturned curl of a lip. The Dorchester girls sucked their teeth — one long thin whine of displeasure — tossed their heads, and then their gaze flitted away again.

I wanted more than anything to know what they were thinking. I knew that, for just a moment, I had entered their consciousness, but how and where I entered I could not tell. They looked at you like they knew a secret about you that you didn't even know yourself yet. Like they'd picked up some scent that you didn't know you carried, emanating from some sincere and deeply embarrassing gland, secreted away in an obscure fold of your skin, pushing out an unfiltered, humiliating stink that bloomed with rude honesty, announcing the precise condition of your very self.

Courtland County High School was like a tidy office park. It was a slate building, all sharp angles and darkened windows. The lawns out front were the same oppressive green as the woods around the Toneybee. The grass was immaculate: not a single stray potato-chip packet, not even a muddied footprint near the sidewalk border.

Inside, things were just as officious. It was especially odd to have a locker to myself, and even stranger that the lock worked, was not angrily bent over on itself by some unknown fist.

In homeroom, the teacher, Mr. Carroll, made me stand up in front of everybody and introduce myself.

"Charlotte Freeman." I began to sit back down.

"And you're from Spring City?"

Half crouching in the desk I turned to the class at large. "No," I announced. "Courtland County."

Mr. Carroll frowned down at the list in front of him, checking up to make sure I wasn't lying. When he bobbed his head I saw he had a little ponytail curling at the nape of his neck. The sheet must have had my address listed because he looked up again eagerly.

"Oh yes," he said. "I've heard all about you." He raised his voice, "Everybody, please listen carefully."

The room became only slightly quieter.

Mr. Carroll announced, "Charlotte lives at the Toneybee Institute. Charlotte, tell the class."

The faces nearest me were bored. The kids farthest from me still weren't paying attention. I said to the shifting, coughing mass of them, "I moved here from Boston last month. I live in the Toneybee Institute because my parents work there."

"On something very interesting," Mr. Carroll prompted.

"Yes."

He waved his hands. "What is it?"

"What's what?"

"What is it your family is working on?"

"We're living there and my mom is teaching sign language." I sat down with a bump of finality.

"To whom?"

"What?"

"To whom are you teaching sign language?" Mr. Carroll was smiling knowingly now.

"To a lot of different kinds of people." Each word sounded much sharper than I wished it to be. The room was paying attention now — a few of the girls looked expectantly at the two of us.

Mr. Carroll tipped his head back until the tip of his pigtail grazed his collar. "That's enough, Charlotte." Then he turned to the blackboard and started writing.

My palms pricked with shame. I thought I was going to cry. I'd never been openly rude to a teacher like that before. I told myself that this was perhaps the start of being better — the triumphant denial of authority. But when the bell rang and I stood up, nobody would meet my eye.

The next class was biology, with a Ms. Simpson, who asked me no questions when she read my name from her roster. I started to take the lab station at the front of the class, but I stopped myself, moved one seat back. I didn't want to seem too eager. The room filled up, some kids three or four to a lab table, but the seat beside me remained empty.

We were fifteen minutes into class when one more student walked in. To my dismay, I saw that she was black.

"Adia Breitling," Ms. Simpson declared, "is late."

Adia mumbled her apologies, slinked toward the lab benches. She didn't choose to sit next to me. Instead she took the empty space in front of me. She dropped her canvas tote bag down and spilled her books and papers across the table and bent her head over the mess she'd created.

I studied the back of Adia Breitling's head and I prayed that none of these white people would compare her to me. Her scalp was shaved into a boy's fade, with two quick lightning bolts nicked above her left ear. Ms. Simpson had a stack of handouts for the class and gave them all to Adia, to start the round. Adia turned to pass the stack to me and I saw her face fully for the first time. She'd kept a crop of close-knit curls just above the center of her forehead. I also saw that her face was beautiful. High cheekbones; full lips; wide-set, hooded eyes. Even

Adia Breitling would not look directly at me.

She turned back around. The purple feather earrings she wore brushed her shoulders. Even for the Berkshires, these had to be out of style. I touched my own brass bamboo bangles. She hunched over and I studied the back of her baggy black T-shirt: a long list of cities with dates beside them and the name of a band, Living Colour, stenciled over the top. She had a long, patchwork jean skirt that stopped right above the steel toes on a pair of violet Doc Martens. The whole class, I read the length of Adia Breitling, from the curling ankh to the flop of that heavy skirt, and I thought that I knew her. I knew, at least, why she was alone in biology lab. To be that beautiful and also that willfully strange did not make sense. It was certainly unfair, almost an insult, I thought. Either way, it meant I could never be friends with her. I was determined to leave strangeness behind at the Toneybee.

Adia turned my way when the bell rang, lifted her heavy eyelids, and pointedly read me over. She took in my too bright hair elastic, my white tennis shoes, and the pin straight braids that ran orderly down my back with the one bit of hair left free at the front. That morning, I'd pressed that scrap of hair around a pink foam curler, forming it into a stiff, fat egg roll to match the bangs that white girls wore on TV. Adia did not take the brass bamboo earrings into account and narrowed her eyes at the bangs. She saw the eagerness in my disguise and she thought she knew me, too.

When she finished her appraisal, she raised her eyes to meet mine. I pointedly gazed ahead of her. I didn't want her to get the idea that we should be friends just because we were both black.

As I walked through the halls to my next class, I felt the sinking stone of loneliness. In Boston, at least, my unpopularity had been accompanied by a running commentary of jibes and sharp observations. The other girls called me bougie, would loudly critique my clothing, cataloging every uneven hemline and accidental spot of food. But Courtland County felt worse. Nobody outright tormented me, and this was the problem. The most I got were glances made up of equal parts pity, curiosity, and indifference. I didn't matter enough to be called out.

I saw my father in the hallway up ahead. He was talking to a group of four older boys, two of them were much taller than he.

They were trading jokes back and forth: one of the shorter boys would say something and then glance quickly up at my father's face to see if he laughed. Sometimes he did. He wasn't paying them much attention, only steadily scanning the hall as people walked past. I ducked into the bathroom before I was spotted.

Inside the bathroom, the facade of Courtland County High School broke. Scraps of toilet paper littered the floor, piled into great heaps, as if some bird-boned freshman, harried with the task of making a nest, had savaged every roll in every stall, collecting the softest bits for herself. The bathrooms in Dorchester weren't this dirty — but then, we weren't allowed toilet paper. When you had to use the bathroom there, you had to ask a teacher for four squares, which she would begrudgingly give you from a drawer in her desk.

I went to the biggest stall, the handicapped one, and I locked the door behind me. The schedule on the inside of my binder said I had English next, but I already knew I wasn't going. There was no place to sit in the stall except the toilet, so I took down my pants and sat on the cold ring. I rested my chin on my hands and studied my leggings where they lay in a tangle at my feet. I stretched my shirt over my bare knees and hunted for the stain Charlie pissed into it. Even in the flickering fluorescent light of the bathroom, I could make out a dark patch at the front.

Maybe, I thought, I should become tougher to get the girls here to like me. I would have to get better at swearing out loud. Abandon the signs. The girls back in Dorchester had a way of swearing that sounded like music. Obscenities made them more girly. They'd say five dirty words really fast, so fast you almost missed them, and then hold out one really filthy syllable as long as possible, making it sing. "You dumbass, motherfucking, deaf dumb bitch," they'd sometimes say to me, and that last word, even with its lone, hard, bitter syllable, sounded like the top note of a love song.

My behind was getting cold. I corrected myself in my head: my *ass* was getting cold. I circled my ankles first one way, then the other. Very low, I was sure it was under my breath, I started chanting the words to a Bell Biv DeVoe song. I'd never heard the song myself, but all the girls in Dorchester quoted it with a fervor that boarded on the religious. Around them, sometimes it seemed that everything that happened in

159

the world could be interpreted through the lyrics of "Do Me!" I tapped out a stuttering beat on the fat of my thighs and chanted, far, far off rhythm: "The time was six o'clock on the back porch, No time to kill, can't be late, got a date, whoooaa . . ." This last part I sang into my cupped hands, trying to hear a little echo. Before I could finish the verse, another girl's voice called, "Hello?"

I cradled my knees to my chest, scrabbled with my pants still hanging low to the ground. I balanced on my hip bones and gathered all the fabric up so that all of me was hunched in an awkward U, no part of me visible from under the stall door.

"I heard you." The voice was coming from right in front of my stall. I looked down and saw a pair of purple Doc Martens squarely pointing at me. The door rattled.

"I know you're in there," Adia said.

I held my breath and squeezed my eyes shut. It did not seem fair that I'd spent the entire day mostly invisible only to be discovered now.

I could hear her panting. It echoed off the tile.

She wasn't going to rush the door. In Dorchester, she would have rushed the door by now. But this girl maybe didn't have the nerve.

"If you're gonna be like that . . ." She left the threat unfinished.

My arms were beginning to shake with the strain of holding up my legs. I slid on the toilet seat again. I thought I had won.

But then I watched, with alarm, the skirt above the Doc Martens begin to pool on the floor, then the black T-shirt came into view, then the unsmiling, beautifully somber face of Adia Breitling, who craned her head beneath the bathroom door to gaze up at me, huddled with my pants down on the toilet. She didn't even smirk. She only said, her voice hushed and serious, "You got the words wrong."

"What?" I tottered uncomfortably, too startled to lower my legs.

"The words to the song. You messed them up. You did a mondegreen."

I lowered my feet. "What's that?"

Adia put her hands on her knees and sighed. She stood up, so I could only see her shoes again. "It's when you mess up the words of a lyric, like you just did." She said it with such disdain, I felt a flash of shame for misremembering the words of Bell Biv DeVoe.

She stayed beside the stall door for a few

moments, as if waiting for me to apologize. When I didn't, she sighed, and then I saw her purple Doc Martens shuffle away. When I was sure I was alone I pulled my pants up and flushed the toilet, just to hear the water in the bowl clap over my shameful exit.

In the cafeteria, there she was again, sitting alone at a table, watching the door for my entrance, staring me down as I made my way through the lunch line. The empty seat in front of her was a challenge. I took my tray and walked straight toward her, holding her gaze the whole time. She sat up a little straighter as I approached, but when I put down the tray and pulled out the seat, she hunched herself over until she was almost lying on the table and cast her eyes down to the sketchbook in front of her, began circling huge, sprawling curlicues across the blank page. I ignored her and began to eat.

Adia gouged at her sketchbook with the broad side of a thick pencil until she sat up suddenly, sucked on her thumb, and began rubbing at her drawing.

To the paper she said, "You smell like a zoo."

"Excuse me?"

She kept rubbing steadily. "You heard me. Like the zoo does when you get too close to

162

the animals. Nobody's told you that be-fore?"

I bit into my hamburger. I chewed very, very slowly, my eyes stinging the whole time. My mother always made us count: thirty-six chews, to make sure we digested correctly. Charlie, of course, couldn't be taught to chew thirty-six times.

Thirty-three, thirty-four, thirty-five, thirty-six. I swallowed. I took a long sip from my carton of milk. Adia smirked. She knew I was stalling. I swallowed and sat my empty carton on my tray.

"That's rude." I crushed the empty milk carton. "It's not my fault I smell like a zoo. It was an accident."

"You smell like a zoo by accident?"

"Yeah."

Adia scratched at her notebook some more. I moved on to the limp salad on my tray. I looked up and Adia looked back down at her paper. I pierced a tomato with my fork, brought it to my mouth, sucked in its sour seeds.

Adia shut her notebook, hunched herself even farther forward. She rested her chin on her elbows, fixing me with a hard stare.

"You're from Spring City."

"No," I said. "Why do people keep asking that? Isn't this Courtland County High

163

School? Wouldn't that mean everyone is from Courtland County?"

"No," Adia explained patiently. "All the black kids here live in Spring City. They get bused in. Well, the good ones get bused in. All the white kids live in Courtland County."

"But there were white kids on my bus today."

"Those were the poor kids. They take the bus. Them and the black kids."

"So you take the bus?"

"No," Adia said. "I live in Courtland County." She was so definitive that it seemed impossible to challenge her earlier logic that only white people lived there.

She closed her notebook. "What type of music do you like?"

The test. Always the test. Invariably, I failed it. I would flail around, naming anyone and everyone who had ever graced the cover of my father's *Jet* magazine: the Commodores, Roberta Flack, Richie Havens — each one somehow wrong. Or I would accidently name the artist who was secretly white. "Whitney Houston!" was shrieked back at me, in disbelief.

I cleared my throat. "I don't really listen to music."

"You don't listen to music?" Adia made

that sound worse than a mondegreen.

Annoyed at her, annoyed at myself, I pointed to the front of her T-shirt. "I changed my mind. I like Living Colour."

Adia looked down at the band logo on her chest, looked up at me. "Nah," she snorted. "That's funny." She allowed herself a real smile. "What do you like?"

Adia was so beautiful when she smiled that, despite her hostility, it made me want to please her. But I had no good answer. I sighed, resigned myself to the snorts of laughter.

"Prince, I guess."

Adia narrowed her eyes slightly, but she nodded, let it slide. She was working up to her real question. She barked, "What did you mean when you said smelling like a zoo was an accident?"

"You heard me." I grinned now. I knew I had her. It was about the wrong thing, but it was the first spark of curiosity I'd gotten from anybody my own age all day. "An accident."

The bell rang. We walked side by side to the trash can. She shoved her garbage in first, then turned on her heel and abruptly walked away. I walked quickly in the opposite direction. I didn't want it to look like she was the one leaving me behind.

■ ■ ■ ■

"I have one teacher. Her name is Miss Lowry and she made me talk about Charlie." Callie took a swig of her fruit punch. My mother sat beside her, signing everything Callie said in Charlie's direction. She'd asked us each to recount our first day of school to the dinner table.

Callie sat down her glass. She had a faint red sugar mustache across her upper lip. She took a deep breath. "So I told them all about Charlie and how he's a chimpanzee and how he's like a little brother. And one of the kids asked if he was my real brother, like, if you gave birth to him, like, that kind of brother, and I said, that's impossible, people can't give birth to chimps, but he said maybe he was my real little brother and everybody laughed."

My mother stopped signing. "A boy said Charlie was your real brother?"

"Yeah."

"And then the class laughed?"

"Yeah."

"Do you think he was making fun of you?" my father asked carefully.

Callie thought for a moment. "No, I'm pretty sure he's just, you know, slow. I think maybe they're all kind of slow." She rubbed her upper lip with the back of her hand. "I think all the kids here are maybe stupid. Anyway, I had two hot dogs for lunch. They let you get seconds at school here. I think I like geography the best."

My parents looked at each other.

"Charlotte, you're next," my mother said.

"It was fine." I kept my head down, held up one hand to lazily sign *fine* in Charlie's direction.

"Just fine?"

"Yeah."

"Did you make any friends?"

"No." I took a bite. "This chicken tastes nasty," I announced.

"Charlotte, if you can't describe something in a way that is acceptable to everybody at this table, you can't talk."

I lifted my right hand, signed *fine* again. Charlie worked his way through a bowl of rice, five grains at a time. His lips moved up and down slowly, and he opened his mouth too wide. I could see the pink and black of his gums, the cakey yellow of his front teeth, all of that mashed up with the white of boiled rice. I caught my mother watching him, warily.

"What are you going to do about that?" I said.

She sighed. "We're working on it."

Charlie pinched his second helping of chicken breast between two fingers and tried to fold it into his mouth, but the piece was too big. It flopped out of his hands and fell onto the tray of his high chair. My mother snatched up the extra meat and placed it on her own plate to cut it for him. Charlie watched her steadily, then bowed toward her, opened his mouth, and snapped his teeth at my mother's hand. It was just a feint, but he was pleased with himself.

With one swift movement, my mother leaned over and lightly bit Charlie back, behind the ear. He screeched.

Callie gasped, rapturous. "Oh, do it again."

My father was queasy. "You did that real fast, Laurel."

And it was true. She bit Charlie as if it was the most natural movement in the world.

My mother said, "I'm a quick study."

CHARLES

In the calm right after the last bell, green shadows from the trees outside wavered and rippled and splashed across the bulletin boards on Charles's classroom's back wall. He loved that. He loved the green. He loved the country: he always had. He'd grown up in an overstuffed double-decker house on Chalk Street in Cambridge, Massachusetts, on a block that his parents had come to as children from Barbados. Everyone on Chalk Street was from back home. On Chalk Street, the houses drowsed into one another and the people inside them kept a careful watch out the windows — everyone was lovingly guarding their lives there. Family was his mother and father and older brother, Lyle, and hundreds of cousins, always asking for favors. You went to Boston and to places where white people were for work, not for life. Life moved from the Chalk Street front porch to Mayflower Meat

Market to the bus stop on Mass Ave. and back again. Anything outside this circuit was not to be considered real.

But Charles always yearned for wide open spaces. When he was six he'd announced he wanted to be a farmer. His parents were appalled. They hadn't left Barbados only to have their son turn around and work his way back down into the dirt. No one understood it; his older brother and their friends laughed about it for years.

He hadn't really known that black people in America could live outside a city, could grow in wilderness, until he found Laurel. When they first met she still smelled like fresh pine sap. It was subtle, most noticeable right behind her ears and under her chin. He'd told her and she'd been mortified and then insisted he must be joking. But he wasn't. She had always smelled like wide-open country to him. He made her tell him everything about her home: the tree farm, the hills. Once, she mentioned picking fiddleheads from the weeds in the woods behind her house, brushing off their paper veils and secretly biting the fresh curls till they burst into green in her mouth. "My mother said they'd make me sick, but they never did." She did not find that wondrous at all, thought him odd for thinking so. "It was just stuff you eat as a kid on your way to school, like chewing on hay," she said, as if chewing hay were normal, too.

The farm was gone by the time they met. Her parents mortgaged it to send her to college and then her father died of pneumonia shortly before her graduation, followed by her mother a few months later. In the wilds of their early love, Charles promised Laurel he would buy it back for her, and she'd said, "Don't bother." She told him about the oblivion of Maine, the cotton balls in her ears, the breath suspended. But that didn't put him off. It made him want it more. Even the racism up there in the country seemed bucolic to him. Much better than the squawks and loud calls of the college students in Central Square who liked to mark their territory by catcalling insults at him from the doorways of bars he'd walked past for years. He considered it the major failure of his and Laurel's life together: that at the end of their first decade of marriage, he still hadn't made enough money to get them to the green.

Laurel knew that, of course. She'd used it to her advantage, when she'd started the long, slow haggle of convincing him to move to the Toneybee. She mentioned the money, and the teaching gig at the high school already lined up for him, but they both knew the real selling point was the woods and the trees and the streams. The selling point was the green. The rest of it: the monkey and the book and the stories, those awful stories about the place, didn't matter.

Charles erased the ashy chalkboard of all the equations he'd written that day. He turned to his desk and began to pack up his things. He would like to have driven home with Charlotte, but she was doing her best to pretend she didn't know him, a fact Charles found funny and sad. "We're the only two black people in this place with the last name Freeman," he'd told her gently. "They know you belong to me." Charlotte was tricky. Maybe she would laugh at that, maybe she would be mortally offended. He'd caught her on a day when she was mortally offended — she'd rolled her eyes at him in a panic of embarrassment.

He walked out of the office toward the parking lot and the Toneybee's Volvo. He could never think of it as his. He did not like to drive it, though he knew it made Laurel proud. Lyle, Charles's brother, called Laurel a snob, said she would ruin him. And Charles knew what Lyle saw — Laurel had a desperation on her, a desire for better that sparked off her like sharp gleams of light. If you didn't know her, you'd mistake it for base ambition. But it wasn't, Charles knew that.

When they were first dating, Laurel worked at a city hospital. Her boss put her in charge of a patient named Ned. Ned was seven but the same size as a two-year-old. He'd been found tied to a metal post in a barn in Vermont. His teeth were rotten, nearly mush. He had never tasted solid food. "His family fed him on one carton of whole milk, tossed into the barn at sunrise every morning," Laurel told Charles, her eyes shining.

Ned had a birth defect: a soft opening at the back of his skull that never closed, only opened wider as he grew. Ned's parents weren't bad people. They kept him in the barn for his protection, they claimed, and tried to overlook the problem of a hole in the head. As for feeding him only milk: they were worried the strain of chewing might upset the gap. By the time the proper authorities got ahold of him, it was too late for Ned to learn to speak and Laurel was supposed to teach him to sign.

Laurel told Charles that every night Ned was in her care, they lay together side by side, his back against her front so that he wouldn't roll over in sleep and crush his gap and die in the spoils of his own brain. She held Ned tight, careful not to brush his head. She clasped his hands, muffled in hospital mittens, between her own, to keep him from scratching. While he slept she studied the hollow in his head. "I forced myself to do it," she told him, and Charles knew then that he loved her.

"It used to scare me," she told him. "It was so open." She could see, under the whisper of Ned's bright blond hair, the mysterious whorls and lines of his brain. "I could look at it all day," she told him. She thought she could see Ned's brain pulse.

"It's like, it's like," she'd sputtered, searching for the right words.

"It's like love," he'd supplied her, and she'd smiled, grateful. That's when he knew they would make it together. "Yes, it's exactly like love," she replied. And then she'd thought a moment, corrected them both. "No, it *is* love."

She finger-spelled into Ned's palm and told Charles excitedly about seeing flashes of recognition in his eyes. She bathed him twice a day, attempting to rid his skin of the dried mushroom musk of the barn, but it never completely went away.

"I just want him to survive in this world," she'd said.

And Charles had understood. He wanted Ned to live, too. The world would prove to be a kinder place, a bigger place than the circuit of Chalk Street and Maine's blinding whiteness, if something like Ned and his hollow lived in it. Charles wanted him to prove how boundless the world could be, and when Ned choked to death trying to swallow his own shoelaces, they both cried for what was lost.

Charles started the car now and began the drive back to the Toneybee. He rolled down the window and breathed in deep, slow, swallows. The world was bigger. Ned had died, but the world was bigger and Laurel had found that for them.

"You don't love Charlie yet," Laurel accused him the other day, and he had not been able to deny it.

"I don't know if I would use that word for him," he'd said diplomatically. But she was angry, oh she was mad, and she'd seemed to miss the point entirely. He'd said, "That monkey doesn't love me, either," and he'd gotten her to laugh at that, at least, because it was true. Charlie understood him as a rival for Laurel's affections, which Charles found funny, and he could only laugh when Charlie would tilt his chin up and stare, glassy eyed, just over Charles's shoulder.

Up ahead, Charles could see the gates of the Toneybee. He had never imagined, back in his bedroom on Chalk Street, that he would end up here, with a woman like Laurel. She made things magic for him. It was a weird kind of magic: it did not bring him anything recognizable, any sort of understood glory. It brought something deeper, something that he did not know he needed until it was in front of him. He didn't particularly care for Charlie — he'd never liked animals much — but he did care for this, for the drive rolling out before him and the large house in front of him that was definitely not Chalk Street. He cared for what was beyond the limits of his understanding. He'd broken through, somehow, gone past his block and reached a different country. It was strange, it was new, he could not say yet whether or not it was *good.* But it was something he could never have imagined, and for that, he was grateful.

CHARLOTTE

I was the one who found my mother and Charlie together.

I still couldn't sleep in Courtland County. Instead, I would go to the living room, lie across our borrowed, bumpy couch, and look through my father's record collection, imagining myself on the album covers: inside Pink Floyd's floating prism; bathed in the same blue electric lights as a chubby Donny Hathaway; getting tangled up in the swirling ribbons of color on the front of *Bitches Brew*.

It was during one of these nights on that couch, staring at the cover of a Labelle record, that I heard the tiniest gasp. I wouldn't have caught it anywhere outside of the overbearing hush of Courtland County. The gasp was so content, so satisfied it was almost smug. I stood up. I saw a dim gray light coming from under Charlie's door. I got up and put my hand on the knob and was surprised when it turned easily: his door was usually locked.

Charlie's room was different at night. The space was filled with a dirty, watery glow, the diffuse glare from the overhead fluorescent light placed on the dimmest setting. I squinted and then I saw them. In the corner farthest from the door, my mother sat cross-legged, Charlie laid out across her knees. I would like to say I didn't know what they were doing at first. I would like to say I didn't understand. But I understood instantly. Something in the way she held herself was sickeningly familiar. I'd seen her back curve like that before. Some part of me remembered from when Callie was a baby.

This was the worst part. My mother heard the door open, but she made no move to cover up or turn away. When I could bring myself to look at her face, her chin was slightly raised. Something threatened to break in my throat, something small and muffled, too embarrassed to be a full outcry. At that sound, Charlie lolled his head away from my mother's chest, his lips coming off her nipple with a pop. Now Charlie, my mother, and my mother's nipple were all staring at me.

"Mom," was all I could say. Again and

again, "Mom."

She had the strangest look on her face: proud, then, as she realized my unhappiness, apologetic and frightened. She pushed back her hair with her free hand, made a slight face, and I could see she was a little bit annoyed at being interrupted. She scooped Charlie up and struggled to stand. When she'd managed to get both of them upright, she came to me. "Calm down, Charlotte." She brushed my arm. "I'm going to ask you to calm down now."

"No," I protested. I should have been yelling, but I wasn't. For my mother, I kept whispering. "I will not calm down."

"It's really okay, Charlotte. He needs it."

She tried to smile. Charlie rested his head on her shoulder and closed his eyes, content to listen to the rise of her voice. "You remember what he sounded like that first night? You remember how badly he cried?"

"Yeah," I said reluctantly.

"You remember how heartbreaking that was?"

"Yeah."

"Imagine if we had to go through that every night, Charlotte. Imagine if we all had to get that upset every single night." She paused.

"Yeah."

"So you see why I have to do it?"

"Yeah."

"And you see why we can't tell anyone about it? Not yet? You're still uncomfortable. Imagine how everyone else will feel. It will just make everything so hard."

"Yeah."

"So, it would be best not to tell anyone else. Not yet, anyway. I want to get Dr. Paulsen used to the idea. And I want to talk to your father about it, too. I should really talk to him first."

"Yeah."

"He has a right to know, everyone does, but it's a sensitive subject."

"Okay," I said, to get her to stop. Charlie opened his eyes and raised his hand to her cheek.

I backed toward the door.

"Charlotte," she said, stopping me, "I was surprised when you walked in on us. I will say that. But I think this could be a good thing. I think it could be good to have a secret with each other."

"Yeah," I said.

Charlie plucked drowsily at the front of my mother's nightshirt, held up his hands, cupped his fingertips together, brought them into a kiss. The sign for *more*. She gazed down at him. She didn't even care if

180

I saw what passed between them. She began to unbutton the front of her nightgown again. I turned and opened the door, left before I could see any more.

There was a squall at the back of my throat when I woke up in the morning, something snarled and contrary, rising up from my stomach. I told myself I was being stupid and that I didn't care. But I did care. I wanted someone else to know.

I nearly told Callie in the morning, but she was too open and bright, smiling at Charlie and my mother, and I couldn't do it. I was too scared to tell my father. I thought of Max, but telling him would make it mean something else, would take it away from me and my mother and Charlie and I knew that was wrong. I didn't think of Adia until I actually saw her.

I sought her out at lunch. I'd been avoiding her since she insulted me on the first day of school. She sat at the farthest table. She didn't even have the pretense of a lunch tray in front of her. She was drawing again. When I put down my tray, she didn't look up. I followed her lead, knowing she was waiting to talk to me. We sat that way for the next twenty-five minutes, me eating, her drawing.

The five-minute warning bell rang. I drank the last of my milk and felt the scratch at the back of my throat again. I had to say something. I reached across the table, put my two hands in front of her face and signed *more*.

"What was that?" She still wouldn't look up from the paper.

"What do you think?"

"I think you're somebody who wants a lot of attention."

I sat back down and waited. Adia drew some more and then she gusted out a loud sigh, as if getting past the heaviest pain in the world. "All right. Just tell me. What was it?"

I signed, *I have a monkey for a brother. He talks.*

"What's that?" Adia said.

It was coming out all wrong.

Adia tried and failed to feign disinterest. "What's that, with your hands?"

"It's," I said, "It's . . ." And then I told her about the Toneybee. Not about my mother. Not yet. Because as I talked, Adia got more and more excited until she cut me off.

"We have to tell Marie."

Marie, Adia's mother, was a fine-arts professor who taught pottery classes at Courtland County Community College. "The four Cs," Adia called it, as we walked to her house. It was after school, and Adia had insisted I follow her home. I still hadn't figured out how to tell her the rest. The rest of it, all of it, sat hard and cold in my neck, and I only wanted it out. Going home, seeing my mother with Charlie wrapped around her, would only make it worse, would make me choke and drown. I was sure of it.

Adia and her mother lived on Courtland County's tiny, preserved Main Street. Everything downtown was brightly painted and porticoed and kept as close to the early twentieth century as possible. The Breitlings had taken over an old general store. The facade was painted a deep, shining cherry red with white trim, and there were old murals for Coca-Cola and Alka-Seltzer fading on the side of the building.

We entered through a screen door at the back and stepped into a long, narrow, gutted room. A battered countertop with three cast-iron taps stood at the far end. It was an old soda fountain. The rest of the space was taken up by pottery wheels and wire baking racks tottering with blocks of clay. Near the soda fountain was a small, gruff kiln. Everything was powdered with brown and white dust. The floor itself was wooden and deeply scarred and all around us were precariously balanced towers of books and papers and magazines. Crumbling *New York Times*es, a tide of *New Yorker*s, a pile of old *Crisis* magazines and a slick, sliding deck of *Essence*s and *Vogue*s. There were even a few *Final Call*s, but it seemed like someone had been using those for an art project: the fronts were nicked with holes where an Xacto knife pruned the typography. There was a stack of *NME* magazines, almost completely torn apart, as if they had been snatched and delivered to the Breitlings by smugglers.

But the centerpiece of the room was the enormous stereo system: two felted speakers with a complicated rig between them, crowned with a turntable and a cassette deck. And in front of all that sat the most beautiful woman I had ever seen, more beautiful than Adia, legs parted, bent over a running wheel.

She had a gold front tooth and a nose ring. She wore her hair in a complicated wrap, a swath of ragged cotton dyed bloodred. She had Adia's features, of course, but they were different. Adia was beautiful, but there was something stubborn in the set of her face, as if she dared you to admire her. Her mother wasn't ashamed of her beauty. She wore it plainly, without apologies, and this made her even more hypnotic than her daughter.

"This is Charlotte," Adia announced, with the open pride of a cat bringing a bird to its master.

Marie held out her hand. "Pleased to meet you," she said. Adia began to talk excitedly at Marie, something about consciousness raising and shelter and the Toneybee, and Marie only lifted her eyebrows, her lips slightly parted to flash her gold tooth at us.

I thought she would send us away or roll her eyes, but it was clear that she took Adia just as seriously as Adia took her. They were equals. She believed every word Adia said, and when I realized this, I felt my stomach tilt with unease.

Marie got up from her seat and moved to the window to light a cigarette.

"You have to tell her where you live," Adia prodded.

I did, shyly. Marie listened, smoke streaming from her nostrils.

"Well," she said with an exhale when I finished. "That's quite a story." Adia watched me now, made some calculation. I had passed a test and Adia had decided I was one of them.

At the Breitlings, it was never quiet. Their two great passions were rhetoric and music. Adia and her mother were rhythm heads. My father loved music, too, but the Breitlings were different. They were not collectors and they were not merely fans. Their passion for music was both religious and profane: they revered and craved it at the same time. Their stereo was on from 7 a.m. to 1 a.m., when Marie's wheel did its final revolution of the night, and she gave the poor, overworked motor of the turntable a break.

When it was just me and Adia, she chose the records. If Marie was there, she was the one in charge, constantly changing discs to keep up with the unending mix in her head. Nina Simone and Sly and the Family Stone — the only records she and my father shared, besides Labelle. Marie even allowed rap music, a fact that astonished me. My parents hated rap and I thought that hatred was shared by anyone over thirty. The only thing Marie banned was any white singers. White composers were fine, she said. She loved classical music. Bartók was her favorite. But, she confided with a laugh and a shrug, she couldn't stand the sound of white people singing.

"Except for Joni Mitchell," Adia said.

I snorted.

"What's so funny?"

But I could never explain it to her.

It was exhausting to be with the Breitlings. Black people could love Joni Mitchell but still claim to hate white singers. It was one of an elaborate set of rules that Marie imparted to Adia, who parroted them back to me as if I had not been in the room at the same time she heard them. It was a long list, the work of many years' worth of debate.

We'd had our own version of these rules back home in Dorchester, but they had been rules of what you weren't supposed to do in public, what you weren't supposed to do around white people. Laugh too loudly, show anger, dress raggedy, show any sign of disorder or chaos. Fit perfectly — without strain — into space.

The Breitlings' list was different. According to them, these were the things black people did not do: eat mayonnaise; drink milk; listen to Elvis Presley; watch Westerns or *Dynasty;* read *Time* magazine; appreciate Jack London; know the lyrics to Kenny Rogers's songs; suffer fools; enjoy the cold or any kind of winter. Here were the things black people did do: learn to speak French and adore Paris; instinctively understand and appreciate anyone from a small island or a hot place; spank their children; obsessively read science fiction and watch *Star Trek* episodes; prefer sweet foods to salty.

The debate over whether or not black people were natural swimmers was a very old one between the two of them, an argument that was full of in-jokes and constructed of rhythms I could not follow.

Living in all-white Courtland County, Marie gave her daughter these specifications so that Adia could spot a real black person as soon as they came along, avoid all the mirages. That's what I thought it was at first and it put me on the defensive because surely, in this analogy, I — in my tennis shoes and wannabe white-girl bangs — would be the mirage. And who would ever want to think of themselves as not really water but actually a trick of the desert?

As I got to know them better, I realized the rules were for Adia herself as much as they were for the world around her. Marie nursed Adia on a bitter pabulum of omnipresent, always-lurking oppression. To ready her daughter for the assault on her rights that Marie was sure was coming, she had given Adia a very simple list of instructions on how to be black. All Adia had to do was follow them and her whole self would be secure. It was intoxicating. I wanted them to tell me their rules forever.

And yet they never could give me the straightforward answer of how they got stranded in the blizzard of whiteness that was Courtland County. Sometimes they called Adia's father a jazz musician, sometimes a physicist, sometimes a planetary scholar, sometimes a poet.

What was clear was that Marie came to Courtland County with the man who himself had been lured there as an affirmative action hire at Courtland County Community College, in whatever was his true discipline. "But this place was too much for him," Marie would say, smoke streaming from her nostrils. "He had to go back down south."

They claimed he sent periodic interplanetary dispatches — whether this was a metaphor or something they believed had truly happened was always unclear. He also sent money, which covered the rent for the Main Street storefront, and the records and the magazines.

For a long time, I couldn't figure out why they didn't follow him down south. I think they stayed because, by the time I met them, they had comfortably settled into the roles of professional angry black women and the idea of living anywhere else was unimaginable.

Marie took on the burden of talking about race for Courtland County. And for her part of the deal, she got this one scrap of land where she could dictate all the rules. The troubling thing, of course, which Adia and Marie never mentioned, was the lack of actual fellow black people. The black people in Spring City didn't count. Marie and Adia only mentioned them when decrying the segregation that caused that town's existence.

Marie's loud protestations about the lack of black history celebrations in town had resulted in a sheepish and hastily thrown together assembly each year at the public library, where all the white children and Adia sang praises to peanuts and open-heart surgery and air-conditioning underneath a store-printed banner that read THE WONDERS OF BLACK INNOVATION. Even the high school, in a misguided but genuine attempt to appease Marie, put on a turgid adaptation of *The Wiz* the previous year, which Adia, with her profound gift for contrarian gestures, refused to take part in. Without her, the cast was all white and deadly earnest. Marie attended every performance anyway, a good sport, and cheerfully lacerated the poor cast members after each show for their inveterate cluelessness.

"You children can't help it, of course," she told them, and they accepted her criticism with a comforting humility.

Courtland County bowed to Marie's demands because the people there, like well-meaning decent and caring people anywhere, were loath to think of themselves as racists but also loathe to think of race at all.

Among the three of us it was different. Marie and Adia liked to quiz me about all the signs I knew.

In their front room one afternoon, the two of us helping Marie as she mixed glazes, Adia said, "Show me the sign for bougie, Charlotte. I bet you know that one."

"There isn't one."

"You're telling me there aren't any black deaf people?"

"Of course there are," I said. "We've got our own signing. Black Deaf Sign Language."

"Marie," Adia called happily. "Listen to this. Tell her, Charlotte."

Marie was just as amused as Adia. They did not find the idea sad or isolating or frightening. They were delighted.

"There has to be a sign for bougie," Adia

insisted. "There just has to be. You know we like to come up with ways to call each other out."

"What do you mean?"

"That's what black people do. We like to call each other out. We don't suffer fools."

"Show us deaf Ebonics," Marie said.

"Show us country signing," Adia said.

"Show us how we do," Marie said.

"Show us ghetto signs," Adia said, and Marie abruptly stopped laughing.

"That's enough," she said sternly. "That's offensive. That's what they would want you to say."

"They who?" I asked.

I had failed them again.

"White people." Adia rolled her eyes. "Duh."

"That's enough," Marie said again, then sat at her wheel and began working. We'd been dismissed for being too rowdy.

In her room, Adia threw herself across the mess of blankets she used for a bed — "Mattresses are colonialist," she'd pronounced when I'd first seen it — and buried her head under a bundle of sheets.

"Sometimes Marie just can't take a joke," she muttered.

I slid down beside her. "Duh," I said.

Adia only grunted.

She put her head on my knee.

"It's just . . . there can be so much more, you know?"

I could feel the bell of her voice vibrate against my shins. I reached out and took her hand in mine and began to spell the alphabet. She didn't move. After a few seconds, "What are you doing?"

"It's all your letters. So you can sign any word you want."

I held my breath. But Adia only allowed, "That's true," and I felt her hand ease into mine.

Adia's skin was much softer than I thought it would be. She liked to use her hands to gouge and sketch and scratch so it was a surprise that her fingers were pneumatic and smooth. In the warm dark of Adia's room, we began to practice the alphabet. I crooked her fingers, made them swoop through the air. She sat up on one elbow so she could see my hands move. We went through it once, twice, but she kept tripping on some letters and she finally threw her arm over her eyes in mock despair, "Oh, lawd te day, I'm blind.

"Yes, yes, lawd," Adia continued. "Lawdy, lawd. I'se is deaf, dumb, and blind."

Then she laughed. To keep the joke going, I took her hand in mine again. "This is how

193

the blind learn to sign." I finger-spelled the start of her name into the soft flesh at her shoulder.

"Like Helen Keller?"

"Yeah," I said. "Like Helen Keller."

I moved my hand to the hollow in the middle of her chest, pressed it to the skin there. The joke wavered, it threatened to break and become serious. Adia held her breath, whether to stop laughing or not, I didn't know. I started to move my fingers to make her name again: the hard fist for *a*. When I pressed my little finger, held up at attention for the letter *i* against her chest, Adia squirmed.

"That tickles."

"Sorry."

But I kept my hand on her chest for a few seconds more, until Adia shrugged, rolled a little bit away from me, and said "Good night," pretending to sleep while still pressed against me, while I slipped my hand down farther, still spelling all the way, while in the last little bit of afternoon light I watched her form beside me, felt her breath rise and fall. I focused — as I spelled into her skin, into wet — on the curve of her skull, the two perfect hollows at its base.

I went to Adia's every day after that, for the

push of her skin and for revolution. Adia talked to me about change and uprising and power till she made herself hoarse, and then she lay beneath me and went quiet while I spelled into her a different kind of speech, a truer one, I thought.

Always, after, Adia kept still. Her mouth closed, her eyes muted, she was finally, briefly, smoothed over.

I lived in this lull, when it was just our breath, just our two bodies sliding very slowly away from each other. I thought it meant that we had broken into something new. Something that existed outside of the Toneybee Institute and Courtland County and what black people could and could not do. When we pressed together, when we moved our fingers against each other, we spelled past doing to simply, unquestionably being. We fell out of time.

I told myself the gibberish that I spelled into Adia's body had become a language that we shared between us. That maybe I was being too cautious. That maybe I could open my mouth and speak and name what passed between us for what it was — love.

I was wrong about that one.

Adia spoke about what we did only once. One afternoon, all slick and warm, the bare trees scratching on her window, the faraway hiss of her mother's kiln downstairs, Adia rolled her head off of its resting place on my knee and propped herself up on one elbow.

"Black people don't know how to love," she said.

I snorted, "C'mon, Adia. Another rule? Black people can't love? That's pretty messed up."

"No." Adia stuck her swollen lower lip out, made a show of pouting at my derision. "We can do it. We just don't know how."

Marie had recently been reading Neruda's love poems and so that meant Adia was reading them, too.

"Marie says our ancestors were the greatest lovers," Adia continued, unembarrassed.

I thought of Marie, her golden tooth flashing from behind her stout lips as she pronounced the word *lovers* with relish. I flushed.

"In Africa, we were kings and queens." Adia was warming to her subject, to the sound of her own voice. She stretched, and I watched all the smooth round muscles of her back contract underneath her brown skin. I wanted to reach out and kiss them, each one, but I knew she would shrink from me now, would be annoyed at any interruption. I sucked my teeth instead, rolled my eyes.

"Kings and queens," I murmured.

"Yes." Adia, impatient now. "Marie says the men loved the women fully and wholly and the women accepted their love. Like a tribute. You know, Cleopatra on the Nile and all that. In Africa, it was the man's job to offer love and the woman's job to accept it. But all that's ruined now. Marie told me." Adia sighed.

Her skin was still damp, her bare arms flexing. "But we're getting it back," I said shyly.

She snapped up as if I'd pinched her.

"You and I will have to learn," Adia told me. "Marie says so. We'll have to find kings." I thought maybe this was another kind of flirtation. Adia looked slyly at me through her lashes. Then she said, "We don't want to go queer like white girls do."

I reached for her to make her stop. I began again to finger-spell against her skin, to find our way into that other existence, but while my fingers worked I made sure to kiss Adia hard, to bite her on the lips and tongue until they swelled, so that when we were finished the quiet would keep and she could not talk us back into history.

■ ■ ■ ■

That night when I went back home to the Toneybee, my own lips were bruised and smarting. I ate dinner and I brushed my teeth and I lay in bed and I thought about what Adia told me. After a while, I got up and went to Charlie's room.

In the dimness, I didn't see him at first. But then, in the farthest corner, I saw some rustling in a mess of blankets. Charlie sat up. I moved toward him. He tilted his head and scratched underneath his arm. He sniffed loudly. I could smell him and I realized with a start that he could smell me, too. I watched his nostrils grow wide. I heard his stomach rumble, heard him make a tiny swallow at the back of his throat. He yawned, blinked languorously.

I held up my hand and signed to Charlie the one thing I knew for certain.

I love Adia Breitling. I like girls.

Charlie blinked again, more quickly. And then he raised his hand and signed it back to me, his fingers swift and nimble: *I like girls, I like girls, I like girls.*

The game played by younger siblings everywhere. I repeat what you say until you cannot take it anymore, until you are enraged by your own echo. He'd done it to me before and it had made me furious.

But now, as I watched him reflect my love for Adia, I felt only the overwhelming need to touch him. But I knew the moment I reached out for him, he would bristle. So I sat, grateful, watching his fingers mirror mine until he stopped.

He yawned and scratched his cheek and blinked again, and then he pushed himself up onto his haunches and away from me. He made a point of turning his back, busying himself with his nest of blankets, until he threw himself on the floor with a groan and covered his eyes with his hands, ready for sleep.

I stood up, careful not to step on his blankets and closed his door behind me.

CALLIE

Callie didn't care. If Charlotte didn't want to come home anymore, that was her business. Callie would watch all the Westerns with Charlie.

Westerns were Charlie's favorite kind of movie. Callie didn't like them, but that was not important. Callie was the family member that Dr. Paulsen trusted to take care of Charlie's collection: videotapes of *The Man Who Shot Liberty Valance; The Good, the Bad and the Ugly; Johnny Guitar. Johnny Guitar* was Charlie's favorite. He sat as close as possible to the TV set during every Joan Crawford close-up and would purse his lips into a kiss and press it against the screen, fitting his own fleshy mouth over her bloodred trembling one. But what he really liked best about the Westerns were the sound effects: the hollow thud of horses' hooves and the whistling theme songs. He would sit back on his haunches and rock back and forth, yes yesing the gunshots with a perpetually nodding head, riveted from the opening scenes of big empty gray sky to the closing monochrome sunset.

Without Charlotte, the only sounds in the apartment after school were gunshots, the soft purr of the gears turning over in the VCR and Charlie's heavy breathing. If Joan Crawford wasn't on the screen, he busied himself with grooming Callie. It's why she sat beside him. *I hate* Johnny Guitar, she signed into the arm of the sofa as Charlie raked his fingers through her hair. His palms got greasy with activator spray and the familiar musky scent of her scalp.

Charlotte didn't smell like home anymore. Charlie's nostrils flared and Callie flared hers, too, hoping to pick up whatever he did.

"God," Charlotte would say. "You don't have to sniff like that."

And Callie would turn away.

The first afternoon when Charlotte was late she had still cared enough to bristle at the rebuff. "Well, hello to you, too," she'd said.

Callie made a brief little flutter of annoyance in her seat. Charlie, also annoyed at the interruption, rearranged himself at her back, burrowed his fingers deeper in her hair.

Hello, Callie signed. She reached for the remote and turned up the volume. Charlie tugged appreciatively at a snarl at the nape of her neck.

"Look," Charlotte started, "I'm sorry."

Callie gazed at the TV screen. Charlotte put her backpack on the ground and sat down next to her on the couch.

"I'm sorry," Charlotte said again. "I'm sorry I have a friend."

"I have friends, too," Callie said. Too quickly.

"Who are your friends?"

"Charlie is my friend."

The sadness of that sentence sat between the two of them until Charlotte stopped it. She flipped over her hand. "Charlie doesn't count. Who are your human friends?"

"Charlie is a hominid."

"Callie, he is not your friend."

"He is. Charlie is my friend. Max is my friend."

This was even worse than claiming Charlie's friendship. Callie knew it as soon as it was out of her mouth, the wrongness of it. And Charlotte, of course, drove it home.

"They pay Max to be here. He's not your friend."

"Well, then, you don't have any friends, either." Charlie had moved from grooming her hair to grazing at the lint on her sweater. She focused on keeping her arms limp, on the feel of his fingertips through the weave of the cloth.

"I'm sorry," Charlotte said again.

Callie shook her head. "Shh." She pointed to the screen. "We're trying to watch."

"Well, good for you." Charlotte got up from the couch.

"I'm doing what we're supposed to be doing here, Charlotte." Callie kept looking at the screen as she spoke. "I'm doing my *job.*"

"What are you talking about?"

"Max tells me all the time. Dr. Paulsen does, too. They say that being Charlie's sister is the most important part of the project. So I'm doing what I'm supposed to do, but you're not doing your job." And then she turned to Charlotte, her face set smug and triumphant.

"You're being so stupid right now," Charlotte said.

But Callie wasn't. That's what she couldn't understand. Or she couldn't understand how Charlotte didn't see it. *Without you, I have nothing.* They had slept side by side every night of her life and now they didn't anymore. But maybe that didn't matter. Maybe it didn't matter that Charlotte's breath was no longer the first thing she heard in the morning and the last thing she heard at night. Maybe it didn't matter that she and Charlotte no longer signed to each other in love, only contempt. It didn't have to matter now that she had Charlie.

But Charlie didn't want her. What Callie felt for him was messy and sweaty and desperate, and it drove him away. "Chimpanzees are social animals," Dr. Paulsen told her. "They need hierarchies to be happy and they are discerning."

"What does discerning mean?" Callie asked.

If Charlie lived with other chimps he would have been the beta, Max explained. He would have been the one cringing in the corner, the one who ate last and got teased first. But what was wonderful about the experiment was that nobody teased him here; Callie only hugged and clapped for him. Here, Charlie ate first. Callie knew that should have made him loving. But it didn't. "Chimpanzees want to dominate whatever social group they are in," Max said. And Callie asked, "Even humans?" and he had told her yes, even humans, delighted that she was catching on. "They will try to challenge each member of the group until they win or until they are bested. They're not dumb about it, either. They're strategic. They start off with the weakest member of the group and work their way up," Max said.

Callie only nodded.

Every affection she gave him was met with a pinch. His kisses had teeth. He swatted her hands when she tried to sign to him. Sometimes he groomed her hair with perfect kindness, carefully trailing his fingers through the grease at the back of her neck, and sometimes he took the strands of her hair between two of his fingers and twisted and pulled until it was ratty and scratched at the scalp. He raked his fingernails across her skin when she held him. He spit into the palms of her hands. But Callie always forgave him. She couldn't back down. If she didn't have Charlie, if she didn't believe that every pinch and slap and bite and loogie were signs of love, then she didn't have anything.

So she began to eat. At first, it was to steel herself against Charlie. A cut, a flick of a nail, were easier to bear when her blood was all mixed up with sugar. When he turned his back on her, she could suck stray cereal dust off her fingers as a balm.

When Callie reached the Toneybee in the afternoons, before she went upstairs to the apartment, she would sneak into the cafeteria. She pressed herself close to the cereal dispensers, cupped a hand to their funnels and turned the plastic dials to fill her open palms with stiff marshmallows and oxidized raisins. She turned the dials carefully: she didn't want the rush of cornflakes against plastic siding to give her away.

She would crawl over the serving lines, hoist herself up to the bar reserved for hot plates, press herself against the chafing dishes, feel briefly the hot, unclean breath of the heat lamps, inhale the stench of floor wax and industrial gravy, and marvel at her own invisibility.

Once she was over the serving trays and into the kitchen proper, Callie could really eat. Cold pasta salad from Saran Wrapped silver tureens, dehydrated flakes of mashed potatoes from the box, handfuls of croutons and bread crumbs from the canister. In the walk-in freezer, she carefully tore at the cartons of concentrated fruit juice. She bent her head to each smooth surface and with her two front teeth, shaved bits of ice off into her open mouth, all that sugar mortifying the taste of loneliness. For the rest of her life, Callie would search for something as sweet as frozen orange juice held underneath her tongue, in the chilled, mildewy air of a refrigerator at three o'clock on a school day afternoon.

The meat, she saved for last. Row after row of naked chicken legs, the skin prickled with oversized pores, sausage links coiled like cornrows and pounds of ground beef. This was her favorite. She scooped small bits of it out with her fingers, then patted and smoothed the mounds whole to cover her tracks. The taste of raw ground beef was sharp and metallic, like eating gold. Callie would lick the tips of her fingers until the corners of her mouth shined with oil.

The first time she went upstairs, lips glossed with grease, Charlie had bounded to her and grasped her head between his hands. His grip was strong; she could not have moved her head if she tried. She felt afraid of him, for the first time. She heard her mother shriek, Max mumble something, and Callie thought: Charlie's going to bite my lips off. She didn't struggle. She sighed, gave into her fate, breathed in the dead milk on Charlie's breath as he bent his mouth to hers. But he did not bite. Instead, her eyes closed, she felt the softest whiskering and then something unbelievably warm, something vibrating with heat, brush against her face. Charlie was very slowly and very carefully licking the last little bit of raw meat from her mouth. After that, Callie made sure to eat the ground beef every day that she could. It was worth it, to feel the warmth, the delicate delay of Charlie's strength, as he kissed the greed off of her.

It didn't seem possible that she could get so big from all of that. It genuinely surprised her when she did. How much was a ten-year-old supposed to weigh, anyway? She did not, honestly, see the difference between 100 pounds and 150 pounds. All Callie knew was that now her thighs chafed to-gether when she walked, rubbed themselves raw on each stride. She had always been chubby, but now little pellets of flesh grew on her arms. Skin tags, that's what Dr. Paulsen called them. Her mother asked her to examine Callie before she took her to an actual pediatrician. Dr. Paulsen, in her green rubber gloves, poked at the sagging undersides of Callie's arms. "Skin tags are common among the obese," Dr. Paulsen explained, and Callie started at that word. The thousand humiliations of the flesh, be-ing stuck in a form that did not feel like yours. *It must be horrible to be Charlie.*

As Callie grew heavier, she became invis-ible. She had always been ignored at school but now, even at home, she was an overfed, slightly grimy ghost. The only two people who really paid attention to her were Dr. Paulsen and Max. Both of them were as embarrassed by her bulk as the rest of her family, but instead of politely ignoring it, they gave her aggressive compliments.

"Look at the camera, please, Callie," Dr. Paulsen would direct. "You've got such a pretty face."

"You look nice today, Callie, terrific," Max said, even when the stitching on the thighs of her pants was split, even when a blouse broke open along the seams of the fat on her back.

The compliments made Callie uncomfortable. She dutifully waited for them, and she always said thank you but she knew something was wrong. When Dr. Paulsen and Max told her she looked nice, her mother never echoed them. She busied herself with Charlie or some piece of equipment in the room when Callie was being praised.

But none of this made her less eager. *Charlie loves me more.* She knew he signed to her the most, she was sure of it.

Charlie didn't sign much with any of them at first. Her mother said he was too shy, but Callie knew it was because he was proud. He didn't like the questions her mother and Max asked. Anyone could see that. "Where is the blue ball? Is the rice tasty? Where is the red ball?" Those questions were boring. No wonder he didn't answer.

Callie's questions for Charlie were better. *Do you miss your mother? Do you ever wish you were someone else? Do you think you have brothers and sisters? What did you dream about last night?* Charlie didn't sign back, he would only fix her with his distant stare, but Callie did it anyway. She was patient. She had time.

She was the first person who saw Charlie do it. He started to sign with his hands behind his back. He did this only occasionally, but when he did, it sometimes went on for hours. Her mother, Dr. Paulsen, Max, none of them, could figure it out until Callie told them all, "He's telling us what happened a long time ago. When he signs behind him, he's telling us what happened in the past." She'd learned it by catching one of the litanies of signs, something about a ball, and realizing it described a misstep in a game of catch he'd made the evening before.

"You're a genius," Dr. Paulsen said. And her mother smiled. "Think of that, a chimp with a sense of history," her father joked. And Max said he didn't think it was possible, it was beyond what any one of them had imagined when they'd started. "But you could imagine it, Callie."

She'd flushed at that, a real compliment. Overwhelmed, she ducked her head and turned to Charlie. She signed to him, *You're so smart. You are beautiful. You are the smartest brother in the world.*

But Callie knew none of it mattered because Charlotte didn't care.

CHARLOTTE

"You don't think it's creepy when Charlie does that?" I asked Max.

He laughed. "Why is it creepy?"

But I couldn't explain it to him.

It was after dinner. Max had dinner with us every night, after Callie's big discovery. Sometimes he had a bulky video camera riding his shoulder, but he didn't like that, you could tell it made him uncomfortable to film us. He was always jerking his face back from the eyepiece so that he could look at us directly and he turned the camera off as soon as everyone was done eating.

Dr. Paulsen was trying to be nonchalant about it, but I could tell she was excited. Every time Charlie signed behind his back, she would stop talking and just watch.

"Maybe you're jealous," Max teased. "Charlie's getting a lot of attention."

"You don't think it's possible he's just fooling you?"

What was most unnerving were the things Charlie placed in the past: some were references to games and toys he had, but there was also a string of nonsense — all the signs we'd taught him, but out of order.

"That's pretty cynical."

"You're going to ask Charlie about his past lives? Reincarnation?"

"Maybe."

This was the problem with Max. He was no good to play with. I found it insulting. It made me want to poke at him more.

Max began to pack up the camera. I followed him to the door.

"Well, you guys better hurry up with all this stuff so we can move back to Boston already."

"It doesn't work like that," Max said. "Besides, I thought you were starting to like it here."

"What's there to like?"

He shook his head. "Good night, Charlotte."

It wasn't until closer to bed that my father noticed Max left behind his camera bag. "Just bring it up to his office and put it outside his door," my father told me. "Hurry up, now, before you go to sleep."

Max's office was on the floor above our apartment. It was a wide room with too-tall ceilings with murals painted across them. It wasn't his office, actually: it was Dr. Paulsen's, and Max worked there at a smaller desk beside her large one.

My father told me to leave the camera bag outside his door, but when I got there the lights were still on. I pushed open the door. I put the bag on Max's desk. And that's when I saw it. A book titled *Man or Beast?* and then a semicolon holding back a spill of words I did not understand, *sublimation, subaltern,* a whole pool of words above the author's name: Dr. Frances Gray. Printed across the very top of the book, in block letters UNCORRECTED PROOF. I probably would not have picked up the book if it didn't have that portrait of Julia Toneybee-Leroy as its cover.

I flipped through the pages — a lot of chapter headings with more confusing words, like *liminal space* and *hegemony* and *appropriation.* In the middle of the book was an insert of pictures. It was hard to tell what they were supposed to be at first. Each one had underneath it, written in tiny, cramped script, *Study of Nymphadora by Dr. Terrence Gardner.*

At first I thought it was a drawing of two enormous peach pits, side by side. They were done in carefully wrought red ink, the lines sharp and small and eager and frantic. In the corners, up and down the sides, were equations: sines, cosines, brackets.

I stared at them for a long time until I knew. I recognized the slope of a back and the insides of legs. And then I felt sick. I looked and I looked, turned more and more pages, and then I began to cry.

Nymphadora of Spring City, 1929

"Do you know I can only play one song on the piano?"

That particular session, I was lying on my side, my arm held straight along my hip, my knees bent only slightly. The pouch of my stomach lapped at the tops of my thighs. When I first lay down, Dr. Gardner had reached out and very carefully placed my hand on my hip. It was the first time he touched me. He said something about finding a "balance of form."

My skin sprung a thousand little needles when he touched me, and so I asked that question, apropos of nothing. Dr. Gardner moved back to his seat on the floor. "You can only play one song?"

"Yes." I was becoming an expert at unfocusing my gaze, letting my eye muscles go limp and keeping my lids only half open, letting the sunny room devolve into one yellow haze. "I can play 'Für Elise.'"

"How did you learn it?"

"We had a piano. My mother bought it for me. She paid the lady schoolteacher to give me lessons. I used to feel so bad for Miss Gaines. She seemed so thin and sorrowful all the time. I thought for certain I would never grow up to be an old maid like her."

"You aren't an old maid." Dr. Gardner said this underneath his breath, but he said it emphatically, and this made my whole skin feel warm.

"How did you afford a piano?"

"My mother was very industrious. She scrimped and saved for it," I lied.

I curled up my fingers and then let them go, rested them back on my thigh.

"A woman named Timothea Hartnett used to always trick Pop out of money. She'd say the dose he gave her was incorrect, or the medicine had made her son sicker. Once she even brought her daughter, who everyone knew was born bowlegged, into the shop and tried to argue Pop set her ankle wrong when she sprained it. But my mother made right work of her. She'd stand on the church steps on Sunday morning and dog Timothea Hartnett out for her lies." Mumma's voice had been measured and low. Not mean. Just ruthlessly correct.

217

All those years of hounding people for bills: another reason it would have been intolerable to be discovered bankrupt. Too many people to smile when my parents were brought low, to say, "You see how it feels now?"

Dr. Gardner couldn't hide his discomfort. "Your mother took pleasure in bullying a woman poorer than you?"

I stiffened. Then I narrowed my eyes. "She was not a bully."

Dr. Gardner didn't say anything. I could tell he didn't agree.

Defensively, I began to list the meager luxuries that Mumma gave me. She bought me a set of watercolor paints; no other child in Spring City had them. I had silk stockings, which our neighbors always borrowed, and sometimes she dressed the ends of my hair in grosgrain ribbons, cut from the dusty, barely used spool in Pop's store, paid for with our own dimes put back into the till.

"That's probably what your Miss Toneybee-Leroy does." I tried to keep my voice light. "She probably got a million perks from her father's rubber factory, like free bouncing balls and tennis shoes."

"Perhaps," allowed Dr. Gardner.

I waited a while longer. Dr. Gardner

began giving me a listing of his various academic accolades: a medical college in Scotland that was supposed to be prestigious, and then study at Harvard. Someone there had passed his name to Julia Toneybee-Leroy when she put out word among her social circles that she needed someone who excelled in the study of evolution and who was comfortable working with live animals.

"Harvard has the only scientific ape colony in the whole United States, down in Florida. I worked there for a year, getting used to them. They aren't so bad. Poor Julia —" And here he stopped himself, as if remembering who he was talking to.

"Poor Julia what?"

"Nothing," he said. "She just needed help in her management, as anyone would. Who knows, instinctively, how to take care of an ape?" And then he changed the subject, made me recount my day in the classroom, all the squabbles between the children I had to mediate.

When the session was done, I stood up and put on my clothes and clambered back into the bush behind his rooming house. I felt, as I crouched down into the shrubbery by the road, a burning ache in my chest and the sudden desire to punch something. I pinched a handful of leaves off the nearest bush and was rewarded with a sting in my palm. As I walked through the woods, doubled over to rub my hands against the length of my skirt to get the nettles out of them, I thought about Dr. Gardner and Julia Toneybee-Leroy. He'd badmouthed his entire race and declared himself an outcast, but he wouldn't speak ill of Julia Toneybee-Leroy. I decided I did not like Dr. Gardner so much after all, and I resolved to hate him from then on.

But it was not as easy as that. I knew what Mumma would have said. "You cannot trust a white man. Tread carefully, Nymphadora, and make sure that your way is true. Think not only once, but twice before you act and speak." But I didn't. It's shameful to admit here, I cannot even write it down without my hand springing to my face and covering it in my shame, while the other one writes the humiliating truth out plain. I was lonely. I was so very, very lonely. And though I knew it was dangerous to think of Dr. Gardner as a friend — "Does he think of you that way?" I could hear Mumma jeer — I couldn't help it.

I'd gone two years in Spring City surrounded by Stars but without one single friend. The Stars of Spring City are not ironical. They do not appreciate sarcasm. When I say something I mean to be clever, they think I'm being snide. I overheard Nadine tell some little acolyte whom I made cry with an offhand remark, "Don't mind Nymphadora being nasty to you. She's just smelling herself." They believe wit is a symptom of bitterness. They don't laugh like Dr. Gardner.

I have never seen Julia Toneybee-Leroy in person, only a very grainy photograph of her in the *Courtland County Mercury,* which was less a newspaper and more a kind of oversized yearbook for the various wealthy white New York and Boston families with estates in Courtland County. The paper published her picture a few years ago, after she left on safari. A print had been sent back from the ocean liner in Boston, showing Julia Toneybee-Leroy stern and small on the deck of the ship. In the photo, it was hard to get a sense of her actual face. All I could tell was that she was slight and thin and dressed in white. Everyone said she was beautiful, but this didn't really mean anything. She was rich enough to be called beautiful no matter what she looked like. I knew I couldn't tip my hand with Dr. Gardner and ask him outright to describe her, so I settled instead on imagining her.

In my mind, she had a short pert nose and a very wide mouth and small beady eyes framed with thick black lashes. She resembled a more attractive, hairless, white version of one of her apes. She wore a flouncy pink hat, like the one I'd seen in the newspaper photo, but her dress was too big and her neck swam out of the collar. I decided her voice must be high and shrill, used to making only demands. And despite all this, in my perverse imaginings, I thought Dr. Gardner was wildly in love with her.

Our next sitting was marred by Dr. Gardner's irritation. He put on a show of posing and reposing me. "First here," then "Here." He did this for forty minutes, had me get up and resettle myself against the floorboards like some mangy old dog, until the flesh at the backs of my thighs was wrinkled from the slats pressing into it every which way. At the end of it all, I was so annoyed, so exhausted, I would agree to almost anything. Which I think had been his plan all along.

"I think I've got it," he said finally. "If you'll do it."

"Just tell me."

The pose he wanted was this: my feet planted wide apart on the floor, so my knees fell open, so he could see all of me.

When he asked me to do it, he said please again. He called me Miss Jericho. And he looked me full in the face, very friendly and professional. He smiled. He asked me to pose like that and I said yes because I was tired, because I wanted to get out of the room and back to my own, because I was deadly lonely and he was the closest I had to a friend, because I wanted to prove I was more daring than an heiress who could order apes from Africa for her own amusement.

I did what he asked. I posed like that. And don't you know, don't you know, he was kinder to me than ever. He kept up a running list of questions. "You've never told me, Miss Jericho," he asked, "how your family came to Spring City."

"We were born here like everyone else."

"It's strange there are Negroes here. I mean, all the way out here. You don't think there would be."

"We're everywhere, when you think about it."

"It doesn't seem so."

"Well, I know there are Stars of the Morning in every state of the Union, so we have to be everywhere. We're probably everywhere in the world." We are not supposed to speak our group's name to any man who is not a Saturnite and certainly not a white man.

He laughed at this, enchanted. "What is a Star of the Morning? It sounds very poetic."

And so I told him about the Stars. Not everything, I still had some pride. I explained that we were a women's help organization.

"But we are a secret." I was drunk with his interest. "We even have secret names."

"You have a secret name?"

"Yes."

"What is it?"

"I couldn't possibly tell you that."

"What do you mean? Aren't we friends?"

And I couldn't help it, I grinned straight into his face at that and he grinned back. I almost forgot how I was posing. "I still can't tell you."

"Was your mother a Star, too?"

"Yes."

"Well, what was her secret name?"

"She didn't have one."

But Dr. Gardner was still caught up in the novelty of it. "Oh, please, Miss Jericho, please oh please tell me your name."

"No."

"How about when the drawings are done? I'll give you one if you tell me your name."

"Why would I want a nude drawing of

myself? It's indecent."

"No, it isn't." Dr. Gardner was hurt. "I explained. It's a great monument. You'll want it as a souvenir."

"Not a good enough prize to get me to tell you my name."

He said nothing and I was scared I had offended him. My knees made an odd, creaking sound as I kept them bent. Finally I said, "Nymphadora."

"What?"

"My name is Nymphadora."

He smiled at this. "Don't you scrimp on my gift now," I said, pretending to sulk. "I expect a full copy of the drawing when you're done."

"Of course," he said.

That night, I dreamed I was in the Toneybee Institute for Great Ape Research. I wore a white lace nightgown and I walked up and down the halls and all around me was the cologne of Dr. Gardner — animals and pencil shavings and blood. In the dream, I walked until my feet were sore and then I found a resting place, a window seat with a view of all the forests in Courtland County and Spring City. As my eyes shut I felt a sharp pain in my chest and my eyes flew open and over me stood Dr. Gardner himself with a long silver knife. He was stabbing me in the heart.

And this is how I knew, when I woke up, that I was in love with Dr. Terrence Gardner.

I had never been in love before. I'd flirted with a few boys from town when I was a very young girl, but none of that had ever stuck. I'd joked to Mumma that I was just a cold fish, not meant for this world, singular and odd, and I had thought it true.

The prospect of being in love made me giddy. I was now a lover and I tried to convince myself that the dream was really a good omen. That my spirit was so twisted and broken by my parents' demise, I had managed to turn what was a wonderful blessing into a nightmare. It did not matter anymore if I was odd or restless or perhaps disturbed: I now loved and, I allowed myself to hope, was maybe loved in return.

As the day went on, the dream didn't leave me. It became more vivid, stronger, so that at times I became actually quite afraid that Dr. Gardner was about to leap from behind a bush or fence with a dagger to finish the job. But I told myself, in a kind of frenzy, that this fear, too, was a good omen. That it was just the stutters of a shy and bashful heart and further proof of my love for Terrence Gardner and his very real affection for me.

That night was our Star of the Morning meeting.

After we went through our rites and called our names, we came to our order of business and Nadine Morton told me, "You've got to talk to that white doctor again, Sister Nymphadora."

I felt a pang of guilt. "What do you mean?" I feigned ignorance, felt only panic.

"Sister Methuselah, tell her what you told me."

Methuselah, better known as Jane Hall, came to the front of the room to stand beside Nadine. Jane Hall was new to the Stars: her mother was not a Star, had been one of those loose women my mother warned me about. But Jane was a hard worker, sober as a judge. She didn't go in for drink like the rest of her family, so we'd invited her to join. She had a husband, Graverly. He wasn't from Spring City, he came from down south. He'd come here for a summer — serving one of the rich families and he'd fallen in love with Jane, a laundress, and stayed. Neither of them had any money. Graverly was always without a job. He would travel around the county, looking for work, leaving poor Jane alone for weeks at a time. Jane was smaller than I, and younger, and much prettier, with big clear eyes and full, round lips that pursed like a baby doll's when her mouth was closed. But she was scared of me because she remembered the power my mother had. She stood up at the front of the room now and avoided my eyes.

She began, "You all know the trouble my Graverly's been having finding work? You all know how hard that is?"

The Stars murmured agreement.

"Well," she said, "he told me he got offered some work up at the Toneybee. He said Dr. Gardner's been dropping by the barber shop —"

This was a shock. I did not like to imagine Dr. Gardner wandering Spring City without telling me.

"He came by the shop and he offered all the men there work. He said it would be easy. Graverly said he told them it would all be work of the mind. And Graverly thought this sounded good enough. He didn't see anything wrong with that. But the other men, they said they wouldn't go because what was this work the doctor was talking about? They said it didn't sound right. They said they didn't want to go to no monkey house. But you know my Graverly. He needed work. He's a good man, he just needs work —"

"Get to the point, Sister Methuselah," Nadine prompted. "Just say to them what you said to me."

"So he went there. He went to the institute. And he thought the work would maybe be, you know, cleaning up or something like that. Something janitor-like. Maybe pick up after the monkeys — he was fine with that, Graverly's not too proud for that if it's honest work —"

"Methuselah," Nadine chided.

Sister Methuselah turned her pretty little head to Nadine, like an obedient child. She nodded. She said, "Well, the point is, my Graverly, he just wants honest work. So Sister Nymphadora, you've got to talk to that doctor again and tell him if he's going to offer work it's got to be honest."

"Wait," I spoke slowly, "please, Sister, explain what you mean."

"That doctor doesn't have honest work. Instead, he asks Graverly up there for tea, in this room with only two chairs and one big mirror in it. And while they're drinking it, Graverly says he gets to feeling all sort of funny, all sort of light-headed, see? Almost like he's been drinking, but he knows he hasn't touched a drop, has only drunk Dr.

Gardner's tea. And then when he's feeling good and woozy, Dr. Gardner brings out some little cardboard cards, some little cards with all these queer pictures on them, and he holds them up and he asks my Graverly questions. He'll hold up a picture of two different shapes and he'll say, 'Which one is disease?' Or he'll hold up a picture of different colored squares and he'll say 'Where does sin lie?' " And at first, Graverly, he thought it was easy work. He thought he was getting away with it. But, oh, Sister Nymphadora, it's just getting queerer and queerer.

"It's making Graverly uneasy, and he thinks maybe the doctor is unbalanced. And he doesn't know what he's doing with all these answers, the doctor is just writing them down in a book. And at the end of it that doctor, he shakes his hand and says, 'Good work,' and tells Graverly to come back again. He asks for Graverly again and again. And Graverly is afraid, because each time he goes back the tea gets stronger and each time he drinks it he gets lighter-headed and the questions, they get queerer and queerer. The last time, that doctor, he showed him two boxes, a red one and a white one, and he said 'Which one is the soul? Which one is the mind of god? Which one is beginning and which is end?' and my Graverly, he tells me, the hairs on the back of his neck stood up. And he couldn't even answer, his mouth had gone dry and he says his head was swimming and then, and then . . ." Sister Methuselah brought a slim, chapped hand to her pretty little mouth. "My Graverly, he swears, he saw, out of the corner of his eye, he saw through the mirror, another man, in a lab coat like Dr. Gardner and a big monkey. And the monkey was looking at the same pictures as he! And after that, he said his head hurt worse and worse and his gut, it began to feel like it would burst, and he begged Dr. Gardner to let him leave and he came back home to me and told me all about it. And he thinks, well, you know my Graverly is not a godly man, but he thinks, he's pretty sure, that what that doctor is up to up there is un-Christian."

Sister Methuselah stopped to take a breath. She looked around at all us Stars, who were listening to her, transfixed. "Graverly thinks it's unnatural," she added, taking a weak triumph at the rightness of that word.

All fifteen of us Stars were quiet for a bit, taking in her story.

"Well, thank you, Sister Methuselah."

Nadine looked pointedly at me. "Graverly's not the only one. You all know I work up at the institute. For the last two months, I've seen buses, the doctor has been renting school buses, and he brings up young colored men. I think they're from Boston. They have to be. The bus comes very early in the morning, before light, and then it takes the men back at night. It's never the same ones. New men every time. Don't speak a word, come in and out like ghosts, every last one of them haunted. It's like they've died inside when he's done with them. The few I've seen, they don't even know enough not to meet my eye and hide it. They just stare straight ahead at me, like he's taken something out of them. Like he's taken something out of their heads.

"And you see," she said, abruptly turning to me, "that's why you must ask him to stop. You got him to stop drawing us. He obviously can listen to reason. What he's doing is evil, but he's maybe a logical man. We wouldn't be Stars if we didn't try to ask him to stop. It's our duty."

The wood bench was hard and ragged and cold underneath my seat. I could hear it creak. I nodded. My mouth had gone completely dry.

"Sister Nymphadora, you know him. You

can get at him, even though he's peculiar. You need to get him to stop this nonsense."

"I don't know," I said. "I'm hardly the right person. Why don't you write to the Negro League in Boston or —"

"He won't listen to them. And once you get them involved, you get that girl involved, too. Julia Toneybee-Leroy is a little girl but she's rich and she's powerful. She has enough money to shut up any league she likes. As soon as you get any of that political nonsense involved, it may as well be over. They'll pay it no mind and do what they like.

"But if it's just between us . . ." Nadine tried hard to make her voice sweet. "Just between people who know each other . . ." She was careful not to use the word *friends*. In Nadine's mind, in the minds of all the other Stars, to call a man like Dr. Gardner a "friend" was a perversion of the word. "It doesn't have to become about politics or race men at all," she continued. "He'll stop listening if you bring that up. He'll listen to you, he's listened before. You need to come with me on my next shift. I'll let Dr. Gardner know you are coming to speak to him. You need to ask him what all this means and get him to stop."

"Tell him," Sister Methuselah said suddenly, shrilly emboldened by the success of her story, "tell him there's not enough money in the world for us to sell our souls to him. Tell him we're good Christian people here. Tell him we can't be bought."

"All right." The words were bitter in my mouth, because I very obviously could be bought, was already bought, for a few foreign cookies and kind words. "All right, Methuselah, I will try."

CHARLOTTE

"They're all racists."

"Who?" Adia asked.

I had caught her before she went into school. It didn't take much to get her to skip. We'd snuck back into her house while Marie was out teaching her morning class, and now we sat huddled together underneath the blankets in her room.

"The Toneybee Institute." I slid the book toward her. "It says it right there."

Adia flipped the pages and slid it back to me. "You're gonna tell me what's in it, or you're just gonna sit here and watch me read it?"

"The lady who wrote this book. She came here and talked to the lady who made up that institute, the Toneybee Institute. She interviewed her." I tapped the cover. "Miss Toneybee-Leroy. And she found out about it. They used to do experiments. In the 1930s. This doctor, Dr. Gardner, he did experiments on black people and chimps, and they did this one horrible, disgusting thing with this woman, this black woman who lived around here, and one of the chimps —"

"What happened?" Adia said, confused.

"It's in the book," I said again. "It's there."

"Are there, like, pictures if I don't want to read the whole thing?"

I showed her the inset of photos: a black-and-white shot of the outside of the Toney-bee; a hazy reproduction of Julia Toneybee-Leroy's oil portrait; and then a few old pictures of what must have been Miss Toneybee-Leroy again, young and in a blouse and a pleated skirt and a cloche on her head, with a chimp riding her hip. The chimp wore an identical outfit, right down to the skirt and the hat.

"Those don't look so bad," Adia said faintly.

"Just wait."

She turned the page.

"This is it?'

I nodded, gravely.

"I don't get it. It's a still life, right?"

I closed my eyes. "No."

"Well, what is it?"

"It's . . ." I thought I couldn't say it. "It's backsides. This one" — I pointed to the one on the left — "is the backside of a woman. They just know her name is Nymphadora. That's all they could find in the archives. And this" — I pointed to the other one — "is the backside of a chimpanzee. A girl chimpanzee."

Adia frowned. "Why?"

"Because," I said, "they're comparing."

Adia was still looking at the drawings.

"They did the same thing to men," I continued. "Not pictures or anything, but they did, like, brain tests on the black men who lived in Spring City and messed up their brains and then compared them to chimp brains. And they forced this woman to pose, they forced her to do it and then they made up a name for her so we can never find her. They're evil, Adia. They're all racists."

She closed the book and I finally began to cry.

Adia and her mother warned me for weeks that the world was like this. Here was proof that it was worse. I wanted her to save me, to explain, to wax sharp and go hard.

I breathed in the balm of Adia and her mother and what I'd counted on as their superior knowledge. It smelled like flaking newspapers and the brown milky slip in its bucket.

"Don't do that." Out of the corner of my eye I could see Adia's hands fluttering helplessly. "Please don't do that." She pushed on my arm and then she said, with uncharacteristic optimism, a terrible miscalculation, "Charlotte, maybe it's not that bad."

I cried until I couldn't breathe, could only choke out, "I don't believe you."

Adia leaned across and kissed me on the cheek. She bent her head, kissed my dumb hands clenched into fists. "I'm sorry," she said.

It was early in the afternoon and we still hadn't gone back to school. Beside the stereo system was a tall standing brass lamp with a piece of red gauze foolishly stretched close to the bulb. Adia and I sat in the dusty light, she was curled around my knees. I'd folded my hands, very primly, and set them on my lap and Adia rested her head on them. My fingers were beginning to go numb. Soon Adia would lift her head and my hands would feel weightless and light and electric again. She just had to lift her head. But she didn't. Adia pulled at a bit of T-shirt wrenched up underneath her. Then she settled back down.

"So, what are you going to do?"

"I don't know."

"Yeah, I mean, I guess that makes sense." She was quiet again, but I could tell she was waiting. "Because," she said carefully, "I've been thinking. And I think what you should do is, confront them. Confront them and shut it all down."

"I'm not going to do that."

Adia finally lifted her head, shocked. "They're terrible people."

"I have to tell my mother about it first."

Adia lay back down. "Don't you think she already knows?" she said carefully.

My mother had to know. It hadn't occurred to me before, but I understood it now and felt sick. "No," I said, "of course she doesn't."

"So you give her the book and you show it to her and the two of you go out together and tell the Toneybee off. You stand up for what's right. You stand up for your rights. You do it."

"I don't know." I knew my mother would never do that, but it hurt too much to admit that to Adia.

Adia sat up. "How can you not know?"

"I should go home."

She stretched.

"Wait till I tell Marie about this."

When my mother pulled up to Adia's, she

239

didn't even park the car, just honked from the street. I'd waited for her outside the Breitlings' front door. I didn't trust Adia, was certain she would denounce my mother the moment she saw her face.

I buckled my seat belt. My mother said, to the windshield, "What is the matter with you? You can't be skipping school like this. We thought something terrible happened to you."

"Well, it didn't."

"Honestly, Charlotte, that's all you can say?"

The whole car smelled like Charlie. His scent had become my mother's: the whiff of animal, but something sharper as well, oniony and frantic, the stink of raw nerves.

"Well, you're not even going to apologize?" She pulled out into the road.

I leaned over in the seat, unzipped my backpack and pulled out the book. I placed it on the dashboard between us.

"Charlotte, take that off, it's just going to slide around and fall off and hurt somebody."

I reached up and turned on the overhead light. She started to complain about the glare, but then she saw the book's cover and she understood. She did not even glance in the rearview mirror — we were back on the turnpike by then — she simply swerved to the side of the road and turned off the car.

The only sound was the engine cooling into pops and the wind in the trees. The overhead light was still on, so bright it made outside the car black, no woods, no turnpike, no nothing.

My mother was calm. "Where did you get that?"

"I found it."

"Where?"

"Nowhere."

She tapped the cover of the book with her finger. She would not pick it up. She said very carefully, "How do you feel about it?"

I didn't trust myself to answer.

"I bet you feel very angry with me right now," she began. "And very confused. That's right, isn't it? You probably think you hate me and the Toneybee, and you're confused."

"It's all here in the book. The Toneybee Institute is racist and they're evil."

"There's a lot of things in that book that aren't true."

"There are pictures —" She shook her head, one brisk no at the word *pictures.* "There's proof. I saw it."

She was quiet for a minute. Then she began to argue with the glass in front of her again. "It was a long time ago, Charlotte. Over sixty years ago. A lot can change in sixty years."

"Not that much," I said. "You don't even care."

She turned to me, her eyes bright, her voice shaking. "You know what, Charlotte? You're right. I don't care. I don't care what that book says. I don't care about anything written in there."

She saw my face and her own softened. "Look," she continued, a little more slowly. "Charlotte, I love you. I love you and I love your sister. And I love Charlie. I love this experiment. You're right," she said. "I don't care about anything that book has to say. *We*" — she took her hands off the steering wheel, formed a fist, and moved it across her chest to the left, to rest right above her heart, signing the word — "*we*, Charlotte, we're bigger than all of this. What we're doing with Charlie now? What we get to do? It's realer than any history and it's better than anything written in that book. It's realer than anything this book" — she tapped it again with her finger — "could ever imagine. But us, you and me and Dad and Callie and Charlie? We're bigger than this, Charlotte. We're bigger than history."

"So what are you saying? You're telling me

you knew about this all along?"

My mother took a deep breath. "I don't care why the Toneybee brought us here. Maybe they hired us because we're black, or maybe they hired us because we can sign, or maybe they hired us because they liked us, or maybe they hired us because we're the best, or maybe they hired us because they think they're using us to make them look good. I'm telling you, Charlotte, honey, please believe me, it's the best lesson you'll ever learn: none of that matters. It doesn't matter why *they* think we're here. What matters is we're here."

She reached up, turned off the overhead light. Without the glare, the woods came back, the fence for the turnpike, the soft street lamps of downtown Courtland behind us. She started the car now: she didn't bother to take the book off the dashboard and neither did I. It just sat there for the rest of the ride, sliding back and forth across the vinyl between us.

When we got to the gates of the Toneybee she stopped the car and said, her voice low, "Just, please, don't tell Callie."

I started to laugh. "You've got to be kidding."

"I'm serious, Charlotte. Don't tell her. She's not going to understand. You don't understand, either, but Callie's just a little girl."

"What about Dad?"

"He knows," she said quickly. "He already knows everything. He's not happy about it, but he knows this is important. As should you."

"So," I said, "I can't talk about crazy racists and I can't talk about you and Charlie, you know, Charlie feeding off of you. Is that it? Is that the whole list?"

"We can tell Callie. Eventually. And we can tell them about Charlie nursing eventually. Just not now, when we're doing so well. It could ruin everything. It's not just you who's affected, you know. It's the whole experiment. They've spent hundreds of thousands of dollars on us already. Do you know how much money that is?"

"Sure. It's hundreds of thousands of dollars."

"Don't get smart with me. If that number doesn't mean anything to you, then I'm raising you wrong. Things like this don't happen every day. There's actually something to lose here. There's a lot to lose here. The woman who wrote this book? People like that don't even understand the concept of having something to lose."

"Adia says we are all in this one struggle

together. Her mother says that black people have to help one another and we start by knowing our history."

"That's bullshit," my mother said. She saw the look on my face. "You want the truth from me and I'll give it. Listen very carefully. The woman who wrote this book and your friend, Adia? People like that just love the trouble. They live for the breaking down. They don't know anything about the building up. They can't even conceive of the building up. They just move on to the next breaking down. Your life isn't like theirs, Charlotte. You and me and your father and Callie, we have a lot to lose if this goes wrong. You start in on this, you decide to make a statement and play the victim on this and it's not just you who ends up hurt. You're being selfish if you think it's just you."

I was quiet for a long time. "Fine," I said.

"And you have to stop talking to Adia."

"No." I shook my head. "No. I'm not going to do that. If you make me stop seeing Adia, this is all off. This whole thing. I tell everyone, and tell Dr. Paulsen and Dad, and I'm selfish. If you stop me from seeing Adia, I'll be selfish."

We were at the gates. We could see Lester Potter through the window of the guard-house, peering at the car, curious about why we hadn't moved. "Fine." My mother flashed her lights at Lester, a signal that things were fine. "But not a word."

I nodded and then I swung the car door open and stepped out on to the gravel drive.

"Charlotte," my mother called, her voice finally panicked.

"I just want to walk up the drive by myself."

I heard the passenger door slam and then the chug of the engine, the crunch of gravel as she maneuvered past me. In the dark, I walked up the drive and threw my head back. The elm trees scratched against the dark sky. It smelled like earth and trees and leaves somewhere, far away, burning.

When I got to the grand steps of the Toneybee, I stepped off the gravel drive onto the cold lawn, toward the heavy double doors that were the staff entrance. I made it through, but then instead of walking up the stairs to our apartment, I stopped and stood in front of the picture of Julia Toneybee-Leroy and her monkey.

I gazed up at her face, and at the bones beside her, shot through with sticks. I leaned close to the painting, pressed my nose against the canvas, kept my eyes wide open until the whole image dissolved, first into muddy colors, then into brushstrokes, into the pimpled skin of the canvas.

I breathed in deep the old oil and dust and my own tears. I pressed my forehead deeper into the canvas, opened my eyes wide to stop crying, let the colors in front of me swim out of focus.

"In times of strife, revolutionaries must offer their homes to comrades in hiding," Adia told me, days later, sitting on the floor of Marie's studio.

"You think so?"

Adia looked at me gravely. "History is a weapon, Charlotte."

We were in from the cold, listening to Marie work the wheel at the end of the room. Adia had just finished reading to Marie from a copy of *Man or Beast?* My mother had made me give Max's copy back to him, and Adia had first tried to order another for Marie to see, but both the Courtland County Library and the bookstore in town claimed that the book was unattainable. Courtland County Community College claimed the same. Marie had finally asked a friend in Boston to send one. Adia and I read the book together, and after every chapter we finished she wrote a letter to the editor of the *Courtland County Mercury,* but none of these were ever printed. She was convinced that we were being censored and blocked by the Toneybee Institute at every turn.

Adia was winding herself up now. "We're gonna fill you up with so much knowledge," she told me, "so much consciousness, this experiment can't bring you down. They wanna hide the truth from us? Well, you're just going to stop participating. You're going to disrupt the whole thing. But we need that book because you have to do it with knowledge and with style and with grace. Right, Marie? You've got to make a statement."

But Marie, serene behind her wheel, called to us, "You cannot do anything."

Adia turned to her, incredulous. "We have to do something."

Marie only sat back and lit another cigarette, smiling maddeningly. She inhaled and when she spoke her voice was beautiful and deep and grave, "Doing anything is impossible."

I felt my stomach dip. "But that's the whole reason why I keep coming here," I said.

Something flashed across Adia's face, but she lowered her eyes before I could make it out. When she raised them again, she was merely angry. Marie was sketching out her argument of inaction.

"It's not real. It's psychological," Marie went on. "That mess at the Toneybee, what your family is messed up in, that's not a real problem. It's the symptom of a larger metaphysical disease. It's a metaphor, and as a metaphor it can only be fought metaphorically, not with actual actions."

"That doesn't make any sense," Adia said, seething, and Marie laughed back at her.

"Of course it doesn't make any sense," she told us. "Nothing about racism makes sense. If it made sense, it would mean it was real, it was the truth. It's ironic," Marie pronounced, savoring the word. Despite this, it still sounded wrong to me.

"My family is real. I mean, I really live in the Toneybee and it's really terrible."

Marie only shook her head sadly. "Your family, your parents and sister and that chimp, you're just as unreal as all of it. That's why it's not possible to 'do anything,' as Adia puts it." Marie sat back and stubbed out her cigarette in a bucket full of potsherds.

Adia cried, "We need marches and signs and we need to write to the outside papers. We need to lie down in the street."

Marie was quizzical. "That book will so be out in the world. It will embarrass the

Toneybee, and they will care. And maybe some people in Courtland County will care. But it won't shift anything monumental in our collective consciousness. There's nothing more we can do here, Adia. And I'm sorry to tell you this, Charlotte. But I don't understand why you girls are getting so upset about this one thing. It's clear that here in Courtland County you can't get a fair shake. They'll suppress the book and anyone who speaks out against it, so why even try? The world is so much bigger and so much worse than this. You throw yourself into Courtland County and you're just working on Charlotte's family. That's only four people —"

"Plus the chimp," Adia added.

"All right, yes, and him. Think of the larger picture, both of you. I know it's hard on you, Charlotte. Please think of my home as a safe space. But agitating against this one thing when your energies can go to something so much bigger — you're young. You can do better. The book is enough. Just let time take care of it."

Marie stood up from her stool, crossed over to the stereo, and put on a record. It was a song made up of just one creaking horn.

At the sound of that horn Adia drew

herself up, grabbed my hand, and took me upstairs to her room.

My mother was right. These people were useless.

Adia raged and cried, but she did not give up. A few weeks later, when I told her that Dr. Paulsen, excited by the progress of the experiment, had insisted on a Thanksgiving dinner with Julia Toneybee-Leroy herself, Adia became excited.

I was more mystified. Adia and I had talked about Julia Toneybee-Leroy and underlined every mention of her in *Man or Beast?* But still, it had been easy to forget that she was a person and that she was alive. It was as if Dr. Paulsen had pulled a ten-dollar bill from her pocket and pointed to the engraving of President Jackson and said, "Make him up a plate."

Quick-thinking Adia coaxed me, "Now's your chance. You get to look her in the face and confront her."

"I'm not doing that."

She moved away from me. We were in her room again, like always, lying side by side.

I was scared of looking like a fool in front of my father's family. Dr. Paulsen insisted that they be invited, too. I'd gotten excited at the thought of maybe embarrassing my mother for once, but my uncle Lyle and aunt Ginny would only see rudeness, not protest.

Uncle Lyle and Aunt Ginny lived in a clapboard Victorian back in Cambridge, on one of the little streets that cramped up between Central Square and the banks of the Charles River.

When we lived in Dorchester, every Sunday afternoon we drove across the bridge and ate dinner on Chalk Street. Every meal there ended with the same lament. Right around dessert, right before the men, Kool cigarettes tucked between their knuckles, disappeared out the back door into a cloud of mentholated smoke, Uncle Lyle would lean back in his chair and say, "Laurel's got you beat, boy. Who ever heard of living in a building with strangers when you could live with family? You think you're better than us." As if our apartment in Dorchester was impossibly chic and not stained with watermarks and seeded with lead paint. It was always that way with them — my father and Uncle Lyle passing some unknown jealousy back and forth, as easily as they traded loose cigarettes from pocket to pocket.

Beside me now, Adia dipped her head and kissed my arm, something she rarely did. I flushed. "I'm going to call you afterward to make sure you do it."

"You're crazy."

"Just think of how good it will feel." She rolled on to her side and flung one arm across my chest.

We lay like that for a long time, me breathing in the sharp acrid scent of Adia, she breathing into the hollow of my collarbone until I said, heady and overcome, "Okay, all right. I'll do it."

She kissed my neck. "I knew you would."

Late November was when Courtland County became truly beautiful. That busy, condescending green that greeted us a few months before softened and deepened until the whole world, despite the winds, despite our breath hanging frozen in the air, closed in around us and felt warm.

It was so beautiful it hurt. Even Adia felt it. The day before Thanksgiving, dismissed early from school, we walked to her house, both of us gathering up handfuls of red-and-orange ombred leaves and scattering the bouquets across her bedroom floor, until her sheets, her hair, her skin, smelled like seeded earth.

I took the early bus from Adia's house and made it to the Toneybee just before dark. I pushed through the institute gates, past

253

Lester Potter in his guard hut, and walked up the drive, watching the bricks in front of me turn from red to black.

Thanksgiving morning had arrived and our whole family was running late. But Uncle Lyle and Aunt Ginny were early. Lester Potter sent word at noon that they were already coming up the drive.

My mother was struggling to get Charlie into a pair of pants, so it was me and my father and Callie who went to find them in the Toneybee lobby.

Callie walked ahead of me, a sweater tied around her waist, the belly of it trailing down the backs of her knees. She hadn't been able to get the zipper on her dress closed all the way. She'd given up and let it sigh half open, so that the expanse of her back — from the tops of her white tights, rolling down below her hips, to the chubby wings of her shoulder blades — was exposed.

I caught up with her, reached out to tug on the zipper, but she shrugged off the touch of my hand and scowled at me.

Go away, she signed.

Your dress is open.

She angled her hand behind her, felt her bare skin there.

Leave me alone.

"What's your problem?" I called after her, but she only walked faster. When she got to the end of the hall, she untied her sweater from her waist and, with a flourish, snapped it over her shoulders.

In the pocket of my own dress was a piece of notebook paper twisted and twirled around a pencil. In Adia's room, the afternoon before, surrounded by broken leaves and bedsheets, we had written a long screed full of denunciations and pleas for the forgotten. The plan was that right after grace I would stand up. I would turn slowly to Miss Julia Toneybee-Leroy and I would recite the words on the paper. I would hold up my hand and sign out the most important ones so that Charlie could understand. "After all," Adia reasoned, "he's oppressed, too. Kind of."

She underlined those words in red so that I would remember.

Lyle's Jaguar idled in the Toneybee Institute's front drive. It was a 1970s model, a discard that always lurked around Lyle's garage, but Lyle and Ginny had made a point of driving it to Courtland County and showily parking it at the Toneybee's front steps. When we found them, Ginny was still in the car, peering up at the building from

255

her window, and Lyle was leaning against the hood, smoking.

My father and Uncle Lyle looked nothing alike. My father was better-looking, but Lyle was the sharper dresser. He spent most of the day in coveralls with oil and dirt beneath his nails, so when he was out of the garage, Lyle always dressed up. He wore a heavy gray cable sweater with a white dress shirt buttoned up underneath and discreetly checkered pants. On his feet, penny loafers, two fresh coins winking out of the leather slits. He was shorter than my father, he only came up to the middle of his chest, but that didn't matter because Lyle's voice was hoarse and booming.

Callie ran to him, and he pressed his hand to his chest, staggered back. "Cal, what happened to you?"

She wavered.

"Your hair," he said.

"I like it," Callie tried.

He reached out and gently crushed a stiff curl between his fingers.

"She likes it, Lyle," my father said, a little sharper than Callie had.

"Gin, you see this?" Uncle Lyle called to his wife.

Ginny, still in the front seat of the car, let her gaze drift over the top of Callie's head, then back to her husband. "It's all right," she said coolly. Ginny always wore her hair the same way: two heavy braids curled into ram's horns on either side of her head, one resting above each ear. On her lap was a white casserole dish, the sides crusted over with trails of brown sugar, the whole thing wrapped up in a threadbare tea towel. Ginny seemed undecided on what to do with the dish: whether to stick it, ungracefully, between her two feet on the car floor and force herself out of the seat, or whether to hold on to it and somehow manage her way out of the car without the use of her hands. Unable to make up her mind, she stayed where she was, eyeing me and Callie.

She blinked at Callie's widened face. She eyed my legs. I had sinned in her eyes and appeared outside without stockings. Ginny's own skinny legs were wrapped up in white hose, the weave on it so thick I couldn't even see the brown of her skin.

She raised her eyes from my legs to the front of my blouse, trying to gauge if it was too tight. I passed muster. I think the ruffles confused her. But still, she couldn't resist saying pointedly, "You've grown, Charlotte."

Inside, Lyle made a big show of inspecting all the brass and chandeliers. He touched the oak paneling and whistled theatrically. "Bet it's a bitch with the humidity in the summer."

"That's the beauty of it," my father smiled. "Laurel and I are here rent-free. We don't have to worry about that stuff. Not even utilities."

Lyle nodded grudgingly. "Good, good."

In the hall, we stopped in front of Julia Toneybee-Leroy's portrait. Callie pointed out the baby skeleton in the picture and Uncle Lyle began, with operatic overindulgence, to praise it. "Well, that's something," he said, "That's really, really something. Baby brother, they make portraits of whole monkey skeletons here? They really do?"

My father ignored him. Lyle moved farther down the hall, eager to discover more to flatter into contempt. He was walking so quickly he nearly matched Ginny's long-legged stride. She pressed her casserole dish close to her chest. She waved off my father and Lyle when each of them offered to carry it.

"What did Laurel make?" she said. "I called her about the sweet potatoes, but she didn't call back. I guess she was too busy?"

My father let the dig slide.

"I made them anyway," Ginny continued, "but I don't know if there's enough. She didn't tell us how many guests."

"That's our fault." Then, trying to repair it, "Don't worry, Gin. The menu is on us."

Ginny shifted the casserole dish under her arm.

We reached the apartment door. I watched Uncle Lyle's face as he walked inside. His eyes brightened, his mouth opened slightly wider. All his jealousy left him when he saw Charlie.

There was my mother in a peach chiffon dress, her hair dampened with activator spray and glistening in the overhead light. There was Dr. Paulsen, who'd dispensed with the lab coat for the day, in a tweed skirt and a shirt with a collar.

And there was Charlie, in the green pants my mother had wrestled with. He wasn't wearing a shirt, but he was so calm, his bare chest and round belly appeared dignified. Charlie's hands hung in his lap, and when we came through the door, he didn't screech or grasp at my mother or even grin. He merely tilted his head back and flared his nostrils.

"Ha," Ginny said behind us, dryly.

Max hustled his way toward us, made for the corner of the living room where he'd set out the camcorder. He eased it on to his shoulder and pointed the lens and the mounted dirty, fuzzy mic at us. He said,

"Just pretend I'm not here," but nobody responded.

Lyle moved toward my mother to kiss her on the cheek. Charlie eyed him warily. "Just wave for now, please," she said.

Uncle Lyle frowned.

"He doesn't know you all yet. It's just going to take a while for him to get used to you."

As she spoke, Charlie got down off the couch. He stood awkwardly, expectantly, arms stretching forward. Then he dropped to his knuckles and loped across the room. He ignored my father. He ignored Callie. He hesitated near the tops of my Mary Janes and I felt certain he was going to spit on them. But he kept going. He made it all the way to Aunt Ginny, who still held the casserole dish in her hand.

He reached out a finger and ran it up against the thick white nylon of her stockings. Ginny shivered. Charlie peered at her knees. Then he reached out his finger and did it again.

"Oh." My mother was embarrassed. "I'm sorry, Ginny."

"It's all right." Ginny's voice was strained. She held the casserole dish a little higher.

Charlie touched her leg a few more times. Then he held his fingers to his nose and

260

took a loud sniff.

"Your monkey's coming on to my wife?" Uncle Lyle said to my father, and this made nearly everyone — Max, Dr. Paulsen, my father — laugh. The only ones who didn't were my mother and Ginny. My mother said, "He's just investigating his environment."

"Is that what they call it?" Uncle Lyle said.

Ginny still hadn't moved. Charlie touched her legs again, his fingers quick. He swept them as far as the tops of Ginny's calves. He stopped at the hem of her skirt. He did this until he collected enough of whatever he needed on his fingertips, and then he crammed his fingers into his nose and sniffed them again, hard. Ginny half closed her eyes.

My mother, alarmed, got up and took the casserole dish. "I think it's your perfume, Gin."

It was the scent Ginny wore, her one concession to fashion — rose oil that she rubbed on the back of her neck and her bony wrists several times a day, until the very essence of Ginny was the rank breath of dead flowers.

Ginny nodded shyly. "Yes."

"Gin, I told you you were going a little overboard this morning, didn't I?" Lyle pinched her elbow, still amused.

Ginny, her hands free now, reached up, uncertain, and rubbed the back of her neck, at the spot where her two heavy braids met. "It's not bad, is it?"

"It's fine, Gin, it really is," my mother answered. "He's just not used to it. I don't use any perfume and neither does Dr. Paulsen. I don't even think Max uses after-shave."

"I don't, it's true." Max leaned his head back from the viewfinder.

Ginny nodded. Charlie was sitting at her feet now, very gently stroking the fronts of her brown leather pumps. He looked up at her, through his thick lashes. Ginny crooned, "Oh, but he's beautiful."

My mother beamed. "I think so, too."

We were interrupted by a knock at the door. Dr. Paulsen sprang to her feet, dropped her chalk in her pocket. "It's Miss Toneybee-Leroy," she said.

Julia Toneybee-Leroy arrived with an attendant, a black nurse nearly as old as she was, who creaked slowly beside her. I could not see Julia Toneybee-Leroy clearly until she sat down, regally, on the couch, and then the room went quiet as we all stared at the woman from the painting, brought to overwhelming life.

She was the oldest person I had ever seen. Her skin lay in great folds over her ropy muscles and tapered bones. Her hair was an ancient blond, colorless until the light hit it a certain way and then it gave off dying blinks of color.

Of course, she was not wearing the gown from the oil portrait. Instead she wore a baggy sweatshirt, slightly stained and printed with apples, and bright blue stirrup pants. The casualness of her outfit was strange, but as she watched each of us it was clear she was not put out by our finery. She did not seem to think it the least bit odd to be wearing leisurewear for a Thanksgiving dinner when everyone else was in hose and dress pants. She took it in as her due.

The nurse was dressed similarly to Julia Toneybee-Leroy: the same cheap cotton pants, the same bilious sweatshirt. Her gray hair was pressed and slicked close to her head.

My father shook the nurse's hand first. He asked her name and she replied in a gruff voice, avoiding his eye, "Nadine Morton."

"Nurse Morton has worked with me at the institute for over sixty years." Julia Toneybee-Leroy interrupted before he could ask the nurse any more questions.

Miss Toneybee-Leroy's eyes were more unnerving than her hair or her skin. Her eyes flitted between all of us, with the tip of her tongue resting between her half-parted lips, her expression less like an old woman's and more like a very wrinkled little girl's. She looked at us all as if she already knew us.

I watched her watching my family and I tried to steel myself, like Adia told me to. "She's the cause of everything," Adia had coached the night before. But I could hear the breath leave her lungs from across the room. And it was hard to hate a woman who gazed at my sister with such affection.

I put my hand in my pocket, just to remind myself of the speech there, when Miss Toneybee-Leroy raised her arms above her head and suddenly began to making a harsh, high hiss from the back of her throat.

We all stared at her. Only Nadine Morton was undisturbed — she sat back, arms folded, unimpressed.

Julia Toneybee-Leroy was calling for Charlie. When she started making the noise, he came and stood beside her, almost against his will. She sunk her fingers into his hair, and began to forcefully pet him behind the ears. Charlie closed his eyes.

My mother watched as Charlie caved, until she couldn't stand it anymore and brusquely turned to Ginny.

"Give me that, Gin," she said, taking the casserole dish. She retreated to the kitchen, giving up Charlie to Miss Toneybee-Leroy, for now.

When Miss Toneybee-Leroy had petted Charlie into submission, Lyle sidled up to her.

"So, ma'am, such a lovely young ma'am as yourself." Lyle took her papery hand in his and pressed it.

"Why've you got my lovely only nieces in the world, my only flesh and blood, with that there monkey?" He said it to make her laugh, and it worked.

"Your only flesh and blood — they're going to be famous." Her eyes flashed. "You should be proud."

She said it so certainly. She did not seem embarrassed or guilty of any past crime. Adia had said she wouldn't feel any guilt. "She doesn't even know she should." I stopped tearing up the paper.

"Where do you get all these chimps, anyway?" Lyle said, still smiling. "A catalog?"

Miss Toneybee-Leroy's voice was clear and strong, "Leopoldville, originally. The

Belgian Congo. Or just Zaire. I went there and bought our very first chimp in 1929."

"The bones in the picture," Callie exclaimed.

Miss Toneybee-Leroy faltered. "Yes," she said. "The bones in the picture."

She cleared her throat. "My first time in Leopoldville, I was there on safari. I danced at a rumba club. The Leopoldvilliens, black and white, were crazy for rumba back then."

"A rumba club, huh?" Lyle was amused. "You cut a rug, did you, ma'am?"

"I did, Mr. Freeman. The Congo was beautiful," she said very deliberately as if she were relaying a secret message.

Ginny pursed her lips. "Sounds like it."

"You look lovely today, Callie. I love your dress," Miss Toneybee-Leroy called.

"Doesn't she, though?" Dr. Paulsen agreed, relieved at the change of subject. "She really looks fantastic."

"You look great," Lyle said, not to be outdone in noticing things about his own family.

Confused by the sudden flurry of attention, Callie stared down at her shoes and mumbled, "Thank you."

My mother returned from the kitchen with a plate of lettuce leaves, each rolled up carefully into a cigar. Charlie's favorite

266

snack, a blatant play for his affections.

She held out a piece of lettuce to him, but Miss Toneybee-Leroy took it before he could.

"Thank you, my dear," she said. "I can help him if you'd like. I remember."

I don't think she meant to be condescending. But my mother burned with humiliation. She tried to recover. "Of course." She passed the leafy cigar off to Miss Toneybee-Leroy's pinched fingers.

"What about the rest of us?" my father tried to help her recover. "Charlie gets some hospitality and we don't?"

"I thought Lyle and Ginny might like to try it," my mother said.

Ginny snorted. Lyle put a hand on her knee. He kept his hand there while he leaned over and reached for a lettuce cigar himself.

Charlie studied the hand on Ginny's knee. He beaded his head down and raised his shoulders. We all recognized that move immediately. It was Miss Toneybee-Leroy who broke the tension.

"I hate to impose," she said, turning toward my mother, "but really, my dear, don't you think we should go straight to dinner?"

It took a while for all of us to reassemble

in the dining room. Charlie began shouting as soon as he smelled the food, and he got louder the longer he sat with an empty plate in front of him, while the rest of us filed around the table. My mother tried to pass a cloth napkin to Miss Toneybee-Leroy, but Nurse Morton languidly intercepted it. Charlie began rocking back and forth in his chair.

"Should we say grace?" my father asked.

"Yes," Dr. Paulsen said.

My mother hurried back to her place beside Charlie and grasped his hand in her own. "Make it quick, please, Lyle," she said.

Dr. Paulsen reached for Charlie's other hand and he was defeated into quiet.

I took Callie's sticky hand in mine and Callie gingerly placed her free hand in Miss Toneybee-Leroy's.

The only one not holding anyone's hand was Max, who stood near my father's end of the table, the video camera perched on his shoulder, trying to get everyone in the picture.

We bowed our heads.

This was my chance. I waited a moment, then looked up, ready to speak. I found only Charlie and the eye of the camera staring back at me. I decided I would let Lyle finish. I would tear them all down after Lyle had just graced them up.

Lyle began, "Lord of our hearts, make us truly thankful for what we are about to receive. Thank you to Charles and Laurel and the girls and, sorry, miss" — he raised his head and gave Dr. Paulsen's hand a shake — "didn't catch your name . . ."

"Marietta," Dr. Paulsen replied, too anxious to give him her correct title.

"Miss Marietta," Lyle continued, "thank you for inviting us. Gin and I are just grateful to share this day with you. And of course, a thanks to the lady who made it all possible, the lovely Miss Toneybee-Leroy."

Everyone raised their heads and said "Amen."

Lyle winked first at Dr. Paulsen, who dipped her head in confusion. He winked at Miss Toneybee-Leroy, too, but she only smiled serenely back. Wanting a bigger reaction, he raised her hand, which he still held in his own, from the table and gave it a theatrical squeeze for everyone to see. But still, Miss Toneybee-Leroy was oblivious. She gave us all a gummy smile and shook their clasped hands in kind.

Now, I told myself. Speak now. I cleared my throat, but no sound came.

Ginny reached to the center of the table for her dish. "Can Charlie eat these?"

My mother shook her head swiftly. "I'm sorry, Ginny. Too sweet."

"Well." Dr. Paulsen gave a quick, placating glance to Lyle at her left. "It can't hurt him to try a little. I'm sure he'd like it." After Lyle's grace, there was no doubt for Dr. Paulsen. She knew he was a trouble-maker.

My mother handed Charlie's plate over to Ginny. When Charlie got it back, he stuck his finger in the middle of the potatoes, then brought it to his mouth and sucked on it. He blinked in Aunt Ginny's direction and made a kiss.

Lyle cocked his head. "I can't get over that monkey being in love with my wife."

"He does seem smitten," Miss Toneybee-Leroy agreed. "I'd hoped to charm him myself, but I see your wife is already first in his affections."

"What's not to like about Gin?" Lyle agreed. "That monkey's got great taste."

"He certainly does." Miss Toneybee-Leroy turned slightly away from him. Nadine Morton leaned down between Lyle and Miss Toneybee-Leroy and began shredding the turkey on her plate.

While Nurse Morton worked, Miss Toneybee-Leroy gazed serenely in front of her, patently unembarrassed. Following her

270

lead, everyone else pretended not to see Nadine Morton's black arthritic fingers shredding the pale turkey meat, except for Lyle and Callie, who stared openly. Lyle glanced across the table at my father and gestured to Nadine Morton with his fork. My father turned to pass the stuffing to Ginny.

"You know," Lyle said to Miss Toneybee-Leroy, in a loud imitation of a confidential tone, "my wife, she does everything for me, too. We've been married twenty years and she still makes me coffee before I wake up. Still wakes up a half hour before I do to put on makeup, to put on her face, she says. Twenty years and I've never seen Gin without makeup. I tell you, that monkey knows what's what."

"It appears he does." Miss Toneybee-Leroy wasn't smiling at all anymore.

Ginny blushed. She kept her eyes on her plate as they spoke.

I think it was to stop the flow of praise, to take attention off herself, that made Ginny stand up slightly in her chair. "Pass your plates up, please," she commanded the table, and began serving out the food to everyone.

"Marietta," Ginny pitched her voice to be heard over Charlie's shouts, "what do you

271

do here?"

"Well," Dr. Paulsen began. But she didn't finish, allowed herself to be drowned out by Charlie.

My mother was annoyed at Dr. Paulsen's hesitation. "She runs the place, Ginny."

Lyle reached for the platter of ham. "That's right?"

"Yes," Dr. Paulsen said.

"And how'd you get into that line of work?"

"Well," she began. But I cut her off. Lyle had begun to fork pieces of ham on my plate, unasked.

"No thanks," I said suddenly. I'd found a place for my contrariness at last. I felt the spirit of revolution swell inside me. "I don't eat pork anymore." Lyle raised his eyebrows in surprise, then tilted my plate and let the meat slide back on the platter.

Ginny's eyes widened at all of this. My mother very slightly shook her head, letting Ginny know I should be ignored.

"What's this about?"

"Well, it's not right for us to eat pork. I mean, we didn't used to eat pork. Black people, I mean. I mean, like a long time ago." I felt the Breitlings' rules wither away. I couldn't remember the logic. "It's not right." I tried once more. "It's not right as

African Americans."

Miss Toneybee-Leroy's whole face went soft in sympathy. I had not expected that.

"Well, what do you know, Charles. Even all the way out here, Charlotte's gone political," Lyle said approvingly. He lifted his own piece of ham to his mouth and took a bite. As he chewed, he said, "I could never get behind that nonsense the first time it came around, Charlotte, when I was young. It's just an animal. It don't mean nothing."

"She should eat whatever she wishes," Miss Toneybee-Leroy said.

I was confused by this, and annoyed. Julia Toneybee-Leroy was the only person at the table attempting to take my declaration seriously, but I realized, with a sting, that she did it out of pity.

That sting helped. I resolved to remember the bits and pieces of Marie's lectures. "Pork," I began, my voice getting surer as I followed the argument to its conclusion, "is full of all kinds of trash, Uncle Lyle. It's got, like, parasites and toxins, because of the way the animals are raised. Pigs are really unclean. They're some really unclean animals, even worse than Charlie —"

"He's not an animal," Callie blurted. Everyone at the table laughed, relieved. Callie looked at me searchingly, hurt.

I ignored her. "All right, Callie," I said, playing up for the others, "an *individual* like Charlie."

We all turned to Charlie who was signing at Ginny, catcalling her with his hands.

"Compare Charlie to the general pigs they breed to eat. Do you know how they breed those pigs?" It was a leap, but I took it, to try to get to the crimes of the Toneybee. "They breed pigs the same way they used to breed us —"

"That's enough, Charlotte." My mother knew exactly where I was going.

"Ha," Lyle goaded. "Go on. Let's hear it to the end."

I looked at Miss Toneybee-Leroy who still looked at me pityingly. Keep going, her eyes said. And please stop. She wished for both, I saw, and this confused me.

It was the pity, though, that was galling. She was embarrassed for me, though everything in the book said she should be embarrassed for herself. The pity in her eyes made me want to cringe and apologize and stop talking and agree. But Adia's voice in my ear told me I couldn't.

My voice, I thought, was ready.

But I was stopped again by Lyle, this time needling Max. "This must be weird for you, man."

Max jerked his head back from the eyepiece slightly. "What do you mean?"

"Well, it must be a little bit of a study for you, too. To see how black folks act at a family dinner. Our theories and stuff."

Max smiled slightly, unsure what to say next. The room was slipping away from me. I realized I didn't want to hurt her, couldn't hurt her, not while she was in the room beside me.

My mother, across the table, signed to me now, not caring if Dr. Paulsen or anyone else saw, *Charlotte, stop.*

"My brother's worried I'm gonna say something off," Lyle spoke patiently to the camera lens. "But don't worry, Charles. I'm not going to say a word."

"Does the not saying a word start now or after dinner?" my father said. "Because you aren't doing a very good job of it now."

"I'm just curious." Lyle stretched back, directed his grin to Miss Toneybee-Leroy. I stood up slightly in my chair, gripped my fork. I know, without a doubt, if Lyle were sitting beside me I would have stabbed the back of his hand with it. He was canceling me out.

"You strike me as an intelligent lady," he continued. "A smart female such as you are, ma'am."

Miss Toneybee-Leroy reached for her water glass. "I don't like it when men call human women females."

Lyle clucked. "All right, a woman such as yourself. Can I ask you, as an intelligent woman, doesn't this all feel a little weird to you?"

"I'm not so sure that I understand what you mean," Miss Toneybee-Leroy said distinctly. Nadine Morton put a hand on her shoulder. "And honestly, Mr. Freeman, I'm not so sure I like you so much anymore." She flashed her gums at him. "I am sorry to be rude."

Lyle was not intimidated.

"Well, I assure you, I like you, ma'am." He laughed. "All I was trying to say before I offended you, and I am truly sorry to offend you, ma'am, that was not my intention, what I was trying to say is, don't you think it's odd you white folks, no offense to yourself or Miss Marietta, of course, no offense to the young man with the camera, I've forgotten your name . . ."

"Max," Max said.

"All right, okay. Yeah. You. Don't you think it's odd to watch my baby brother and his family as hard as you watch Charlie? With that nice young man's video camera and all?" Lyle said.

I gouged the tablecloth with my fork, praying for Lyle to shut up and cede the floor. I felt my heart beat fast in my throat. It was almost too late. If I yelled over him, my voice would sound flat, the speech itself would disappear, leaving behind something thin and flat and headache inducing, like a whiff of spilled gasoline.

"Don't you think, Miss Toneybee-Leroy," Lyle continued, "that we're all, me and my wife and my brother and his family, don't you think we're just as much of a specimen at this dinner as that monkey over there?"

Dr. Paulsen stood up. "Miss Toneybee, if I may?" she said, but did not wait for approval. "Mr. Freeman, that was never our intention. And I do not like what you're insinuating. And frankly, what you are implying is insulting to everyone at this table. We are all working extremely hard. We would do this with *any* family, really. Your family just happens to be black."

Lyle snorted at this.

"It's a descriptor of your family who is participating in this experiment. Not an identity," Dr. Paulsen said, firmly.

"Like how Charlie just happens to be a chimpanzee?"

I'm not sure whether Lyle knew exactly what he meant by this, but even Dr. Paulsen

277

knew enough not to challenge that one. She sat down. Lyle took a swig from his water glass.

"You're making a fool out of yourself," my father said quietly.

"I'm pointing out the truth."

"Since when have you cared about any of this?" my father said. "Since when have you ever cared about being conscious or whatever you want to call it? You're wearing a cravat, for Christ sake."

Miss Toneybee-Leroy's head was high and her eyes were burning.

"I'm just saying what I happen to see in this room," Lyle retorted. "A whole bunch of black folks eating dinner provided by white folks, interacting with a monkey, so that this nice white lady," he gestured to Miss Toneybee-Leroy, "and that young man behind the camera, I'm sorry, son, what is your name again?"

"Max," Max said miserably.

"Max over there, can film it all. And take some notes. And it isn't exactly clear where these notes end up. I'm just speculating here."

"It is odd," Ginny began. My mother shot her a look and she stopped her from going further.

"Yeah," Lyle said, "like, is this a Tuskegeetype situation or —"

"That's enough, Lyle," my father said, more forcefully.

Ginny gasped. Miss Toneybee-Leroy's eyes shot open. During this whole exchange, Charlie had taken the opportunity to reach one of his long arms behind my mother's chair and begin inching his fingers closer to Ginny. With everyone preoccupied, Charlie took his chance. He swiped forward and yanked down hard on Ginny's sleeve, tore free a good piece of silk. He snatched it back to his side of the table, to hold over his nose, the fabric delicately shuddering with each breath. Then he opened his mouth and began tonguing the rag. As we all watched, before any of us could stop him, he stuffed the whole bolt of cloth between his teeth and began lolling it around with his tongue.

"Oh my," Miss Toneybee-Leroy gasped out with a laugh.

"That's disgusting," Callie said.

Poor Ginny touched her ripped sleeve, her newly bare arm. She gazed up at all of us wonderingly. Charlie hadn't taken his eyes off her the whole time, and when she looked at him, he brought his free hand to his nose and sniffed his fingers, then opened his mouth to show us all the spit-dampened silk. He pressed his lips closed and ran his fingertips around their edges.

Ginny covered her face with her hands and began to cry. My mother at first ignored her, reaching for Charlie, but Dr. Paulsen was already beside him. "Go to her," she told my mother. "I can handle him."

Lyle also decided on laughter. He got up grinning and stood by Ginny. "Oh God, Gin, I'm sorry." He tried to sober himself, put his hand on the back of her chair. "I'm sorry, baby. You okay?"

She jerked away from him, pushed her chair back from the table. "Come with me." My mother caught her elbow. "We'll find you something new to wear."

Ginny followed her down the unfamiliar hallway. We heard the click as the lights turned on for them.

"Max," Dr. Paulsen called, "a little help, please."

Max put the camera down on the floor. Charlie was now slowly pulling the piece of cloth out of his mouth like a magician pulling scarves.

Miss Toneybee-Leroy called out, "There's no way you'll calm him down now. He's far too excited." She caught Lyle's gaze. "And this night, perhaps, has been too much for me. Marietta, calm him down. To the rest of you, I'll have to take my leave."

We stood up and filed out, leaving Dr. Paulsen and Max crouched around Charlie's chair.

In the living room, Nadine Morton brushed off my father's attempts to help and put a dingy down overcoat first across Miss Toneybee-Leroy's shoulders, then an identical one across her own.

My father offered, bravely, "I'm sorry for this."

Miss Toneybee-Leroy replied evenly, "I've had worse directed my way."

Finally, Lester Potter was at the door, ready to take them to their car. Miss Toneybee-Leroy gazed at me and Callie with damp, avid eyes. "Good-bye, girls," she called, and then she was gone, taking any hope of retribution with her.

When they were gone, my father crossed to the liquor cabinet and poured himself a glass of brandy.

Lyle sat down on the couch, rubbed his hand against the deflated cushions. "I can't get one of those?"

"Not after all that." But my father poured a second glass anyway.

Lyle swirled his brandy before he took a sip. "You know I'm right, Charles. I may have been obnoxious about it, but you know I'm right."

"We're not gonna talk about it now," my father said.

"This is a ridiculous situation," Lyle said. "I don't care how much they're paying you. You have to understand my point of view. You're my own flesh and blood —"

"Lyle." My father cut him off, gestured with his glass to where Callie and I stood. "Girls," he called, "go find somewhere else to play."

"But," I began, my insides raging. I took the tattered speech from my pocket and cleared my throat. It could still count if I read it now, I told myself. The important part was the action, the action had to be made. The audience was gone, but I could still make the action.

"When in the course of human events . . ."

It had been Adia's idea to crib the opening lines from the Declaration of Independence. We'd been studying it in history anyway, and Adia liked the roll of the words. "They won't even know," she'd said. "At the very least, the old lady will get it."

"When in the course of human events," I began grandly, my voice only breaking a little in anticipation.

"Charlotte, so help me God, get out of this room right now," my father breathed and pointed to the door.

I made a show of following Callie out of the room, but once we closed the door, we turned around and leaned against it, listening.

"All right, Lyle," I heard my father say. "You've caused enough trouble."

We heard a scattershot of clinks as they set their brandy glasses down on the coffee table, readying for the next round.

We heard Lyle say, more loudly now, "No amount of money in the world is worth this. Look at Callie. I mean, my God, look at that girl. She was always a little bit bigger, but she's getting obese out here. That can't be good."

Beside me, Callie blinked, rolled back on her heels, took the hit.

"I don't know what you're talking about," my father said.

"And Charlotte. She's older, so she's probably handling it better. But how long is this experiment supposed to last?"

"What's that got to do with Charlotte?"

"I mean, she's a young woman. Learning how to be a young lady. She's a freshman in high school. How is she supposed to have any sort of a life, an adult life, if she's the only one out here?"

"You can stop your grandstanding," my father said. "That old white lady can't even

hear you anymore. You can stop performing."

"That's just it," Lyle said, "You're proving
my point. Their every move is watched.
They're always performing. They've got
twenty-year-old white boys who don't know
their heads from their asses taking notes on
them."

"It's not for you to decide," my father said.

"It's not for you, either." A glass coming
down again on the coffee table. "This isn't
your house. It's that damn monkey's house
and you know it."

"You know what you are." My father's
voice was cold and deliberate. "You are jealous. Laurel always thought you were, and I
said you weren't, but now I see it."

We heard the springs of the Toneybee sofa
squeal. Then Lyle's voice.

"I know you don't mean that, little
brother. I know tomorrow morning you're
gonna wake up and you're gonna want to
call me and make a joke and tell me you
were tired and Laurel's sorry and that
monkey really meant well. But you know
what? I'm not going to pick up the phone."

"Fine," my father nearly shouted. "Don't
pick up the phone. Don't talk to us. Don't
come back."

We heard the stomp of Lyle's penny loafers. Then the hallway door swung open. The movement made the overhead light click on, and Lyle started for a moment, startled by the sudden sight of me and Callie.

He leaned his hand against the side. "One of you go and get Gin for me." He caught at Callie, held her close to his middle. "Charlotte, you go get my wife."

I walked to my parents' bedroom. When I got there, I found Ginny sitting on the bed, staring steadily into space. My mother stood at the open closet door, trying to pick out a blouse for her. There were a few already discarded on the carpet. My mother held up a dark green silk one with brass buttons. Ginny turned dully and shook her head.

My mother pursed her lips, annoyed.

Ginny rubbed at the bare flesh on her arm, where the sleeve was torn away. "What I can't understand," she announced, "is why did he tear up my sleeve? I would have given it to him. I would have let him kiss my hand if he wanted to. He didn't have to get nasty about it."

My mother held up another shirt. Ginny shook her head.

"It's like he didn't really care about me at all," Ginny said. And then she started crying again.

My mother shot her a pitying glance. Then

she caught me in the doorway. "What is it now?"

"Uncle Lyle says he's ready to go."

"We don't have anything for Ginny yet."

"I think that's really okay."

"Can you tell him she needs some more time?" She saw my face and misunderstood. "Don't be scared. She's just in shock, that's all. It's okay."

"I'm not scared."

My mother studied my face, still didn't understand. "Fine," she said with a sigh, giving up. She knelt by the pile of clothes on the floor.

"Mom."

My mother looked up at me.

It's Lyle, I signed.

"What did he do?"

Ginny was now toeing at a few of the discarded shirts on the ground.

They had a fight. It's bad. They yelled about Charlie. I don't think Uncle Lyle's coming back here anymore.

My mother's hands fell to her sides. She looked at Ginny one more time. Then she went over and helped her to her feet. "Gin . . ."

"Ginny," Ginny corrected her. "I don't like it when you call me Gin, Laurel. You know that."

"Ginny, I'm going to have to ask you to pull yourself together, please."

Ginny lowered, wounded. "I am together, Laurel."

"Good. I need you to pick one of these shirts and put it on. And then I need you to walk with me down the hallway and we are going to go into the living room and figure out what's going on." My mother spoke in the same clear, bright tones she used when directing Charlie.

Ginny stiffened, offended.

"All right," she said, "I'll take the green one you just showed me. The garish one."

My mother ignored the insult, picked up the blouse and handed it to Ginny.

"A little privacy, please."

My mother stood beside me at the threshold, ready to close the door.

"You know what your problem is, Laurel?" Ginny called as the door swung shut. "Your voice. It's too proud."

In the light of the hallway, my mother suddenly looked very tired. Her curls lay dried and scattered around her face. She brought one hand up to her forehead, pressed her wrist there.

I caught her other hand and signed into her palm, *It will be over soon.*

From behind the closed door we heard a

muffled shriek. "Lord, what is it with that woman this time?" my mother said through her breath.

Ginny had worked the blouse over her shoulders, but she hadn't buttoned it up all the way. She pinched the lapels between her fingers, turning the front of the shirt inside out to show its cotton lining.

"There's blood in this shirt, Laurel. Here, in the lining."

"Now, Ginny, calm down." My mother took a step closer. She hesitated only slightly, only for a moment.

"I don't see any blood."

"Quit lying, Laurel. It's there, plain as day. Right here, see it?"

"I don't."

Ginny rubbed the cotton lining between her fingers. "See. It's smudging when I touch it." She held up a finger to my mother, who jerked her head away, disgusted. Ginny faltered. Then she turned to me.

"Charlotte," she called. "Come over here. Do you see it?"

I stood between her and my mother and looked at the shirt lining. There were two small full blooms of blood, right where the tip of a breast would press up against the fabric. Ginny's fingers were shiny with faint traces of the blood and something else, something translucent. I realized, with a lurch, that it was the grease from the cold cream my mother rubbed into her chest, to keep her skin from chapping after Charlie fed there.

I glanced at my mother, but she was looking steadily down at the dress. I started to speak.

"It's a trick of the light," my mother said firmly.

"It's blood and you know it," Ginny said.

My mother still wouldn't meet her eye. Ginny's face softened. "What is it, Laurel? You in trouble?"

My mother drew herself straighter. "I think we're all just getting overheated right now. I'll find you something else. Give me back the shirt."

Ginny watched my mother a little longer, waiting for her to break. Then she shrugged the shirt off and balled it up. She stood there, unembarrassed in her underclothes, the heavy beige bra that started somewhere just above the ends of her ribs and reached up nearly to her collarbone, her skirt and stockings still on right and proper.

My mother took the shirt and tossed it in the corner. She went back to the closet and took out another. Ginny ran her fingers again along its lining, watching my mother the whole time, then pulled it over her head.

"It really is time to go now, Ginny," my mother said in those same patient tones. Ginny nodded, slipped on her brown leather pumps and followed her out the door.

In the hall, we came across Dr. Paulsen and Max. Dr. Paulsen cradled Charlie in her arms. She had just gotten him to calm down. He was not asleep, only sedate. When he saw my mother, he stretched out his hands. She went to him immediately, she couldn't help it, even over Dr. Paulsen's protests, "We just got him to stop."

"We're just saying good night," my mother insisted, and Dr. Paulsen stepped back.

Charlie draped his arms around my mother's shoulders and rested his forehead against hers. She closed her eyes. Then her expression changed. Her eyes flew open, her lips parted as Charlie had worked his fingers down the front of her shirt, reached for her breast, and curved his lips into a nursing ripple.

"Oh my," Dr. Paulsen said. "He's really misbehaving tonight." She and Max both reached for him.

Charlie tried to angle his head into the right position. He felt the hands of Dr. Paulsen and Max on him, and in desperation he tried to grab for the ends of my mother's hair. But they got him off in time, so his fingers grasped at nothing. He began to twist and shake in their arms. It took both Dr. Paulsen and Max, holding on as hard as they could, to still his body. They shuffled him back into the dining room, Charlie shouting his objections.

The front of my mother's blouse was askew, the hem of a buttonhole caught on the edge of her bra. Ginny and I could see the swell of her left breast. My mother was so stunned, she didn't even notice. She touched her hand to the back of her hair, patting it down in place.

"Laurel," Ginny said, gesturing to the front of my mother's shirt, "he got you."

My mother stuck her hand into the cup of her bra, fished around so the flesh set right, then pulled the blouse the right way around.

Ginny figured it out. I guess it was how my mother did it without thinking, her finger run through the inside of the bra. Ginny's face fell. She looked down at the front of her own shirt. Then she took off down the hall, my mother and I hurrying after her.

We got to the living room just behind her, just in time to hear her shout, with her eyes squeezed shut, "She's feeding him with her titties."

Everyone looked up at Ginny, and then at the doorway, where my mother and I stood.

"She's lost her mind," my mother said. "She's in shock."

Ginny shook her head furiously. She turned to my father. "Charles, she's got bloodstains on the inside of her dress, where the —" Here Ginny paused. She was taken, for a moment, with the audacity of what she was saying. My mother glared at her. Her hostility gave Ginny courage. She took a deep breath. "Where the *breast*" — this word she hissed under her breath — "goes. And just now in the hall. He lunged at her. And tried to eat from her. Like a baby would. She's *feeding* him. She's sick," Ginny finished, triumphant.

As Ginny spoke, my mother's shoulders slumped and her jaw went slack. I couldn't bear to see her headed for defeat. When Ginny called my mother sick, I couldn't help it. I declared, "She's only trying to help him."

They all turned toward me. My father put his glass down slowly. "I think, Lyle," he said, "you and Ginny have done enough" — he searched for the right word — "accusing here tonight."

Uncle Lyle, though, was not going to let this chance pass. He got up, put his arm around Ginny. "Accuse?" He said. "You calling my Gin a liar?"

Ginny shrugged at the weight of his hand, but Lyle only gripped tighter.

"I think your wife doesn't know what she's talking about."

"Your own daughter confirmed it —"

"I'm going," my father said very carefully, "to ask you both to leave right now. I'll walk you to your car."

My mother had not lifted her head the whole time. My father didn't look at her. I kept my eyes on the ground. Then I heard the door close behind them.

Callie sat up suddenly. *Is it true?* she signed.

My mother didn't move her hands.

"Yes," I said.

Callie's hand began to shake. "Why didn't you tell me?"

My mother crossed to Callie, tried to hold her. "There's nothing to tell."

Callie shrugged her off. "You told Charlotte," she managed to say. She blinked wildly, trying to stop tears. "Why didn't Charlie tell me?"

My mother tried to catch Callie up again, but she kept twisting away. Finally she stopped trying.

"You know I love you," she said, her arms

at her sides.

Callie took a ragged breath. "No, you don't."

And she ran from the room.

My mother walked over to the couch, sat back on the cushions. The springs squealed. She was not a drinker, but she picked up my father's glass of brandy and drained it.

"Clearly," Dr. Paulsen said when she had finished, "there is much to discuss. But I don't think we can make any headway at the moment." She crossed to the door, Max following her.

"Laurel. We'll speak in the morning."

My mother held the door open for them. When they were gone and we were alone together, I turned to the wall so I wouldn't have to look at her.

"Charlotte —" she started to say.

But I couldn't listen anymore. I got up and walked out the door.

I took the staircase to the left and I climbed all the way up to the top floor, to the practice rooms. I found the broken bass drum and I tried to roll it over me. But my legs were too long and my trunk too broad to fit inside the tear. I curled my hands over my shoulders and began to slap the skin there, first the right one, then the left. I tried to pretend it was Adia's skin I was arguing with. But it was no use, it was my own. I did this over and over again, warming to the sting, until my skin felt thin and hot and watery and my fingers burned. I lay under that drum the whole night and my hands would not be quiet.

What She Said to Me:
An Apology to the
African American People
by
Julia Toneybee-Leroy
NOVEMBER 23, 1990
Toneybee Estate, Courtland County,
Massachusetts

African American people, I am sorry.

It is terrible to think that what I have grown here, what I have dedicated my very heart and soul and self to for over sixty years, has harmed You and wounded You and driven You to rage.

Already, the source of my shame and my downfall is coming. The book *Man or Beast?* has recently been published and will embarrass me and the Toneybee Institute. Embarrassment, of course, is a very small emotion

296

compared with what this book claims I put You, African American people, through.

When I first heard the accusations, I thought for certain they could not be true. I became defensive and a little mean, but as it became clear that everything in that book was correct, I became only very, very ashamed. And guilty.

African American people, guilt is different from shame. It has a different weight. Shame just heavies the bones, in a most insinuating way, rousing them to a dense, salty jelly. Guilt, though, is quick and hot and silvery, and it flashes through you with the regular, metered pulse of an electrical current, animating everything inside you to do something, anything, to make the shock stop. A very queer sensation, to be working through the body at my age. I am eighty-one years old and supposed to be past such obligations as shame and guilt and remorse. The only way I've found to get such feelings out is to do something reckless and big and a little bit desperate, which is why I write this apology to You, African American people.

In brief: the book claims that my Institute has not been happily concerned with language acquisition and chimpanzees for the past sixty-five years. It claims that when this

Institute started, our very first director, Dr. Terrence Gardner, used the African American men in Courtland County and Spring City in terrible eugenics experiments at the Institute. It claims the men who participated were left humiliated and never properly compensated. Worse: the book claims Dr. Gardner took improprieties with an African American woman. She has only ever been identified by a horrible joke of a name, "Nymphadora." Dr. Francine Gorey, the author of *Man or Beast?*, has drawings from my very own archives, she says, to prove it.

After reading an early version of this book, knowing it was soon to be published and my defamation assured, I decided that there was work to be done. It was time to make amends. I hope that You, African American people, will appreciate this.

I ordered the Toneybee Institute's board to hire a public relations man. He came up with a lot of ideas: scholarships, and prizes and maybe bronze plaques, but none of them seemed enough. It was Dr. Paulsen, who hemmed and hawed and finally told me that she had found the Freemans. It seemed miraculous. It seemed fortuitous. I have to say that I knew it was fate when Dr. Paulsen told me about them.

Not very many people know how strongly

I believe in fate. They think I am an arm-chair scientist, and like amateurs every-where, I must be overzealous in my hobby. But I abandon all scientific principles when it comes to fate. Or rather, I believe that fate is a kind of science. I believe it is stronger than history and the past and love and hope. So I agreed immediately to hire the Freemans and I fooled myself, for a while, that this would be enough. That it would make You, African American people, if not forgive, if not forget (I would not expect You to do that! I know You are not stupid!), then at least, perhaps, not be so offended and angry.

But as the Freemans moved in and as they settled down and as that lovely boy, Max, brought me reports of their progress, it did not help. Even when I heard what they got Charlie to do, it did not stop the terrible sinking feeling of utter wrongness in my heart.

And I have lately, just today, had an experience that makes it clear to me that I was a fool to think the Freeman's love could be stronger than fate. Because of that experience, I'm awake now writing this let-ter to You. In my old age, I don't sleep well or often. But tonight, what little sleep I got was interrupted by a sudden low, dull, sensation: as if someone were paddling a mute and rusted dinner bell that woke me with the absolute that I was in the wrong. The Freemans will not be enough. I have to do more to make it right.

I do not think I can make up for any of it, but something within me, perhaps foolishness again, thinks if You could only understand why I started this place, You might begin to feel better and You might begin to think about forgiveness. (But I am not pushing or commanding You to forgive! Please do not accuse me of that!)

As I understand it, You, African Americans, are very much concerned with history. With Your past. From what I gather, You claim to be nameless. You claim that Your history has been taken from You and what is left is a vacuous hole where the words should be.

Do You know, African American people, I understand this? I understand it completely because I suffer from the inverse. I suffer from too much name. You will see, as I tell my story, that to support the weight of a great family name is as much a burden as being nameless. At least, I believe that to be so.

I will tell You, African Americans, what *Man or Beast*? did not.

In short: I am rich and my father was rich and so was my mother. The Toneybees are a very old New England family and the Leroys are an even older French family from Dominica. The Toneybees did not come over on the Mayflower, but they hurried along shortly thereafter. My father's family has been making themselves and, in turn, this nation, rich since the 1700s. We started out with a general store: from there we became involved in imports and exports. My grandfather built one of the first modern factories: a shoe plant on the Lowell River. My father did something special with rubber and developed one of the earliest prototypes for the athletic sneaker. My father cornered the early market on sports supplies. This made him rich enough to afford a wife with plantations in Dominica. They were both proud people and so gave me both their names to carry on. The Toneybee-Leroy family line is rich, but it is not fruitful. I am the sole inheritor of both their fortunes. This Institute is my heir and its scientific discoveries about great apes and language will bear the Toneybee-Leroy name into the future.

So, You can see, as the crimes of the Toneybee Institute become known, it changes how and when and where my family name will enter history. It is a question of whether the Toneybee name will be spat upon and sneered at and pushed down to the bottom or revered and lifted up and allowed to rise to where it should be, which is the top.

Now You, African American people, are wise enough to know that in the great, vast history of this world, of the world that You and I make together, in this sad and wondrous world, not a single person anywhere at any time has ever been able to undo the past. This is the fundamental inaccuracy that that book and its author Professor Gorey bring to me. That book talks about the past and injustice and crimes as if any of it can be undone. And it cannot be undone at all. As if I could somehow do something to take it all back. As if the past has anything to do with You and me.

So You see, African American people, I would never ask of you the impossible. I would never ask you to believe that what's been done can be undone. We understand each other. And from this understanding grows a kind of trust. And so I tell You, African American people, You can trust me to tell the true story.

Right here, right now, I promise You, African American people; I would not, could not, and will not ever, ever, lie to You.

The book that makes my heart hurt is by a history professor named Francine Gorey. She came here, to the Institute, three years ago, to interview me for her project, and though she claims, in writing, to have confronted me with my Institute's worst crimes, I swear to you, African American people, I cannot remember that part of our conversation. And I don't remember doing anything the book says I did. But we will come to that later.

Professor Francine Gorey came to my library and she sat across from me in a leather club chair. She is a little brown woman. Her feet did not reach the ground, and she is so sweetly plump that she could not cross her legs. Instead, she crossed them at the ankles and swung them back and forth, charmingly, just above the carpet, while we spoke.

She told me she was writing a history of scientific institutions. She told me she admired my work. She asked me why I began this place. I trusted her, and here, African American people, I am sorry to admit that I trusted her because I underestimated her. Francine Gorey looked harmless. As I said, she was little and plump and she wore oversized glasses that kept slipping down her nose and her panty hose were an odd, bright tan, too light for her color and riddled with runs. Her voice was very high and when she spoke, her whole soft, inviting face wobbled with enthusiasm, and I found myself instantly at ease. Her face was at once familiar. You see, African American people, I find myself at ease with You more often than not.

Francine Gorey mispronounced *frugivorus*. She said, instead, "forgive-or-us." When I corrected her, she did not become defensive but instead smiled back.

She laughed. "Forgive me. I'm a historian. I'm not a trained biologist."

"Good for you, my dear," I said.

Professor Gorey reported this exchange in her book and wrote about it: "Julia Toneybee-Leroy was driven to found the Institute by a zealous and ingrained belief in upper-middle class European American hegemony and supremacy, so ingrained in her she does not even know it."

Now, when I first read that sentence, I did not know exactly what it meant, but I could tell it was not kind. Max, our research assistant, explained it to me. I was horrified. That is not me. And though I know, because of what Dr. Gardner did, You, African

American people, are, of course, forever in the right — that what Francine Gorey says my Institute did is unforgivable — I have to object and say that I told her why I founded this place and why I wanted it to be. But she did not include that in her book.

That day, Professor Gorey settled back in her chair and swung her ankles and said, "Miss Toneybee-Leroy, can you tell me why you care so much about chimps learning to use language?"

And I said, "Of course, it's true, anyone knows. I started this place because of my love of chimpanzees."

"But why?" Professor Gorey said. "Why do you love them?"

This is the part she left out of the book. This is the part I remember. So I will retell it now in the name of seeking amends. I will tell You, African Americans, the rest of the story.

I started this Institute and I gave it its mandate because in 1927 I stood in the Congo and I shot down a chimpanzee from a tree, and right before she died, she spoke to me.

My parents died when I was young. I did not know them well, only knew the longing for them, sounding deep inside me like an echo. I have always been alone, but I've never liked it. I inherited everything, of course, but it came to me slowly. The first thing I got was the music conservatory — gifted to me when I was eighteen, a present meant to teach me responsibility. I walked through its halls, I listened to tens of violins and horns and cellos sound out their passions. So much need, so much want, all sounding at me. My heart flipped over in terror. I fled.

I bought a one-way ticket to the place farthest away from Courtland County that I could possibly think of: the Belgian Congo. My trustees insisted on giving me a chaperone whom I grudgingly accepted. She was a spinster aunt who was too overwhelmed by life to bother looking out for me. I may as well have been on the trip alone, so wrapped was I in my helplessness. Every day of the journey I willed the ship to go faster, to sail straight into the equator and beyond, into the jungle, where I imagined whatever was wrong could be baked out of me.

My first sight of the Congo, I loved it. I loved the brown of the river. I loved the low trees. I loved the smaller figures I spied on the distant shores: I imagined they were naked and brown, too. I loved the heat.

God! How I loved the heat! You cannot understand, what a shock it was to these cold New England bones to be in that heat. It beat you down and made you want to beat it back. It was a challenge to your heart to go on slapping. All of the other white people onboard the ship complained bitterly about it: it became a kind of game for them to bang on and on about how they couldn't get a proper bath in the ferry sinks and could never get completely clean. But who wanted to be anything as petty as clean when the great dirty stink of the jungle rose up all around you?

You must believe me, African American people, when I tell You I'd never experienced anything like it. The jungle seemed to sigh when I sighed. When I gazed over its rails and down at the river, it felt as if the whole expanse of water had broken wide with my shame, as if everything in the world shimmered mockingly at my mistake, as if the waters of Africa were raging with me. I stretched my arms along the ship's railing and breathed in, really breathed in, for the first time since I'd run away. The air smelled deep and low, like the clay bricks of the conservatory. It smelled like creation.

My first day in Leopoldville, I saw a group of white men from my hotel, crowded around a table in the market, picking up roasted skulls of some large and foreign animal and licking at the inside of the bones until they got out all the meat. I tried to do the same, but my chaperone stopped me.

I saw a beautiful black man in a three-piece suit hurrying down the street in front of me. He turned and smiled, and I saw that his teeth were a brilliant green. I went up to him and offered him cash if he would come with me and grin at me with those green teeth all day, and tell me where they came from, and how he came to dress so well. He grew frightened and only bowed, and pretended not to understand the French I spoke.

One night, I escaped my chaperone and went to a canteen. It was on the avenue Prince Baudouin, a long street that went from the white *ville* to the black *cité.* Some men I met at the hotel bar offered to walk me.

The canteen was at the end of a long dark road and inside everything was lit by spirit lamps in old tin cans. In the canteen, I saw black women in A-line skirts and blouses, their heads wrapped in African turbans, dancing to a black band doing their best approximation of jazz. Their black, black skin glowed in the spirit lamps. The white men I went with, the ones who'd helped me escape my chaperone, whispered to me that the women were prostitutes, hoping to shock me.

I walked up to the darkest, brightest one and I paid her to share a dance with me. She was little and warm and I pressed her too close. I felt her stiffen. I felt the fat of her hips underneath my hands. She told me her name was Marie-Angélique. I imagined that she would breathe to me, as my mother never had, as my father never had, that she loved me. But only if I held her tighter. I held her all night, and when the music of the canteen stopped, I made her sit with me and the white men at the bar. I made her show me how she tied her hair up and I took out one of my handkerchiefs and asked her to tie up my hair, too. She stuck her dimpled fingers into my lank hair. I closed my eyes when I felt them there. But it was no use. All around me the air crackled with the white men's disgust and rage and lust.

I announced to my chaperone that I wanted to go on safari. We left the city and traveled deeper into the forest. I know, African American people, that I sound like every old white biddy who writes about her Africa, but truly, it was uncanny. The trees were really the sturdy necks of great ladies.

The bark on them was smooth and glossy as glass but the darkest pitch I'd ever seen. The trunks were covered entirely in purple flowers and in between the stems sprouted the thickest cobwebs I have ever seen. They were violet in the shade of the jungle, and when we walked past, they trembled so delicately I imagined the trees had budded shivering décolletages. Everything — the flowers, the trees, my own slick skin — was covered in the sweat of the world. I held a gun at my side, and each futile shot I made sent a halo of spent gunpowder above my head.

I wore a suit of barathea I'd ordered special. The only way you can clean that fabric is with gasoline. In the jungle, I spent every night wiping down the sleeves of my dress. The scent made me dizzy and I took it in in great huffs, clamoring to swoon, finding comfort in the fact that I bathed in fuel and smelled like a fuse.

I was an American heiress dressed in dun colors wandering around a jungle floor. I had an inheritance waiting for me that I did not want. Nobody in the world loved me or ever had. I did not know myself.

On the final day of safari, before we were to head back, I shot the chimpanzee.

I did not expect to kill her. I did not even

think I made a direct hit. I'd been aiming wildly at the leaf cover above me and only occasionally jerking my trigger finger. After I made the shot, I stepped forward, my ears still ringing, ready to trudge on, and I only knew I had hurt something when, from the corner of my eye, I saw her fall from the tree.

I got to her first, before the others. I took her hand in mine and she did it then. She spoke to me. I leaned very close, until she was breathing right up to my ear. So close that when she parted and closed her lips, I could hear the knuck knuck knuck of her teeth clacking together. I could smell the rotting meat on her breath, but it didn't smell bad. It smelled sweet.

Her voice was low, with labored, strangled breathing. I knew she was dying. I felt a stumble of a pulse where I held her close. I waited. And she huffed out a few more broken breaths. Then she hissed. Her tongue, thick and gray as old steak gristle, flicked the rind of my ear. She whispered something, one last thing, and I know it was words, I know it. I know how ridiculous this sounds, but believe me, African American people, she spoke to me.

When I told Francine Gorey this, she stopped writing down her notes. At the time, I flattered myself to think it was because she was as moved as I.

"What do you think she said?" she asked.

And this is the whole tragedy of my life. I don't know what she said. I just know that she said it.

And I would give anything, have given everything — my money, my reputation, my happiness — to know what this thing was, what she said to me. I would give anything to be back there, listening closely, and I would make sure to hold up my hand in time to stop the guide from trampling up, crashing underbrush, cracking sticks one two three, and drowning out that beautiful chimp's last words to me.

She was still speaking to me when my boy got there, but I couldn't hear. I only heard dead leaves breaking. I turned to my boy, wildly hoped for a moment that he maybe, with some secret African sense or African better-built ears for the jungle, heard her over his own noise.

"Did you hear it?" I almost shouted at him.

He grinned wide and nervous. "Yes, miss," he said.

I had them pack up her body and took it back with me to Leopoldville. The concierge at the hotel told me he could find a man to stuff her and do a very nice job, but the man he recommended was a quack and what he sent back to me quickly ripened and rotted so that the customs officials rejected it and I had to throw her corpse overboard as we sailed back toward the Atlantic.

I told You, African Americans, when I first heard what people were saying I did to You, I felt ashamed. I recognized the feeling because I have felt it before. That animal's end, and my hand in it, shamed me. My own shallowness up until then shamed me. I can barely tolerate the guilt I feel now, toward You, African American people, so imagine how all that shame felt in my limbs when I was lithe and eighteen, a rubber heiress who feared she killed something miraculous.

Back home, I poured all the money I had into setting up the Institute. I took over the conservatory, threw out the music and its needs I couldn't fill. I let chimps and scientists fray the carpet. I thought I had to make the world over. I was compelled to do something as new and terrible as getting an animal to talk. The bonus, of course, would be if the animal could talk about something relevant. But I wasn't going to get greedy, on top of it all. I spent my millions and would have been happy with just a sentence about the weather.

The very first experiment, I thought that maybe we had done it. I thought we could have succeeded. I had a colony in Florida send me a chimp. Her name was Daisy.

In setting up the Institute, I consulted many experts on chimpanzees and general zoology. One of them had mentioned the possibility of getting Daisy to speak through massage. He said it was just a theory, that nobody had tried it out yet, but that if someone could sit and rub her mouth into the shapes of words and whisper in her ear, it might encourage Daisy to talk on her own.

Francine Gorey says in *Man or Beast*? that these experiments were cruel and unusual punishment, and I think, perhaps, she is right. But the experiments did yield results. Daisy did speak, after a fashion.

As soon as Daisy came to me, I hired an African American nursemaid from Spring City to care for her. She was named Nadine Morton. She is quoted in Francine Gorey's book. She is, at present, my nurse. Today, African Americans, in 1990, it is a kind of comfort that Nadine Morton remembers Daisy's youth much as I do. Nadine Morton bathed her and played with her a bit every day and dressed and fed her.

Every morning, Nurse Morton brought

little Daisy to my room while I was still in bed. She placed her in my arms, and it was me alone who massaged dear Daisy's lips into words, worked her soft and hairy little cheeks with my fingers, coaxing the English out of her.

Francine Gorey calls this cruel, and maybe she is right. But by her second birthday, Daisy could talk. Four words: *Mama, Papa, cup,* and *ball.* My society friends, my board of directors, my scientific observers all toasted me and Daisy with flutes of champagne.

But I must admit, Daisy's voice sounded odd: a far-off hiss that came from the back of her throat, like a gas burner left on in an empty room. Daisy did not so much move her lips to speak but instead opened her mouth wide and rooted her tongue around her billows of breath. While she spoke, she threw her head back and peered at us all from underneath her heavy eyelids.

Each word took Daisy a long time to learn, and she did not seem inclined to put them into sentences. Still, emboldened by her progress, I hired a sound man to record her voice and I wrote away to a few scientists, telling them about her. They were cautiously optimistic: they wanted to know if she could learn more. Here is where my ambition took over and I cannot hide behind half admissions anymore. I know I was in the wrong. I kept Daisy close and I tried to teach her more words, but she was exhausted by the five she already knew.

Nadine Morton complained bitterly about having to spend all day listening to Daisy husk out those words over and over. My fingers cramped — there are only so many facial massages you can give to a monkey. Daisy seemed to sense our disappointment. The heartbreak of her failure was doing the same thing to her every day — working my fingers into the cheeks, sounding out the words, watching her follow my lips, and the results never changing. Daisy held all of that ambition in her breath, and then it died on her lips, fell into nothing.

The last word Daisy learned was *cup,* and then she stopped speaking altogether and only sighed, that same queer hiss of air, which got higher and fainter. When a bout of influenza came around with her third birthday, little Daisy lifted her head and sighed that in, too, and quickly died.

I can say now, though it shames me to my core, I was relieved when Daisy died. I loved Daisy, but I did not know how to mother her. I was not a natural-born mother.

I put a monument to Daisy beside my

parents' grave in the Courtland County Cemetery, but I kept her bones. I had a portrait made of me, in this library, sitting at this very desk, her little skeleton upright, keeping vigil beside me. The portrait painter made me seem much older than I actually was, but he got the skeleton correct.

After Daisy died, I could not bear to think of another chimpanzee. I mourned her terribly. Daisy's bones on my desk, I swear, click clacked to me constantly our whole sad adventure together. So I ordered them packed away in storage, and they are there now, somewhere in a box, in some attic upstairs, yellowing under tissue paper.

Doubled down again with that familiar grief of failure, I hired Dr. Gardner and gave him full range of the Institute. I let him do whatever he wished, as long as he could get a monkey to talk. He promised me he could. And for a long time I did not pay attention to anything he did. So I cannot rightfully be held responsible for it. If You are being fair, African American people.

Dr. Gardner only stayed with us a year and left suddenly — right after the triumph of the birth of one of our first chimpanzees, after Daisy. One of his assistants went to his room and found it destroyed — pages torn from his books, his ledgers dashed with ink and his pencils splintered and scattered across the floor. A few days later, he sent a postcard to the Institute with a postmark from Miami, claiming he would be gone for only a few days. He was never heard from again. Professor Gorey claims that she has traced his whereabouts to a cemetery in Florida, to a grave with an alias on a headstone. She believes he hanged himself in Miami, but it is too sad, too horrible, to imagine such an end for Dr. Gardner, even if he was as terrible as described.

I did not know he was dead until Professor Gorey told me, over fifty years later. At the time, I sat here and waited a few months for him to return, and when he did not, I was crushed again by my own failure. I dismissed his research team and had all his papers boxed up, and I hired other doctors, different doctors, to meet my goal and I didn't think of You, African American people (I hadn't been thinking of You to begin with), until Professor Gorey came along.

So, You see, African Americans, this was all I knew of the story. I can't be blamed. I cannot be held responsible. I certainly cannot be judged for it. My money funded these experiments, it's true, and many people were hurt. But I didn't personally do it. So where does my guilt lie? I feel it, but I don't think it's justified. So I do not think it's a real emotion. But I feel it in my breast just as keenly as I've felt any other sorrow, so I write it out for You, hoping it will be enough for the both of us.

I began my work not out of a wish to hurt. And not to "establish and honor my cultural hegemony," as Professor Gorey would have you believe. Everything I did, even this, especially this letter that I write to you, I do out of love.

I seek your forgiveness, African Americans, in earnest. I've lived long enough to know that faith and trust in the kindness of others is a hard-won oblivion, is a very strong armor. It may hurt, in the short run, to have an open, trusting heart. It may mean, in the short run, that you are weak. But in the long run it can mean survival.

It takes a kind of courage to be kind. So I ask, African Americans, that you be kind to me. That you not blame me for wrongs I knew nothing about and that have nothing to do with me. I hope to play some small part in restoring You, African Americans, to bravery and love. In restoring You to hope. In restoring You to Your trusting nature.

Because You must understand the importance of what I've been trying to do. I've waited over seventy years to hear an ape speak, to finally get it right. And African American people, it's bigger and weightier than anything You think I've done to You.

With love,
Julia Toneybee-Leroy

CHARLOTTE

"You can order whatever you want," my father told me.

We were in a diner in Spring City. I had crawled out from under my drum the morning after Thanksgiving and slipped back into the apartment, where my father was lying on the couch, staring at the ceiling. "Let's go before the others wake up," he told me, and I'd followed him to the car and he'd driven us across the border to Spring City, to the only open restaurant, to a sticky booth that smelled like whitening bacon grease.

I got the shrimp cocktail, because it was the most expensive thing on the menu. I wanted to hear him protest, but he only raised his eyebrow at the request and ordered coffee.

"So." A grubby glass trough of shrimp and cocktail sauce sat between us. "So."

"So."

"Charlotte, I'm not mad at you. You were just being loyal to your mother. That's what good daughters do. You and Callie have been really good throughout all of this. We've asked too much of you."

"I can do more," I said, uneasy.

"We can't keep living like this."

"But I haven't even been trying that hard," I said. "I can try harder."

"It's not a question of trying harder."

The waitress came and poured more coffee. We both stopped talking.

She left and I started to scramble again. "Please," I said. "I won't have any more secrets. I won't cause any more trouble. I can do better."

"Charlotte, after all of this, after what your mother told me. Now that I know the truth about all of this —"

"I told her to tell you. I did."

"It isn't your fault." He looked out the window. "I can't live in that place anymore, Charlotte. I just can't. I can't in good conscience stay a part of that, for lack of a better word, experiment. So . . . So," he said this last bit in a rush, "I'm moving out."

He waited. "You can come with me if you'd like. I want you to come with me. Or you can stay with your mother."

"What about Callie?" I panicked.

"She's too young. She should stay with her mother at least."

"Well, where are you going to go?"

He took a sip of his coffee. "I have the teaching contract for one more year, so I'll be close by until spring. We won't be apart. But," he said, "I'm going to be honest with you. I don't know if they'll hire me again if I'm not, you know, part of the Toneybee. If I'm not part of the game."

"So you would go back to Boston?"

"I can't say yet. It's a while off, though. We can worry about it when we come to it." He reached across the table and touched my hand.

"I really can try harder," I said feebly.

"You have to decide if you want to come with me. And of course you and Callie will visit with me. On the weekends."

"Does Charlie have to visit with us?"

"No."

"That was a joke," I said miserably.

"Oh," he said. "Good one."

Tractor trucks passed by on the highway. The one that passed outside now was bright white, and on the side was a long, splashing river of cola, surging from the back end to the cab.

"You'd really leave Callie there?" I said. "I read the book, you know."

He sat back, truly defeated, his whole face slack.

"She didn't tell me you knew that, too."

"You can't leave us there," I began to cry, furious.

"I don't have a choice," he replied, dully. "Not right now, anyway."

"Why did you bring us here?"

"I thought —" He stopped himself. "Your mother and I thought that it could be different."

"So we're supposed to leave Callie there," I said, sobbing. "And she's just supposed to be stuck, and you and I leave? We're not supposed to care about her at all?"

"Your mother thinks the odds of her doing well with a . . ." He hesitated, then he said swiftly, "A single father are worse, frankly, then being raised with a chimpanzee. I think a little bit differently. But she, and Dr. Paulsen, and the Institute: they won't leave me much of a choice. You know what a contract is, Charlotte?"

"Of course I do."

"So there's your answer."

We both sat for a while, sopping up the bitterness of this statement. He pointed at the plate between us.

"You aren't going to eat that?" he said wanly. "I'm paying good money for shrimp in the Berkshires in November."

"I can't leave Callie."

"I know." He touched my hand. "Good girl. It was worth a shot."

The waitress came back. "Everything okay?"

"We'll take all of this" — he made a sweeping gesture across the tabletop — "to go."

While we waited for her to come back with our bags, I said, "I knew it."

"You knew what?"

"I knew this whole thing was terrible."

"Well, you should have told me." And then quickly, when my face began to fall again, "It's a joke, Charlotte. A joke."

When we got back to the institute, my mother and Callie and Charlie were in the living room, a turned-over Monopoly board on the coffee table. Charlie was holding three plastic hotels under his tongue and wouldn't give them up. My mother and Callie both knelt in front of him, trying to coax his mouth open with the offer of an orange wedge.

Callie turned to our father, pointedly ignoring me.

I tried to force the Styrofoam container into her hands. "Here," I said. "Take this."

She opened it, curious. "You guys got

shrimp?" She glared at this sign of further betrayal.

"Come on, Cal," he said. "Come with me into the kitchen. We can sit down and eat it together. Just the two of us."

She followed him happily.

My mother hadn't turned at first, when we came in. She finally got Charlie to open his mouth long enough to hook her finger and fish around under his tongue and pulled out a gleaming red hotel. She dropped it back on the Monopoly board. She signed, *Good boy.*

Then she said, quietly, her back still toward me, "So?"

"I'm staying. But for Callie, not for you."

"Of course." She turned to me. "You're a good sister, Charlotte."

I shook my head.

She sighed, annoyed that I wouldn't take the compliment. She held out her arms to Charlie and he climbed into them. Then she staggered up, the bones in her knees cracking under the weight of him. "Oh," she said. "Jesus, he's heavy."

Charlie pinched the fabric of her blouse between his fingers, impatient. I got up and left the room before I could see her duck her head toward him.

I went and lay on my bed. I kept the lights

out, listened to my own breath in the dark until I heard the door creak open.

I knew it was Callie standing over me before I turned on the bedside lamp. I opened my arms wide to her, but she stiffened.

"You and me are in a fight," she announced. "We aren't doing any discussions."

"I'm sorry, Callie."

"Everyone gets to have secrets except me."

"That's not true."

"I've got secrets, too."

"Callie —"

"I have a lot of secrets," she sang as if I hadn't spoken at all.

"You're not making any sense."

Her eyes were red and swollen. "Don't ever say I'm not making sense." She breathed. "I am making perfect sense."

I'm the only one in this family who makes sense, she signed.

"You want to know why I make sense?" She put her hands down. "Because I am not a liar. I don't lie to my sister and I don't lie to my father, either."

I got angry at that. "I'm not a liar."

"Yes, you are." She smiled very slowly. "I know all about you."

And then she was gone.

I waited until I heard her close her own

door and then I sat up. I pulled the worn-up speech from my skirt pocket. The greasy pencil markings were smeared, but the words were still legible, written in Adia's surprisingly girly script: big swooping cursive letters that curled with painstaking accuracy around the lines on notebook paper.

I tore it into long, thin strips and let them fall to the floor.

Our father told us it was a trial separation, but we heard the lie. Dr. Paulsen wanted me and Callie to do a round of tests, to assess our levels of depression and possible emotional disturbance, but my mother wouldn't allow it.

Still, Max came around more often with his camera, a fail-safe, documenting.

"Stop sniffing around here with that," I told him. We were in the living room, spending a miserable, snowy afternoon indoors.

"Why don't you just fire my mother already, you and Dr. Paulsen? Why don't you just get her to leave?"

"We can't." Max sighed. "It's complicated. And" — he remembered himself — "you don't mean that. You shouldn't talk about your mother that way."

Down the hall, we could hear her and

Charlie babbling to each other. Max turned, grimaced. My mother claimed, to anyone who would listen, that she was weaning Charlie, but nobody really believed her.

"You're afraid of her," I said.

"I wouldn't say afraid." Max blushed.

"Yes, you are."

"That's very harsh, Charlotte." Max hurried to pull the camcorder back on his shoulder, obscuring his face with the viewfinder so I couldn't read his expression anymore.

I looked straight into the lens, trying to catch Max's eye behind all that machinery.

He didn't move the camera away from his face. Only swallowed. "I'm sorry, Charlotte."

Me and Callie had to visit Dr. Paulsen in her office. We couldn't go together, though. They separated us.

"You don't have to talk, Charlotte." She blinked. "I know you know about the book. I know you know how terrible things have been here. In the past. The things that happened here, they make me sick," she said.

She began to speak, and it was strange, she seemed to be begging me for something. She told me she was determined to save what she could of the experiment. She told me she felt they were close to greatness. She told me we only had to wait a little while longer and good things were coming soon.

Finally she asked me, her yellow tongue soft, to put what my mother had done into perspective. "What she did isn't so bad," Dr. Paulsen said, "when you think of the past. And what happened in the past here — that was an act of malice. What your mother did was an act of love. Do you see the difference?"

She waited for me to nod, but I didn't.

"Think of it in terms of history." Dr. Paulsen ran her fingers across the softened end of the stick of chalk in her fist. "In terms of all of history, what's happening now is not that terrible."

Everything in my heart said not to believe her. But I was weak because my heart was broken.

CALLIE

At least her father tried to make it up to her. Callie knew he would. He took her downtown and he told her to pick out a present. This was after he told her that he was moving out.

She already knew what she wanted. It was on Main Street, in Griffin Books and Occult Supplies.

When she opened the door, a heavy breath of New Age halitosis — incense and crumbling paperback bindings and cat dander — hit her in the face. The books on the front table all called to Callie with the ubiquitous use of *you* and *your* in their titles: *Finding Your Center of Power, Your Personal Magic, You and the Universe.*

But the book she wanted had the loneliest title in the world: *Magick for the Solitary Practitioner.* The first few pages were nonsense: prints of sextants and astrological charts and words Callie did not understand, like *gibbous* and *godhead*. She skipped ahead a few chapters and then she found the one that promised what she wanted: "How to Master Those You Love."

Callie ran back out to the car parked on the curb. She panted on the sidewalk, until her father powered down the passenger window. "Please." She stretched her hand through the gap. "You have to give me forty dollars."

"Forty dollars?" He laughed. "Jesus, Callie, you trying to hustle me?"

"Please," she repeated, urgent, half mad. "I need it for my soul."

Charles laughed again, but it was sadder. He would have given her the money either way, but when she said that, deadly serious, "I need it for my soul," he reached down into his pocket for his cracked and doubled-over billfold and slipped her two ragged, wrinkled bills.

The book said to master your love was to contemplate your love. Callie found this impossible to do. Charlie hated direct scrutiny. A full gaze made him charge. So Callie took to sneaking down to the reception hall of the institute, to look at the bright white skeleton in the picture beside Miss Toneybee-Leroy, to imagine it alive and covered in muscle and hair and spirit, a loving placebo for ornery Charlie. But it didn't work. The real Charlie still didn't love her back.

The next step the book recommended was making an idol of your beloved. Callie asked her mother to drive her back to Griffin Books where she purchased, from the begrudging clerk, a block of soft clay. At night, before she went to sleep, she worried the stone till her sheets and blankets were smudged with mud and her fingers cramped.

It was harder than Callie thought it would be, to first form the top of a head, then the bend of a back, the humps for knees. She pricked the palm of her hand by accident, when she was using a nail file to add a flick of a tail.

Magick for the Solitary Practitioner told Callie that she had to keep the likeness of her beloved with her at all times, sleep with it close by, and memorize its features so that she could manipulate it in her dreams. Callie did all of this, and dutifully dreamed of clay that turned into half-formed monkeys with bulbous noses. But even though she slept with the idol tucked under her pillow for weeks, she mastered no one. Charlie still overruled her and would not love her back.

She couldn't figure out what went wrong, but she was sure it must be her own fault. She went back to the book, to the chapters she'd skipped, and way in the back she found an appendix with a list of magical fabrics. Velvet was at the top. "To summon the magickal," the chapter heading said, "one must feel magick at all times." It was clear: her very skin had to be covered for her new cause. She asked her mother to make her a red velvet cape.

"I don't understand," she said. "What is it for?"

"It's not for anything," Callie said defensively.

"But you must want it for something," she insisted.

"I just want it," Callie said.

Her mother sighed. "I guess, sure. I'll do it."

The first time Callie threw the cape over her shoulders, she felt it. It was just like the book said. She felt anointed. She stood on top of the toilet in the bathroom — because of Charlie, there weren't any other mirrors in the house and she wanted to see the whole length of herself. She balanced on the closed toilet seat and looked and looked for a change.

She met her own eyes in the mirror.

Nobody looked her in the eye anymore — not her father, not Charlotte, not even her mother — she winced when she saw Callie's fat cheeks or the folds of her neck. All of them looked away, like they were embarrassed, like she embarrassed them.

But now, when Callie held her own gaze, she saw that she was stronger than everyone else. Her whole skin went flush with the knowledge. She bunched the red velvet up in her fists and very carefully climbed down from the closed toilet seat, trying not to fall.

"It's good?" her mother asked when she came out of the bathroom. "You're happy?"

"Yeah," Callie said. "It's good."

Their father called the new apartment an "efficiency." Charlotte said that sounded sad, but Callie liked the word.

"You'll see," her father assured them as he drove from the Toneybee to the new place. "It's really fun."

The Volvo stayed at the Toneybee with their mother. When her father picked them up for their first weekend visit, he drove a brown sedan with the name and number for Uncle Lyle's garage painted in peeling white letters on the back fender. He parked it in front of the institute gates, but he didn't get out of the car. He sent Lester up to get them.

The apartment was in Spring City. He had two rooms at the top of a sagging Victorian. The walls were a grease-spotted dingy gray, the kitchen drawers lined with layer after layer of faded contact paper.

The first room had a couch. "It pulls out," he explained. There was a single wooden chair and a small television with a set of pliers duct-taped to a switch where a knob used to be. All around the front room were the moving boxes they'd put together only a few months before in Boston. Her mother's handwriting was still on them: *Books —* *Charles.* The second room held a dresser and a twin bed, as slim and girlish as the cot Callie slept on at the Toneybee.

Charlotte wouldn't put her backpack down. She swung it in front of her and held the sides protectively.

"Where's the kitchen?"

"Well, it's like camping," her father explained. He stepped across the room, stood in front of a closet door. "We're gonna make all our food on this." He opened the door to reveal a plastic bookshelf with a hot plate on the top rung and a toaster oven on the bottom.

"You don't even have a microwave?" Charlotte asked.

"Well, you don't really need it with the toaster oven and the hot plate," he said.

"But what if we want popcorn?"

Her father considered the kitchen in the closet, defeated.

"We'll make it on the burner," Callie said, after a pause. "We'll cook it in the pan. See, Charlotte, it's like camping."

Her father touched the top of her head, grateful. It was good, at least, Callie thought. Things could be good here already.

By the end of that first visit, Callie knew what she had to do. She had to cleanse the place to make it right. It would be her gift to her father.

The next weekend, she smuggled two plastic gallons of whole milk out of the Toneybee cafeteria and packed them in her rolling suitcase. In the efficiency, she took the cartons into the small bathroom and poured them into the tub. There was no way to be secret about it, so Callie took this as an opportunity to tell her father about magic.

"I'm starting here," she called to him. "Because places of water are very powerful."

"Callie, this place is yours. You just have to clean up after yourself" was all he called back.

When both gallons were emptied, Callie pulled on her Mickey Mouse bathing suit, the cartoon grin stretched to oblivion across her stomach, and sat down in the tub.

Her book said bathing in asses' milk and rose petals was a way to ensure a good beginning. But, it turned out, two gallons weren't enough, and Callie ended up huddling over a meager puddle, the backs of her thighs just skimming the surface, her fingers crumbling up petals from a handful of mums, the closest thing she could find to a rose in December.

When she finally got out of the tub, cold and a little embarrassed, her skin had the same rancid smell as Charlie's breath, and she knew, in her heart of hearts, she had not changed anything. She wiped the milk off the back of her legs and turned on the hot water. No matter. This wasn't defeat. She would just have to try again.

Callie could hear the TV blaring as she rinsed down the tub. Her father's TV got terrible reception so he and Charlotte only ever watched the Saturday night movie, spasmodically beamed in from channel 38 in Boston. It was always an action movie, never a romance, never a musical. It bored Callie, but her father and Charlotte never changed the channel. Unstirring, they watched warehouses billow with flames and plate-glass windows burst into shimmering mists and crimes tear whole cities apart, all while Callie went about creating her devotions.

For her next spell, Callie turned her attentions to the bedroom. The book said the most powerful charm was one that included your familiar. Callie tried to cut a few strands of Charlie's hair from the back of his head, but he was too wary. She settled on collecting stray fur from the lint brushes her mother was always running over their coats and sweaters. She gathered all the hair up into a ball and sealed that into a plastic sandwich bag, which she brought to the efficiency, along with a thick red candle she swiped from the holiday display at school. While her father and Charlotte sat in the scramble of light from the TV set, Callie closed the bedroom door and set the candle on the room's one windowsill. She lit the wick and threw the whole mess of hair at the flame. Only a few strands caught. They made a quick, satisfying sizzle before they filled the bedroom with a terrible perfume and spattered one long greasy gray streak on the ceiling.

That streak, the rotten smell, the hiss of the hair burning: all of it had to be signs that the spell would work. But when she came out of the room, stinking of burning hair, she was confronted by the sight of her father and Charlotte, still dormant on the couch, unraptured.

Her supplications grew more intense. She began to speak a mantra, chanted thirty times in a row, at least five times a day. By repeating words, her book told her, your soul called out to what you wanted most in the world and made your desire known. What you wanted most could finally find you and answer you, all you had to do was ask.

So Callie spent all her days asking. She chanted in the morning, during lunch, at night while doing her homework, before she went to sleep. The tip of her tongue hurt from so much chanting. Her jaws popped. When she was alone, she chanted in her full voice, loud enough for the stars above to hear and respond, but when she was around others she chanted under her breath. She didn't want to disturb anybody. At the Toneybee, the sounds of her muttering were washed over by Charlie, who screeched and raged and cooed. At school, her teacher reprimanded her for mumbling and so during the day, Callie chanted with her fingers. *Good things are mine and I am good things,* she signed. She'd made up the words of the mantra herself. She was proud of it.

Sometimes Callie confused the order of the words and then, afraid that this meant the spell couldn't work, she would have to begin the ritual all over again. She repeated it so much that she no longer kept her chanting to only five times a day. She did it nearly all the time. She learned to move her lips at an imperceptible flutter, so that no one could tell she was speaking. Her mouth dried and soured from devotion.

Even when she wasn't chanting, when she was washing dishes or playing with Charlie or walking to the bus stop, her own thoughts would abruptly stop speaking and then it was only the chant, only those words: *Good things are mine and I am good things.* The words made her brain hum. It wasn't a bad thing. It became something she longed for, because those words were better than her own thoughts. They were better because they contained only love: no doubt and no anger, and most of all, no loneliness. She believed with all her heart that these words could fulgurate her family's destitution and she could burn back their happiness.

So her father and Charlotte sat on the couch and Callie chanted for them. Sometimes one of them would reach out for the pliers on the television set, wrench them to the left to turn down the volume of a thousand petty destructions, and listen instead to the drone of Callie's longing as if it were their own.

Nymphadora of Courtland County, 1929

I'd only ever been to the music conservatory the summer of my parents' demise. When I went with Nadine, though, we walked past the green and the garden where the students performed plays; we walked past the front steps and the heavy brass doors. We went around back to the kitchens. Nadine went through the door first; I followed. She took a heavy white apron with a red cross on the chest down from a peg. The cross was so that the other workers knew she was a nurse and not a maid. Julia Toneybee-Leroy had been so secretive about what was happening in her mansion that she hadn't hired anyone from Spring City to work there. Her employees, the cleaning staff and the cook, came from New York City and lived on the grounds. The rest of the staff was all white, and they nodded begrudgingly at Nadine as she swept past them in her red-and-white apron, and openly stared at me. I obviously did not belong. Nadine took me up a narrow little wood-lined staircase, up to a hallway covered in velvet and gilt. I gasped at how fine everything was. As I said, except for Nadine, Negroes were only allowed on the lawn of the Conservatory, never inside.

"It's like a palace," I said just as something, somewhere, began to shriek. I felt it in my bones. I broke out into a cold, sharp sweat, but Nadine merely shrugged. "The apes know it's breakfast time," she said. "And the cook is late."

We walked farther down the hallway, our footsteps getting louder as we moved off the plush carpeting and onto marble. As we walked, I smelled what I'd first noticed on Dr. Gardner. The pungent, commanding stink of wild animal. It got stronger as we moved along the hallway until, as we stood in front of a door with frosted glass, I could hardly breathe. I parted my lips and sucked air in through my mouth.

Nadine knocked.

"Yes," he called. I smiled, I couldn't help myself, at the sound of his voice.

"Dr. Gardner, it's Nurse Morton. And Miss Jericho."

"Oh, yes." He did not sound happy for the visit. "Just a moment."

A faint rustle of papers. Something banged somewhere and I heard him swear, softly, very softly, under his breath, "God damn it."

Nadine shook her head in disgust.

"All right," he said. "Won't you please come in?"

Nadine opened the door and I stepped into his office.

My heart stiffened. The room was large, with a mural of singing angels painted on the ceiling. Dr. Gardner's desk dominated — a large, gilded table stacked high with papers, odd metal instruments, empty picture frames, and old magazines. Behind the desk, Dr. Gardner seemed smaller than he normally did. I realized he was not smiling: that he had always smiled at me when we were alone together. When he was reaching out his hand to draw me from the bush I hid behind, when he was studying my open, naked poses, he smiled. But not now.

"Nurse Morton," he said. "And, of course, Miss Jericho. What is it you need?"

I thought Nadine would leave us alone together while I made my plea. I had rehearsed it in my mind: she would introduce me and then withdraw, shut the door, and I would sit by Dr. Gardner's elbow and rage at him. I thought, with some excitement, it would be our first quarrel.

After that disastrous Star of the Morning meeting, when I had heard what I thought was the worst, I had gone home and lain in my bed and cried until my eyelids itched. I wasn't so special after all. I wasn't Dr. Gardner's only specimen. Yet I thought *I still love him,* and the worst of it was, I wasn't even horrified by this. I was scared at the idea that I might lose him and be lonely again. So I began to imagine, in great detail, our reconciliation. I would yell my recriminations at him, and he would rush to placate me. And then, little by little, I would let him win me over, until I had him telling me jokes and trying to make me laugh. And when he was anxiously trying to please me, I would say, "Some of our less sophisticated citizens" — I would make a joke of it — "some of our unevolved, you know, you're scaring them with your tests. You're making them uneasy. You know how we dislike uneasy. Please, for me, please stop. And what do you need all these questions for, anyway?"

And he would laugh, too, he'd say, "Thank you for telling me, Nymphadora," and it would become another secret joke between us. And he would stop his testing. For me, he would agree to do it and I wouldn't have to be alone again.

But it didn't happen that way. Nadine didn't leave the room. She stood beside me, her arms crossed, as if she'd turned to stone, and Dr. Gardner looked at her, puzzled, but as she was staring at me, he turned his face to mine and raised his eyebrows.

"What may I help you with?" he said again.

"Well," I said. "Well, see, I understand you've been offering the men of Spring City some work —"

"Yes," he said, cutting me off before I could finish. "I thought it might be helpful. Useful. We're in a position to provide employment for many people, so we may as well be of use, don't you agree?"

"I suppose." I'd tried to catch his eye as he spoke, but he directed himself toward Nadine. Eventually he turned back to me and his face was blank. There was a long silence. Nadine glanced at me. I knew what she was thinking: What is wrong with you, Sister Nymphadora?

"Forgive me, ladies," Dr. Gardner cleared his throat, impatient. "But why have you come this morning?"

"Well," I said again. "The work you've been giving the men. It's just, it's not decent." I heard Nadine rustle beside me. She was nodding her approval of that word and I wanted to wince. Dr. Gardner raised his eyebrows even higher.

"Decent?" he repeated. "I'm afraid I don't understand what you mean."

And this was the worst, having him condescend, having him pretend he didn't understand. I pleaded with him with my eyes: You, above everyone else, know what I mean when I use certain words. You, above anyone else, man, woman, or Star, you understand me. Or you did. I know you did. I know you can now.

And he saw me, he saw my eyes speaking to him and he kept his eyes dumb. My heart stiffened again, like an old leathery hide that'd been punched. I wanted to lie back, defeated, deflated, if we had been alone together I would have sunk to the floor, but Nadine, Sister Saul, she was at my side and she was nodding her head approvingly.

So I said, miserably, in what sounded to me like a voice strangled, I said, "The questions you're asking them, the tests you're having them take: they're indecent. And we wish you would stop."

Dr. Gardner didn't say anything for a moment. He let his eyes flit between me and Nadine again. Then he pushed his chair back and stood up. He came around the front of the desk and stood before us. He made a cold, shrewd appraisal. Then he clasped his two hands in front of him, a mea culpa, and bowed low from the waist. It was the most submissive thing I'd ever seen him do, certainly the most polite action I'd ever seen him take, but I felt it sting like a slap to the face.

"Apologies." He raised his head. He kept his hands clasped together. "Your concerns are wholly understandable. But I assure you, ladies, and please also assure the men, they are unfounded."

"With all due respect, Dr. Gardner" — Nadine kept her eyes downcast but her voice was strong — "our people know what they saw. They know what they felt."

"What they *think* they saw, what they *think* they felt. Impressions. I'm sorry, the fault lies with me. I wanted fresh, unbiased impressions, so I did not explain the experiment to anyone, certainly not the subjects. You ladies may not know, but this is standard scientific procedure."

Nadine held her tongue.

"It's my fault for not explaining to the men, in a way they could understand, what I wanted —"

"What do you want?" I had recovered

enough to ask. "What is the purpose of the experiment, then?"

"An excellent question," Dr. Gardner said. "A really good inquiry. It's merely a test about language. Language acquisition. That's all it is. It's a test to see how different kinds of brains understand language. Why, I did it myself, one of my assistants administered the test to me, and I did it myself. Nothing about it is harmful or un-Christian or indecent." He emphasized this last word, though he did not look at me. "But I can see how it may have seemed that way. To someone who was untrained. To someone who didn't know any better."

"So it is about language." Nadine was still suspicious. She knew that this didn't sound right.

"Yes," Dr. Gardner said.

"And you say you've done the same test on yourself."

"And every research assistant who works here. I'll show you the reports. They're somewhere around here."

He turned back to his overpiled desk, sifted about.

"Ah." He extracted a green leather notebook from the mess, handed it to Nadine. She flipped it open, began pouring through the pages.

"There," Dr. Gardner said, pointing. "That log, I believe, has my results. Right beside a Negro fellow from Boston, Percy Davidson, I believe his name was. Side by side: we were tested on the same day."

Nadine studied the names on the page. It seemed to make a great impression on her, the white man's name and the black man's name, one after the other in the column. Nadine shut the book.

"Well, then." She was not satisfied, I could see that, but she was unsure. "You say this was a misunderstanding?"

"Exactly," Dr. Gardner said. "That's exactly what this was."

Nadine eyed him a few seconds more, deciding whether or not to trust him. "Thank you for your time, Dr. Gardner," she said. I knew that she was merely retreating, but Dr. Gardner took her hand as if she had decided he was right.

He still hadn't looked at me.

Nadine shook his hand and smiled falsely. Then she turned for the door and gestured for me to follow. I knew if I left that room with Nadine right then, I would have to give up Dr. Gardner.

Nadine was at the door now, waiting for me, wondering, and so I said, "Go on. I have one more thing to ask Dr. Gardner."

She did not even bother to hide her disapproval. She glared at me, then looked to Dr. Gardner, who raised his hand in agreement. She shook her head once, then was out the door.

I stood for a few minutes, wondering how to begin.

"Well," he said. "What is it?"

Even as I spoke it, I knew it was wrong. Even as the words came out of my mouth they felt oily and slick and sad: like gristle on an old soup bone. I could taste their poverty. This was not how I imagined saying it for the first time to a man would feel. But I am nothing if not stubborn. So I said it anyway.

"Dr. Gardner, I believe that I love you."

I thought he would be disgusted or angry or offended. But he only twitched and his upper lip rode a little higher on his two front teeth. And then he widened his eyes and pulled his mouth into a grin, and I realized with dread that he was going to be kind. He said, "How can you say that, Nymphadora? I don't believe you understand what you're saying."

"But I do," I said miserably. "I understand perfectly."

"Then I revise that statement. I don't believe I understand the words you are saying." He had tried to make a joke of it. I shut my eyes.

"There's nothing more to understand," I said, my eyes still closed. "I am in love with you."

"That's not possible." He sounded puzzled as he said it, as if it really were outside the realm of being.

And then there was a very loud scream. Dr. Gardner rushed toward me and clamped his hand over my mouth. I could see he was a little bit afraid of me, if I was capable of making that sound. Afraid of me, and even still feeling pity for me. I looked back at him, only ashamed. He was still holding his hand to my mouth, believing he had quelled me, when the scream sounded again. We sprung apart, surprised. We'd both assumed the sound had come from me, that I'd lost complete control of myself and was lowing my misery like a broken organ.

On the third scream, Nadine rushed back into the room. "Come quick, Doctor, come quick. Merryweather is going mad." And then he was gone.

I could hear a commotion in the hallways: feet shuffling past and yells and calls for blankets and buckets and help, more help. The screaming got louder. I sank down into Dr. Gardner's chair and closed my eyes.

I heard another shout, an eerie hollow call, so loud and sudden it sounded like it came from over my shoulder. My eyes opened. I jerked up. More footsteps rushed down the hall. I saw a mess of shadows blur across the frosted glass on Dr. Gardner's door. I turned back in my seat, sighed. And it was then that I saw it.

As I write this, I think how lucky I was, that at the very moment Nadine and I were attempting to shame Dr. Gardner, one of the apes threw a fit. She went mad in a swirl of grunts and shrieks that truly were unholy.

So, to that crazed and saddened ape, I owe my life. Without her, I would not have been left alone in Dr. Gardner's office, and he most surely would not have allowed me to discover the drawings.

On his desk a curious curlicue caught my eye. I looked, and looked again. I recognized something. I reached for the sheet of paper and drew it out of the stack and I held it up to my eyes and there I saw it.

I thought at first that the curve I saw was mine, but then I looked at the head attached and saw, grinning back at me, the shivering smile of a chimpanzee.

What my eye had recognized was the pose. She was posed the way I had been, our first time together: on her knees, pressed down on her elbows. Of course, he could not have gotten her to actually pose this way. This could not have been from life: no wild animal would consent to that. Only dumb, lovesick human beings would consent to that. There was a tinier subset drawing, done quickly but with much detail, of a folded-over, secret part of her anatomy: I could not tell if it belonged front or back. I turned the drawing over in disgust and was confronted with myself. There I was, in the exact same pose, a mirror of the monkey on the other side, my elbows and knees ground down.

I began to weep. Loud, loud sobs that luckily no one heard: no one was around the office anymore. I sobbed and sobbed and stood up and began to frantically shift through all the papers on his desk: searching, searching. I found twenty drawings in total: all with me on one side and the chimp on the other. On a few, a name appeared. *Rosalee.* It must be hers, I thought. And this was the greatest insult. He only ever sketched my body in those drawings. Never my face. But the chimp was drawn precisely, her every mood lovingly captured, the wrinkle of a pensive brow, the scurrilous raise of an eyebrow, the pensive suck of lower lip, the large brown eyes soft and inviting. He drew her like he loved her, like he loved her face, and I realized I had been wrong to be jealous of Julia Toneybee-Leroy.

And I saw that he'd written little notations beside me: estimates for dimensions — scribbles of number with double prime marks for "inches." And he'd used my name, my secret name. He'd written *Nymphadora.* I turned the page over to Rosalee again and saw she had the same marks beside her. And on a few, I could see my measurements and hers. And this equation:

$$(Rosalee)(12'') \; / \; (Rosalee)(34'') >$$
$$(Nymphadora)\,(42'') \; / \; (Nymphadora)(36'')$$

That stupid, stupid sign. That little gaping mouth, pointing his love for Rosalee, how he had scientifically determined she was greater than me. I almost tore the drawings in half right then. But I didn't: I turned cold. The same feeling that had come over me when I burned my parents' store started to quake, and I put the drawings back as best I could. I took one close-up detail of Rosalee's face, her eyes full and trusting, I took this with me and slipped it into my handbag. Then I opened the door to Dr. Gardner's office, and I ran down the hallway, trying to remember the way as best I could. I ran back down the little stairway and I ran back down the steps and out of the kitchen and down the long gravel drive. Away and away, I ran and I ran until my chest burst. And I had her face in my pocket.

Dr. Gardner sent me letters in the mail every day for a month. I didn't answer a single one.

Where did you go off to?

Will you come sit for me again?

Tell me how I offended you and give me a chance to defend myself at least, please.

You are being impossible.

He even risked gossip and came to Sermon on the Mount's house and asked if I was in, but I told her to tell him I wasn't home. I watched him walk away from behind my window curtain. I am not proud to say, but following his cringing walk as he made his way down the street, the falsely modest bend of his back, I still loved him even then.

I stayed in my bed all day. Luckily, it was still summer recess, as I don't think I had the will to drag myself from my nest of sheets to face a roomful of students and write alphabets on a chalkboard.

Instead, I lay on my side, my one good blouse buttoned up to my chin, my skirt and drawers in a tangle on the floor beside my bed. I let the hot muggy air wash over me. I only kept on the blouse so that I could wear my pin. I worried that pin constantly, twisting it back and forth while turning over the picture of Rosalee's face. I didn't eat anything for three days: I only sipped at the dull water at the bottom of my washbasin. On the fourth morning, when I woke up sweaty and spent, my fingers ripe and swollen from turning that pin, I knew what I had to do.

I packed up everything I owned. It fit easily into one small suitcase. I left behind only my bottle of scent. I thought for certain I would leave behind my Star of the Morning pin — my fingers were hovering up near my throat, I was ready to take it off. But something stopped me and I let it stay. It was as if the pin had decided, all on its own, that it would come with me.

I waited till night, till I heard Sermon on the Mount creak first one way past my door, then the other. For the past few days, she'd knocked a few times to check on me, and I'd meekly called to her that I was merely tired, and Sermon on the Mount, bless her, bless her, never turned the doorknob. She only called back, "All right, then," and kept walking. When I opened the door and went out into the hall, I shuffled on the sides of my feet as I passed by her bedroom door. I left the remainder of my month's rent on her tea table, tucked under a fine bone saucer. When I opened the front door and tripped down the steps and down onto the street I felt the dark close around me. I kept going, my legs trembling a little bit from the lack of exercise, the muscles shaking until they grew steady and by then I was out of Spring City. I crossed into Courtland County.

That night, my suitcase weighed heavy in my fist and my schoolmarm's boots bit at my heels, and I wished I'd listened to Pop and not Mumma in such matters as the natural world and guides in the wilderness. Mumma only taught me metaphors that were useless now. Knowing the moon was the alias of Diana was not helping me. I kept glancing up at it as I walked, but not once did that cold, fixed stone seem to change place in the sky. At least, I told myself, it stayed bright. At least it didn't dim. And then, when I thought I could go no farther, I was there.

At night, the birch trees and the gravel of the Toneybee Institute glowed and the building didn't squat like it did during the day but seemed, instead, graceful, as if it had suddenly decided to take a deep breath and stand up straight. It was all so pretty it made me bold.

When I got to the kitchen door, I panicked: what if it was locked? I tested the door and was relieved when it swung open without a sound.

Once indoors, I let the smell guide me. I followed the stench of apes up the little staircase and down the hall, past Dr. Gardner's now-dark office, around a corner, down more stairs. Then I came to it. A large door at which I did not even hesitate. I pushed hard and again it swung open for me.

In the dark, I could hear them dreaming. I heard them inhale. Exhale. Sigh for some other place, far away and dim and half forgotten. I wondered how I would know which cage was hers, but again, luck was on my side. When I leaned close I saw, in the hard white glare of the moon, that each cage was tagged.

The first one read BENJAMIN; the second one, JOSEPH. I went past three more cages until I found her. Rosalee. She was farthest from the door and her cage stood alone.

I settled down, tried to make the only sound the whisper of my skirt: the last thing I needed was to startle a bunch of apes awake and raise the alarm. I considered her where she lay. I thought about maybe just picking up the cage and carrying it off, but I tested it and it was too heavy.

I drummed my fingers against my knees and tried to figure out what to do next. And then, I felt the little spark, like static electricity, that one feels when one realizes she is being watched. A flash like sunlight slapping water. Rosalee was awake and her eyes gleamed at me in the dark.

We studied each other for a good while. I had not held eye contact with any being, human or otherwise, for a long time and I found myself, again and again, following the curve of her perfectly made eyes, large and amber, and the very elegant slope of her brow. I thought, with a flash of bitterness and insane panic, Of course he prefers her. All the while, Rosalee gazed steadily back at me, probably taking in my goggled eyes and dead tooth with a curiosity that in a human would be called sympathetic. Then she leaned forward and took a long, theatrical sniff. I held my fingers up to the bars so she could know me better. To my surprise, she grasped my two longest fingers in her hand, brought them close to her mouth and pressed them to her lips.

With my free hand, I rubbed my pin one

more time, good and quick, and then I took a deep breath. I drew my hand away very slowly and then I reached up and unlatched her cage. I waited a few seconds more. So did she. Then I reached into the cage and held out my arms and she crawled right into them, she did not even hesitate, and I embraced her.

The way back was slower. A young girl chimp is heavy. Rosalee nestled against me, draped her own arms around me, held on lazily, as if I were a bridegroom carrying her across the threshold after dancing all day at our wedding. She rested her head on my shoulder.

I tried to be quiet at first, but I realized this meant I could not be fast, so eventually I started moving at a clip. Through the hallway. Past Dr. Gardner's rooms. Out, out, out into the night air. When we were outside under the moon, Rosalee was still holding on to my neck. She raised her head. I realized it had been a long time, possibly never, since she had been out of doors. She took it in stride, the only sign of her curiosity was her dilated nostrils, quivering very slightly, trying to catch the smell of the country at night.

I held her and walked until my arms began to shake and then I found a hollow place for us to lie. We were off the Toneybee estate by then, making our way very slowly along the turnpike back to town. I shambled the two of us down off the road and into a leafy ditch. I knew it was unlikely that anyone would pass us on the road, but I did not want to risk it.

I sat in a pile of warm, moist ground to catch my breath and I held Rosalee in my arms. She nestled even closer. Eventually, her body went slack against mine, and I realized she had fallen asleep. I eased myself down to the ground, until she was lying almost on top of me, her limbs entangled with mine. I tried to match my breath to hers but I couldn't, I grew winded. I settled for breathing in her air, which only smelled slightly sour. Mostly her breath smelled like the grass and the leaves rotting around us. I lay with her for a long time, felt the quick beat of her animal heart against my own. Her skin on me began to feel too hot. I lifted my face up to the sky and imagined lying there with her forever. I squeezed my eyes shut and willed that it could be so. And then I reached up and took her arms away from mine, rolled her gently to the earth, stood up and brushed the dirt from the seat of my skirt, took my battered suitcase in my hand,

and scrambled out of the gully and left her there.

It didn't really occur to me what I had done until I was more than a mile away, almost at Courtland County's train depot. I hadn't planned to do it at all. As I walked away from her, my heart and head separated, floated apart, became two separate entities; my heart stayed in the ditch with Rosalee, but my mind was already at the train tracks, waiting for the next car out. I did not believe what I had just done. My original plan was to take her all the way back to Courtland County with me, to smuggle her aboard the 4 a.m. milk train to Boston, to find a suitable home for her in the city. I imagined delivering her to a delighted laboratory at Harvard or some tidy city zoo. I'd make her life over and then I'd make my life over, too, far away from Stars of the Morning and falsely friendly white men.

But.

But.

She was so very heavy in my arms. And her skin was so hot, unbearably hot, that when I finally disentangled myself it peeled away from my own. And she had so loved the night that it did not seem fair to consign her to the world of people again so quickly.

At least, that is what I told myself to make it right.

The night was warm, she wouldn't catch cold. I knew I had to hurry if I was going to catch the train to Boston.

And I made the train, but when I got to the city, I found my conscience had galloped down the tracks ahead of me and met me there. As soon as I stepped off the train, it hit me, hard, between the eyes and made me flush with shame all over. I took what little money I had and headed to the West End, where I knew Negroes lived, and found a room so similar to the one I'd just left it made me a little bit queasy. I waited anxiously for one full day, and in the morning I bought every paper I could find and scoured the pages for any news items, any mention, some funny little story about a hunter or a farmer or a driver startled by an ape in the Berkshires. There was none.

I bought a paper every day for a week and a half, despite the cost, but still there was nothing. So I imagined an item. I imagined a girl, the paper would say she was from "the Negro quarter of Courtland County," discovering one of the charges of the Toneybee Institute for Great Ape Research in a small clearing a mile or so away from the institute and the mystery of how she got there. And I felt free. I imagined that the girl who found her was one of my students, that she was good and kind, and I thought of her as I wandered around the city asking for work and finding none. I thought, with pride, of that imaginary girl, *She's better than me.*

I think I am going to San Francisco next. There are, after all, as Mumma told me, Stars of the Morning everywhere so surely they've made it as far as that coast. I imagine, I hope very much, I am in fact counting on the assumption, that the golden light of the West and the spacious beaches and bountiful orange groves means the light of the Stars of the Morning is not so harsh there, not so unforgiving. Far stranger things have happened. I have to save up money for it, though, so I'm leaving for parts not yet known. But I wouldn't write down what they were if I knew them.

Before I leave Boston and New England for good, though, I take from my skirt pocket the scrap of drawing I've kept with Rosalee's face. I fold it in three. I put it in an envelope, with this almost confession I've written, this attempt at explanation for my many betrayals of my race and of dumb blameless beasts. I take drawing and confession and I mail it to you, Dr. Gardner, whom I still love, still, despite all, knowing that I should not, so that you may finally know my true name.

But only if you wish to hear it.

CHARLOTTE

The reporter was on us by the end of January. That careening, desperate Thanksgiving dinner badly frightened Miss Toneybee-Leroy. Dr. Paulsen was worried, too, despite her attempts, with cookies and confidences, to hide it. For weeks, her mouth was a blush of yellow chalk dust.

My mother tried to convince the two of them that there was nothing to worry about. Uncle Lyle and Ginny were too disgusted with our family to ever talk. The whole business was just as mortifying to them as it was to us. The ultimate rebuke, for them, was silence.

But no one at the Toneybee believed her. She was not, at that point, a credible source. They decided, in another showing of Dr. Paulsen's clammy, frenzied cunning, to scoop themselves.

After a Christmas spent watching Charlie scrape the wrapping off shoe boxes filled to the brim with Raisin Bran, after a New Year's Eve celebrated in the dim glow of our father's television set while Callie lit a noxious stick of incense at midnight for good luck and prosperity, the cheap oils in the stick bringing in a new year dank and far too sweet, we had a guest for dinner.

All I remember about him was his soft belly that poked through the button gaps of his dress shirt. It made me queasy whenever I caught a glimpse of it. He never announced himself as a reporter and my mother never called him that, either. She said only, "This is Paul, he's our guest for the day. He's here to learn more about the experiment. Please be polite, girls."

Paul played catch with my mother and Charlie and fast-forwarded through Max's videotapes and ate dinner with us, during which he attempted to win me and Callie over with the voice of an adult unused to children — all brightened vowels and sly teasing. I stonewalled most of his questions, but Callie, of course, helpfully and happily chattered away about her love for Charlie. She taught Paul to sign *I love you* and *Hello,* giggling when he bungled the movements.

Paul's article came out in February, just in time for Black History Month. We saw it on a Sunday, on the front page of the science section of the *Boston Globe*. There was a photo Max snapped of us, unaware, months before: me and Callie and Charlie and my parents making spaghetti. To the Toneybee's credit, they did not crop our father out of the picture. The caption read BREAKING BREAD WITH AN UNUSUAL BROTHER.

The article itself detailed Charlie's sign acquisition, his love of my mother, Callie's love of Charlie. There was a short paragraph about the book *Man or Beast?* and a brief quote from Frances Gorey, but these were buried beneath a longer interview with Miss Julia Toneybee-Leroy, who was featured in a full-length photo on the inside page, smiling gummily, the skeleton of Daisy, yellowed now, on the table beside her.

"Everyone's going to see this," I choked to my mother.

"I thought you would like it." She looked pained. "I thought you would be proud." She slowly realized her mistake. "Maybe it won't be that bad," she said hopefully. "How many high-schoolers read the science section of the *Boston Globe*?"

But she was wrong. The reaction at school was surprisingly swift. The biology teacher clipped the whole article out and tacked it to her classroom bulletin board. The history

370

teacher did the same. The principal made an announcement over the loudspeaker at lunch: he mentioned me and my father by name. By second period I found out that a gaggle of freshman girls raided the library and cut the picture of our family out of the paper and taped it to the inside of their locker doors. The girls who did this were not the most popular ones, of course. The most popular could not have cared less. The girls who did this were the quieter ones, the studious ones, the vegetarians, the ones who stickered their political beliefs across their binders. The ones who actually read classroom bulletin boards.

I am not proud to say that I reveled in the attention. I thought it was a bit of good luck. If I couldn't have Adia, maybe I could at least have fans. I thought those girls were outliers, the first to pick up on my value. The more popular ones would come later. Maybe, I thought, maybe I had been wrong to suppress Charlie for so long: maybe the very thing I hated was my ticket to acceptance. At the very least, at the very most, it gave me a chance to triumph over Adia. In the cafeteria, at lunch, I signed for anyone who asked.

What was most surprising was that no one in Courtland County seemed disturbed by the mention of Frances Gorey's book. It was true that her research was only referred to in passing as "unfounded allegations." Courtland County simply believed that this part of the story didn't apply to them. They didn't care about history, only biology, only the deep pleasure of gazing into another living animal's face, only the here and now. Charlie became for them a teen idol, magnified in newsprint.

This did not devastate me. I was, in fact, relieved. I didn't want to explain the Toneybee to anyone and I didn't want to have to feel guilty for living there anymore. But I know it devastated Adia. We still weren't speaking, of course. Photocopies from the *Man or Beast?* she owned began littering the high school: stacked on the tables in the library, left in the cafeteria. She did all this anonymously, but of course it was her work. But they were not censored, nobody swept them away. They were left out in plain sight for weeks on end, patently unread, their edges curling up in disuse.

While Adia tried to tell the world the truth, the Toneybee's version began to proliferate. The *Globe* article was just the beginning: the *Washington Post* and the *New York Times* and a column in *Psychology Today* picked up the story. My mother started a press album where she lovingly pasted a fluttering of clippings from papers across the country. None of these articles mentioned the book, or if they did, it was only in passing. The only article that elaborated on it was the *Boston Herald*. She refused to clip this one: she wouldn't even let the paper in our house. "A tabloid," she said.

The girls at school collected as many snapshots of Charlie as they could. At first, they asked me to annotate them, provide my recollections of when a picture was taken or what happened after a lens flicked. I would oblige, trying to work in a funny story about myself or what I saw on TV the night before or what book I was reading. They listened politely and steered me back to the clippings. A few of them began angling for trips to the Toneybee, but I had enough pride to refuse this. I knew they only wanted to come to see Charlie. When it became clear I wouldn't be introducing him to anyone, the girls backed off. I still sat beside them at lunch, stubbornly willing the conversation in another direction, any direction away from the Toneybee, but they resisted just as stridently.

So I told stories about Callie and Charlie as if they had happened to me. I did impressions. I pulled faces. I made jokes. I was a hit, for a time.

But I couldn't stay ahead of the fad. It twisted and turned and then one day, on my way to the cafeteria to talk, once again, about Charlie, I passed some girl's locker and I saw that she had taken a pair of scissors to her newspaper clipping and cut one straight brutal slit across the photo, straight to Charlie's face. She'd separated his face from his surroundings by cutting it into the shape of a heart. She'd discarded the rest of us. She taped only the valentine, with Charlie's worried, anxious face at its center, back into her locker.

The edit became popular. By the time school let out, my family was missing from all those locker doors and it was only Charlie in the center of a collection of hearts of varying size.

I slid miserably toward my father's classroom. When he saw me in his doorway, he looked surprised.

"To what do I owe this honor?"

"Nothing," I said. "Is it okay if I just sit here for a little bit?"

"Sure." His expression didn't change. He just nodded. "Stay for as long as you like."

He turned back to his desk, began to fill

his briefcase with papers. We didn't talk until the bell rang to tell us to go home.

CHARLES

Last period of the day. Charles had decided that morning that he would talk about tessellations. Last period, they should have been covering sines and cosines. They should have been starting to graph, but he just didn't have it in him. Tessellations were his favorite.

When Charles first met Laurel, he'd told her that. He'd told her how much he loved the idea. "Everything has its place," he'd said. "And when it's in its place, it makes beauty." Laurel said laughingly back, "That's too easy." She didn't like easy. She never had. She liked complication. She said, "If it's not hard, it's not worth it," and he had believed her. It had excited him, it still excited him, that willingness to battle. But he knew the danger of those words now. "If it's not hard, it's not worth it." It wasn't true.

A whole class on tessellations, the subject

didn't deserve a full lesson, but that morning, crumpled on his bony couch, drinking the spit of grounds and lukewarm water that drooled from his secondhand coffeemaker, he'd bookmarked the graphs in his notebook, at the lecture notes he'd penciled for himself in his straight boxy hand, and what was left of his heart had gone out of him. He knew he couldn't bear it. For once, he wanted to speak with love. He wanted to talk in public about something he loved. And since he couldn't speak of Laurel and he couldn't speak of his girls, tessellations would have to do.

It was odd, this desire. It was, of course, he knew, like the ache at the back of his throat and the licks of burn in the pit of his belly and the dryness of his eyeballs and his relentless insomnia — all of it a good doctor, hell, just an especially empathetic ninth grader, would diagnose it as symptoms of the divorce. He didn't like to call what was happening by that name. Charles called it "a separation" for his kids and he called it nothing for the people at work when they asked, after glancing at the newspapers with his picture in them, how he was doing. But to himself and to Laurel, he called it by its true name: the cleaving. He always said it as a sad joke, though. "Should we talk about the cleaving?" But Laurel wasn't having it. "Just call it what it is," she'd say, sad and a little annoyed, and he would answer, still laughing, that that was what he was doing. That was its true name.

She didn't want the divorce and neither did he, not really, not deep down. But she'd left him no choice. She'd shown herself to be the worst of what anyone could think of her, and not just in front of him; they could have recovered, maybe, if he'd been the only one to see her shame. But in front of Dr. Paulsen and that boy Max, and his baby girls, and most of all, in front of his brother Lyle, sneering Lyle, who saw the worst and more, who was proven right after all those years: "That woman is going to ruin you, Charles."

The night of Thanksgiving, the two of them had sat in silence in the living room, after the girls and Charlie were asleep. They'd sat and she kept her head bent low. She'd never bent her head like that before. He'd studied the bend of Laurel's head and then that dumb boy Max had burst into the apartment, used his staff key to open the door. He'd forgotten his video camera, he'd come back, and when he saw them, Max's face flushed with pity, he apologized profusely, he shut the door and turned his own key in their lock, and that had decided it.

Charles said, "I don't think I can live here anymore."

And Laurel had kept her head down so that he couldn't see her cry. She spared him that, in the end, she was kind about that. Her voice was low and strangled, "What do you want to do?"

And now, months later, he knew the answer to that question. He wanted to talk to a crowd about something that he loved. It was a pressing need. He felt it keener than the systematic breakdown of his very body without Laurel. He found, in the months since they split, that he was now embarrassingly earnest. He'd been good at being honest about his feelings before. He wasn't like Lyle, who once told him he only said "I love you" to Ginny on Christmas, and even then, only every other year. No, Charles always prided himself on his effusiveness with the girls. Speaking his feelings was not the problem. It was that when he did it now, it came out deadly serious. He had always prided himself on his humor. This was a list of what he was: a good husband, a good father, a good teacher, and a funny guy. But lately, he was sick of jokes. He was sick of joviality. He only wanted to talk about things that he loved.

In the teachers' lounge, he frightened people. A simple "See the game last night?" set him off. He would discourse on the beauty of a spiral throw, on the intensity of a team's surge. Once he even rhapsodized on the splendor of the Celtics' colors. He knew, even as he was speaking, that his ardor was horrifying. He saw it on the faces of his listeners, how some would widen their eyes and some would narrow and all would eventually turn away, hoping this would get him to stop talking. It didn't. He talked even more. He wanted, he desperately needed, to speak about all the things he loved, to remind himself they still existed in the world, that the things he loved were multitudes, that not everything he loved was locked away from him in the Toneybee Institute.

The first bell rang and he watched the shadows of the trees on the back wall again. He supposed, if he had to talk about something he loved, he could talk about that. How much he loved the green and how much the green was like Laurel.

He stood up and began writing on the board. The secret of teaching was to set up an ever more elaborate series of scenes. They liked it. They loved it when they found you still writing on the board. It was like getting a glimpse of an actor in a dressing room, putting on his makeup before the show. It gave the whole endeavor a frisson of excitement.

On the dull, ashy blackboard he drew a honeycomb. The simplest tessellation. Last period was his favorite because, he was ashamed to admit it, his most devoted students were here. He never understood this waxing adoration. Back in Boston, some years, none of them liked him; many years they outright despised him. But then, sometimes, he would get a group of students like these, who laughed at his jokes, who stayed after class, who seemed to love him. At Courtland County High, it was four boys in the last period on Tuesday, who breathlessly christened him their favorite teacher at the beginning of the year. They were all freshmen and all players on the school soccer team, and they seemed to have adopted him, his jokes, and his class as their own personal mascot. There was Nick and Adam and Seth: all awkward bones and muddy knees. Sometimes he caught a smell off of them, the smell of the terrible loneliness of male adolescence, and it made him want to cry. It smelled like tears. He'd smelled the exact same thing on the boys he taught back in Boston, that same strangled melancholy.

The fourth boy in his fan club was Hakim. Hakim was one of the three black boys in the whole freshman class, bused in, like his comrades, from Spring City. Charles asked Charlotte about Hakim at the start of the year, but she'd bristled at his name, turned up her nose. "He's all right, I guess," she'd huffed. From that reaction, he'd gathered that Hakim, despite his athletic abilities, wasn't popular, but as he watched Hakim over the next few months, he realized he guessed wrong. Hakim was very popular, one of the most popular freshman boys, always in the middle of a press of kids. The three other boys deferred to him, sometimes waiting for him to laugh before reacting to a joke. But if Charles ever happened to pass Hakim in the hall, the smell of loneliness came off him so strong, it made his eyes water. Sometimes, when everyone else was supposed to be busy with some quiz, he would catch Hakim watching him shyly, quickly glancing away when he realized he was caught. He never paid the boy the indignity of acknowledging this. He suspected that Hakim had led the charge in popularizing his class and he was grateful for that. But he respectfully kept his distance from him, which, he knew, made Hakim's heart swell for him more, and which, in turn, made him love Hakim.

There were five girls, too, who always sat in the front row. Megan, Kristen, Jen A., Jen C., and Doreen Harmon. Poor Doreen, saddled with the name of a different time. She didn't even have the excuse of the girls Charles had come up with, who could say their parents weren't from this country, didn't know any better. Doreen's parents were just lost in time. Or so he imagined.

The greatest impression the girls made on him was "hearty." Even their acne was well scrubbed. Down to a girl, the skin on their cheeks was a wind-chapped red and they all wore their hair in scraggly, greasy ponytails, pulled back so tight he could see the knobs of their temples. They wore oversized fleece pullovers zipped up to right beneath their chins, the grubbier the better. They allowed a scrum of dog hair and dust bunnies to nap up their sleeves. This was maybe one of the biggest differences in the students here, besides the obvious one of his old classes being all black and these ones being nearly all white. The girls he taught back in Boston, even the bookworms, would have writhed in mortification if ever caught wearing one of those fleeces. The girls in Boston, it had saddened him to see, wore tighter and tighter clothes each year, growing more swollen, constricting themselves even further in brightly dyed tight denim and greening gold chains. Thank God Charlotte escaped all of that. He hated the Toneybee now, but he was still grateful it let her escape all of that. He didn't like that Adia girl, of course. He found her obnoxious: he had her first period on Wednesdays and Fridays and she made a point of sitting right up front and passionately doodling in a notebook, making a show of being oblivious to the entire class. But he noted with relief Adia's combat boots and heavy denim skirts and oversized concert T-shirts. No danger of too-tight jeans and all they brought with them from that one.

He turned from the board to see that everyone had assumed their places. The girls in the front, his boy fan club a few rows behind them, their fellow students sprinkled in between. In the very back were the louts. This never changed. It didn't matter if you were in Courtland County or Dorchester, Massachusetts, it didn't matter if it was 1991 or 1971: the back of the class was for the lost and showily rebellious. It would be that way until the end of time.

"We're gonna do something a bit different today," he began. "Today we're going to talk about beauty, truth, and light. I'm not talking about a laser show or whatever you kids are into —"

The class chuckled. This was a trick of teaching patter: establish an inside joke and make callbacks to it. In his first few days at Courtland County he'd asked, "Y'all do what around here? Fish in ponds? Make mud pies?" and one of them gulped, "We go to the laser show at the CCC's astronomy lab." And he'd laughed. The kids thought he was mocking the innocence of it, calling it lame, so they laughed heartily, too. But he'd been generally delighted by the answer, by its decency. Now he joked about it whenever possible, it always got them on his side.

"Tessellations are the most beautiful patterns you'll ever see, they have the most truth you'll ever encounter" he began, "and you can find their perfect representation in nature."

As he spoke, he made his way around to the front of his desk and, with a purposeful squat, hopped on the top, swinging his legs back and forth. He could fall apart and cry and call it a cleaving to Laurel, he could feel his throat ache with tears even now, as he lectured, but he couldn't show it. Of course he couldn't show it, he knew, though a part of him wondered why, would forever wonder why. A part of him was always twelve years old. This was the one thing about Charlie that had fascinated him: did chimpanzees, like humans, contain a multitude of selves? When he'd raised the question with Laurel, playfully, one night early on in the experiment, as they lay before sleep, she'd gotten indignant. "Of course they do," she'd sputtered. But the way she'd said it, it was obvious she hadn't thought of it before, was only defending this answer because she loved Charlie and she couldn't bear to think of him as different from herself. That was, perhaps, the source of their cleaving in a nutshell. Laurel could not conceive of anyone that she loved as not being of the same mind as her. That is what she'd said when he'd raged at her about it all: Ginny and Lyle and the breast-feeding and the humiliation. "I never asked because I thought you would agree, Charles. I thought we were of the same mind." Himself, he knew he could love those of a different mind, but even he had his limits.

Anyway, all the evidence, from Charlie's dull glare, demanding grasp, and general obnoxiousness pointed to "no" for his original question. Chimps, or at least Charlie, appeared to contain not multitudes but only one self, stretched thin with need and longing. But maybe Charlie was an exception or maybe developmentally he was stuck at being a toddler or maybe the answer was just that Charlie was an asshole, pure and simple.

"Can someone give me an example of a tessellation in nature?" Charles asked.

"A honeycomb," Jen A. answered.

"A pineapple. I mean, like, the skin on a pineapple," Jen C. added.

"Good," he said. "Those are good examples."

It started from the back of the class. He didn't realize what it was at first. It honestly sounded like somebody retching and he was momentarily panicked: the one thing that dazed him in a classroom was when a kid was sick. He couldn't even stand it when his own kids threw up: he would leave the room and leave it to Laurel. His palms began to sweat at the thought of having to deal with it, all while trying not to retch himself. But that wasn't it. He glanced at the girls in his front row and saw that the Jens wouldn't look at him, instead were slowly blushing. Megan and Kristen were the same. It was only outdated Doreen who could look him in the eyes, and when she did he realized, with a start, that she was crying.

The boys, his fans, looked murderous. Hakim was staring straight ahead in a mounting, unvoiced rage, his fists clenched and vibrating on his desktop. This was what made him listen closer to the sound. It was wordless and bass and hollow. At first he thought maybe it was supposed to be an owl call, and that was weird, why would one of the louts disrupt a lecture with an owl call?

Charles cocked his head and made a theatrical show of listening again. He thought this would stop it, would put the girls in front at ease, but it didn't. The sound grew louder.

It was hooting, he realized. It was supposed to be hooting and then it struck him: it was a really bad imitation of a monkey. He sat back against his desk. He folded his arms across his chest, still trying to control the class, while inside he only wanted to cry.

The hooting grew louder.

It was baffling, how even rebellion came in only one shape: slouched shoulders, head low, insult the obvious. In Boston, it had been to call him a nerd, to make fun of his smarts, but this was so far from an insult it made Charles love those students more. Of course, here in Courtland County, they would go after Charlie.

He had waited, expectantly, for days after the article for something like this, but it hadn't happened. He'd been perplexed by the girls who'd swarmed his desk for news about Charlie. He'd been most worried about Charlotte, but she seemed to take it in stride. It seemed, perversely, to gain her more friends. This saddened Charles, but it seemed to make Charlotte happy: he spied her sometimes, in the lunch room, caught up in a thick mass of girls, telling stories and giggling and nodding enthusiastically. Still he braced himself. He waited. And nothing had happened so he'd told himself he was being silly and let his guard down.

So it was here now. The hooting grew louder and louder and Charles leaned back against the desk, his heart racing, love on his tongue, feigning detachment. He told himself, I am not angry, I am not angry, I am not angry. He would put it aside. It was what he always did. One of the worst things to do was to lose your temper, was to let them see your anger. It was true of children. He didn't like to make sweeping generalizations, but he had learned it was true of white people, too. Anger had to be carefully deployed. Children and white people, they expected you to become angry, they thrilled at it, a little bit. They pretended to be afraid, but it was a game some of them liked to play with black men. His students back in Boston had done the same: he had never wanted to give them the satisfaction of getting angry.

He took in deep, slow breaths. He tried to think of what would be the best next move.

Someone screeched "eee-iiii-oooo" and this gave him something to work with. He turned and smiled brightly and said, concise and clear, "Let's get one thing straight. A bunch of little boys are not capable of embarrassing me. I'm still the one who decides whether you pass or fail. No amount of noise changes that."

There was more rustling. One of the kids in the back leaned forward: a long, skinny tibia of a freshman named Martin Wade. He'd never had a problem with Martin before. In fact, Martin had always struck him less as defiant and more as terminally bashful. But now Martin leaned forward, one oversized Adam's apple bobbing with self-loathing and fear, and he shouted loudly, "Ooga booga, ooga booga," to the laughs of his friends.

And Charles turned around and called back without thinking, "You know, you're awfully lucky you boys are white."

He didn't know why he said it. It had broken out of him. He'd wanted to speak with love: that was all that he'd asked for that day, but now there was a shocked silence. Martin still leaned forward, his mouth agape. Oh shit, Charles thought. I'm fired for sure.

And then, a miracle. The whole classroom broke into relieved laughter. The girls up front giggled through their tears, his fan boys laughed expectantly. Hakim's whole face broke into a proud, wide grin, even though his hands stayed clenched in fists. Even Martin Wade grinned. "Oh, you burned," the boy beside him called out, then swatted Martin's stringy tricep.

How did they get the joke? Charles wondered as he smiled thinly at the class. How did they get the joke?

He let the laughter wash over him. It was the first time he'd spoken truthfully in Courtland County, without pretense. It was the first time he'd spoken the truth without trying to make it a joke. He let the laughter wash over him and he watched the light spattering against the back wall of his classroom, dashing and dappling and turning his classroom walls to mud.

CHARLOTTE

"Jesus," Adia said, "your dad is *good*."

By the end of the day, the whole school knew about his outburst. He had become, in the constant retelling, a kind of folk hero. The same girls who hovered around me at lunch came up to me as classes let out, eager to talk, breathless with my father's transgression. Adia, who had quickly found her way back to my side, glared at them until they backed away.

"I can't believe they don't care." We lay now, curled together in the blankets on her bedroom floor. "They have to at least *care*."

I didn't say anything, only tried to concentrate on her side pressed against me.

"You can't talk to those girls anymore." She settled in closer. "Or if you do talk to them, you have to tell them the truth."

"C'mon, Adia." I played with her fingers. "They're my friends —" She took her hand out of mine. "Or . . . we're friendly. I'm not

392

gonna start lecturing them about this stuff."

"You're just scared." Adia sighed. "You're always so scared."

I slid further under Adia's blankets. "Don't say that," I said, very small.

"It's the truth." Adia sat up. "I think we can both agree you're not a very brave person, Charlotte."

"Neither are you," I said, even smaller.

"No," Adia sang now, "no. I don't think so. I'm much, much, braver than you are." She turned on her side, away from me, and crooked her arm around her sketch pad. "Even your father is braver than you."

She was so engrossed she didn't hear me as I slid across the space between us and kissed the back of her neck, right where it met her skull. I could feel the very slight bristle of her hair, the tiny bit of it left by the errant razor blade. Adia jerked forward as if I had pinched her.

"What was that for?" she said, sharply, glancing over her shoulder.

"I'm braver than you." I kissed her arm.

She pulled her arm away, rubbed the back of her neck, as if she was trying to get off some stain.

"I'm braver than you are," I said again, pushing forward. The only thing to do now, I realized, was to keep going. If I backed down now, she would be right.

"Get away," Adia hissed, but she didn't move. She hadn't turned on her side toward me, either. She was still stubbornly rubbing the back of her head, her face turned out toward the room.

I inched closer to her, until I was pressed up against her back, until I wrapped my arms around her front and slipped my hands underneath her T-shirt. When I kissed the back of her head again, she didn't flinch. She didn't move at all. She went terribly, terribly still, not even a breath, not even a sigh. Then her spine curled into me and she collapsed down and that was it.

She wouldn't get under blankets afterward, though I did immediately, despite the heat in Adia's house. Instead, when she was awake again, she stood up, in only that too-big T-shirt, and began to pace the room.

"I told you I was brave," I said, if only to see what she would do next. If only to see how she would keep the game going. I didn't want it to be a game anymore. I spoke to give her a chance to make it stop but she only nodded curtly. "I've got something better."

I pulled on my sweater. I got up and stood in front of her to stop her pacing. Side by side, she was only an inch or so taller than me. Her eyes had gone all drowsy again, her mouth half open and she breathed sweet, "You're really going to like it."

She knelt down to pick up the notebook she'd been worrying, rummaging through it until she found the page she wanted. She pulled back the cover and handed it to me.

There was my mother, her neat Jheri curl scribbled into a nest of worms. There was Callie, then myself, our cheeks and lips distended, our chests and stomachs and laps doubled into a mass of half circles. In the drawing, Adia gave us both buck teeth, and Callie didn't have any eyes, just two blank discs for glasses like Little Orphan Annie. In the middle of us was Charlie, a tail circled around his midsection. My mother brandished a glass pitcher with a facsimile of the Kool-Aid Man's smile plastered across it. "Who wants grape drink?" she was asking. On the plates in front of us were heaping piles of fried chicken. All of our mouths outlined in wide rubbery, thick red lips.

"Do you like it?" Adia shook my knee. "It's good, right?"

My hands felt too weak to hold up the notebook. "Why did you draw this?"

"You don't get it." Adia laughed. "I knew you wouldn't get it."

"It's ugly," I said.

"It's ironic." Adia nodded proudly, and then she stood back, scanning my face for a dawn of recognition.

Marie's favorite word, and now Adia was adopting it as her own. But neither one had ever succeeded in explaining what it meant to them.

"Why did you draw Callie's eyes like that? And what did you do to my teeth? Why did you make us so ugly?"

Adia assured me that that, too, was irony. "Don't you get it?" she said. "That's what your mom is doing to you. She's making you ugly like that, by making you stay there, making you be in that experiment. That's why she's feeding you the Kool-Aid. I can't believe you don't get it."

"You made us so ugly."

"Because that's how *they* see it. That's how they all see it: Max and Dr. Paulsen and those dumb girls at school, the ones pretending to be nice to you. You're ugly to every last one of them. That's what the cartoon is about."

"But *you* drew it."

Adia shook her head impatiently. "That's what everyone thinks about you, anyway. But they're too polite to say it. That's your problem, Charlotte. You're afraid of making people answer for things."

I just made you answer, I thought to myself. I just made you answer after months of you and me asking the same question to each other over and over again, and you don't care.

Adia was bouncing on her heels, now, beaming. "I gave it to the school paper —"

"You did?" I felt tears in my eyes.

"Yeah, I submitted it, but Mr. Carver said he can't publish it, that it's too offensive. But I could see, deep down, it's what he's really thinking."

"You showed this to other people?"

"So what I think we do now," Adia continued, "is make photocopies. Like, a million photocopies. And we plaster them everywhere. In school, downtown, all over the Toneybee Institute so that everybody knows, gets, it. Everybody is confronted —"

"No," I said.

I took my hand out of hers, pulled on my jeans, and left her room. I walked through the heat of Marie's dark studio, out the door, and onto the cold street and into the night.

I called my mother from the only pay phone on Main Street.

"Where are you?"

"Just in town. Please come get me."

"I can't. I can't leave Charlie with Callie, you know that."

"Come get me, please. Please do it. I need you."

"Can you call your father?"

"No."

"Charlotte —"

"You aren't hearing me," I said. "You aren't listening." I began to cry and I heard her breathe in. She had decided something.

"All right," she said. "I'm coming."

I walked to the cemetery in the middle of the town green. In the dark, I balanced myself on the low iron chain that bounded the graveyard and swung back and forth, shivering off the cold.

When she came, it was just her in the car. I slid into the front seat and she reached across and held me.

"Don't say I never did anything for you." She laughed, gruffly into my hair. "Don't say I didn't listen."

We sat like that for a long time in the car, not moving, not speaking, my face pressed hard into her shoulder to keep from shouting.

CALLIE

"Help me get Charlie together," her mother said. "We have to go get Charlotte."

But Charlie was stubborn. He wouldn't go. He sat down on his hands and whined when Callie tried to get him up.

"We don't have time for this." It was the first time Callie ever heard her snap at Charlie. And Callie knew this was her chance.

"I can watch him," she said.

Her mother was skeptical.

"I can. I'm old enough. You can trust me."

Charlie was hunching over, whining louder.

"You won't even be gone that long, right?"

Her mother nodded, uneasy. "Okay," she said. "All right." And then she was gone.

All day long she'd been waiting for a sign and here, provided by the hand of the universe, like the book said, was one.

She sat down beside Charlie because her

heart was racing. She was so close. To calm herself, she scratched at the collar of her shirt, pulled a single, bristling Charlie hair from the weave on the front of her sweater.

Callie felt her fingers begin to cramp: this happened sometimes, when she was nervous. The very tips of her fingers would want to curl down to her palms. She took her hands out from under the blanket and pressed her right fingers down on her left wrist, feeling for a pulse. They'd been learning to do that at school. She pressed down on the flesh, felt the indentation on her skin but nothing else. Charlie's pulse, when he let Callie take it, was fleet and stuttering and strong. Maybe that was what it meant to be a familiar. He was her better self. He was alive to the world and she was, well, not dead, exactly. Just insulated. As if she were speaking to people and watching people from very, very far away. That was what it meant, she decided. That was what would change. What she was going to do would make it better. She was sure of it.

If she backed down now, it would mean she had the bitter little soul of someone who got the steps wrong, of a coward. Her soul, she was certain, was more expansive than that. It had to be, or else what would be the purpose of her being so lonely all the time?

It would be very unfair of the universe to be all those things and a shallow, artificial soul, too. To be all those things and not strong. They had to balance each other out.

Beside her, Charlie straightened himself out and busied himself with her hair. She held out her arms and he settled on her hip and she staggered with him to the kitchen. Even though she knew they were the only ones in the apartment, she still was careful not to make any noise. She spooned leftover spaghetti from the pot on the stove into a plastic sandwich bag. She poured chocolate milk into a plastic travel mug, printed with the Toneybee logo. Then she walked just as carefully to the bathroom, Charlie still on her hip, and climbed on to the edge of the bathtub to reach behind the towel-covered mirror for the medicine chest, where the cold medicine was kept.

Then she took Charlie and the bottle back to the living room, where she gathered together her school backpack and the spoils from the kitchen. She snapped on the cape with a flourish. Then she emptied her backpack onto the floor, a scatter of balled-up notebook paper and eraser dust, and she put the magic book in the front pocket and slung the bag over her shoulders.

Before they left, the two of them spent a

few companionable minutes eating from the plastic bag of spaghetti with their fingers. Callie let him have the last bite. In gratitude, he allowed himself to lie up against her, and for the first time in a while, they were quiet together. Maybe, maybe, this was all the book meant, Callie thought. Maybe her true self was two stomachs made gassy from too much starch. Maybe this was how the world was saved.

But no, that did not seem right. And anyway, she needed her familiar to help her with the task. Purification, the book said, had everything to do with nature. It also was dependent on the purity and courage of the purifier. But Callie was strong. She was stronger than everyone she knew.

So she put her arms around Charlie and hugged him closer, just for a minute. Then she slipped her arms out from underneath him and reached for the knapsack again. He got excited at the chocolate milk and began clamoring for the travel mug. He kept trying to turn her toward him, and she kept having to shrug him off. She poured one capful of cough syrup into the mug, and the chocolate milk turned a sharp purple and grew a greasy sheen. Charlie was getting annoyed now, slapping her back. He would get more forceful in a minute if she didn't give it to him. She decided she'd better pour the whole bottle in, and she just managed to empty it before Charlie reached for the mug himself and brought it up to his mouth with his own hands.

He drank fast. She could hear every swallow. When he was finished, he let the empty mug fall aside and then slumped up against her again. He burrowed closer into her arms.

She waited a few minutes, felt his belly rise and fall. He wasn't asleep yet, but his eyes were heavy-lidded and his breathing was deep. She sat still for a bit, and then she heaved him again, as gently as she could, onto her hip.

For once, Callie was grateful for her weight. She only staggered a little bit underneath him. If she was as skinny as Charlotte, she wouldn't have been able to carry him so far. Once she got her balance, she had enough heft to hold on to him comfortably. She forced his legs to clasp her waist, and he held the pose, slightly confused. It was as if he had forgotten the measures of the world. This gave Callie confidence.

She stooped to pick up one of his blankets: she didn't want him getting cold outside. She stuffed another blanket into her backpack for good measure, even though it meant she couldn't zip the bag closed. She carried everything — the bag, the blankets, and Charlie — to the living room, where she nudged open the front door and made her way into the hall.

She passed the laboratory wing, heard her shoes hit first soft on the velvet carpet, then loud and clacking on linoleum. The heavy double doors swung open so easily, she took it as another sign. She hitched Charlie up on her hip as best she could, took a deep breath, and led them both out into the cold night.

In the security guard's outpost, down at the front gate, a flashing light and shrill, sharp bell went off where Lester Potter sat drowsily reading his newspaper.

It was the most excitement Lester had ever had at the Toneybee Institute. He began scanning the television monitor in front of him for some kind of clue. He saw the double doors open, no sign of who had moved them.

He waited three minutes, and when he didn't see anything more, he hauled himself up the stairs, to the apartment, where he pushed on the still-open door, stood in the living room he'd watched flicker and snow up for so many nights on his screen, and realized he was alone in the apartment.

He shouted into his walkie-talkie and then he was back down the stairs, to the double doors that had tripped the alarm and out onto the Toneybee's grounds. The full moon was so bright, he would have instantly seen anyone walking across the grass, but he saw no one. His walkie-talkie squawked to life: it was Dr. Paulsen saying she was on her way, warning him not to call anyone else, especially not the police, at least not yet.

Lester Potter stood in his uniform short sleeves on the frostbitten lawn of the Toney-bee Institute and tried to listen above the sound of his own teeth chattering. He could hear the crunch of the ice on the grass whenever he moved. It was impossible that anyone was out here.

That's how Dr. Paulsen found him. "They can't possibly be outside," she scolded. "We need to make a full search of the building."

They didn't see Callie and Charlie on the lawn because they were lying low in a valley of frostbitten grass, just to the left of the swell of earth that Lester Potter stood on. Callie was on her back and Charlie leaned docile against her. While Lester Potter called their names, she tilted her face to the moon in the sky, watched it with wild, darting eyes. Beside her, Charlie's pupils were glassy, his lids low.

They heard the whine of Dr. Paulsen's voice, the distinct click of the doors swing shut and they were alone again.

They sat together, the two of them, and Callie waited for that filled-up feeling she usually had whenever Charlie allowed her to touch him. But she felt nothing. Only the cold. Only smelled starch and sugar on his breath, which seemed wrong somehow. Transcendence and purification should not smell like already-eaten dinner. She sat up, tugged on Charlie, and started them both toward the lake.

The water was beautiful in the moonlight, not the scabby brown it usually was, but silver and inviting. She could hear the waves knocking against the wooden boat on the shore, and the sound, she knew, right then, with all her heart, was the universe calling to her. She walked both of them closer to the water. Even then, Charlie didn't protest, he just held the edges of her cape a little tighter.

She only meant to sprinkle a few drops of the Toneybee's lake on the top of Charlie's head, just wet his hair and maybe behind his ears, and wet her own stiff Jheri curl, and then they would head back inside, united and reborn. But, as she knelt close to the water, as the wavering, sloppy reflection of her face opened wide into a smile, Charlie broke out from under all that sleep and bit her hand, the one that was stretching out to the water's surface, to absolution. He bit her in the palm of her hand, nipping the tough skin there.

She didn't mean to drop him in the water. It happened so quickly and then she was in the water, too, and the two of them were wrestling and panting, Callie bringing her velvet cape over his head and trying to dunk him down, over and over again, while he resisted.

By the time Lester Potter and Charlotte and Laurel and even Max got to the shore, Charlie was under the surface, flailing in the water, and Callie had the cape's edges bunched up in her fists. It took Max and Lester Potter both to get a good grip on her and drag her out of the water. Laurel went straight to Charlie. She took him in her arms and he bucked and gnawed furiously at the air until Dr. Paulsen came rushing across the lawn, running at an awkward, hampered pace because of all the blankets she carried. She made it to all of them, panting, and she dropped the blankets in the grass and stepped in close to Laurel, held out her arms.

"Give him to me, please."

Laurel looked down at Callie, who was huddled now on the ground. Charlotte was beside her, trying to gather her into her arms.

Charlie held the ends of Laurel's hair.

She opened her arms and released him.

Epilogue: Charlotte

Beside me on my desk there's a raw chicken liver in a red velvet jewelry box. The box is just large enough to fit the meat, but a pinch of flesh is caught in one of the metal hinges, and the little gilt clasp that closes the box strains against the hump of liver.

The whole thing — box and liver — softly stinks. This morning, before I sat down at the computer, I took the box out of the refrigerator where it has nestled for the last few days between a quart of raspberry kefir and a plastic pint of alfalfa sprouts. When my wife, Darla, saw me put it on my desk so early, long before I was supposed to take off, she wrinkled her nose.

"Jesus, Charlotte," Darla said, "is that really necessary?"

"I don't want to forget it," I told her, but she knew, of course, I would never forget.

"You could have just kept it in the fridge. I would make sure you took it."

The velvet box is from the Christmas present Darla gave me last year. The present was a necklace made of a flat gold chain. I wear the necklace now, but when I got that present, I was most excited about that box and wished I'd gotten it a few weeks earlier. When we were cleaning up last year, I slipped that box into the plastic shopping bags we keep in the hall closet, stuffed with throwaway bows and scraps of wrapping paper and dead rolls of scotch tape, and I thought about that red velvet box all year long.

But still, I put off getting into the car until the last possible moment, until I will most certainly be late.

Instead, I sit at my desk with my present of chicken liver and answer e-mail.

Before that, I was Googling Charlie and the Toneybee. I only allow myself to do this once a year, this time of year, and every year I find a little bit more. In the years since we left the Toneybee and I have grown and graduated from college and made my small life in the world, the story has moved out of my reach. It's all because of the Internet. Online, there are those who remember the experiment, and those who discover it, and usually those are the people I've learned to avoid: racial militants, animal militants, trivia buffs, fans of great apes, the relentlessly quirky. Once a year, I search and I find our family in posts with titles like "Top Ten Wackiest Sacrifices for Science" and "Fifty-Three Weirdest Childhood Pets." I read the lists and then I will myself not to read the comments.

Sometimes someone finds my e-mail address and sends me a question. They've tracked down the Toneybee's report of the experiment, or they've read *Man or Beast?* for some college seminar. They write to ask if all of it is true. I don't write back to the cranks or the ones with a mission, but I respond to the softball questions.

"What was it like having a chimp for a brother?"

I've learned you can't really answer much more than that. You have to stop the questions there, before things get weird. Things always get weird. Usually people are just ramping up, waiting to steer the conversation toward what they really want to talk about: some form of race baiting or speculation about hygiene or, inevitably, questions about sex. To stop any of that from happening, I make a crack about the smell. I write, "Having a chimp for a brother stinks." I like imagining the groans that greet that awful pun.

"What was it like having a chimp for a brother?" they write, and I write back, "It was a wonderful experience. I would not trade it for the world. It was really something special. My sister and I are grateful."

Twenty minutes before I should leave, I get up from my desk and take great interest in fishing a broken tea bag out of the garbage disposal. When I pass through the living room, Darla says, from the couch, "Just go already. You're making it worse by stalling."

Darla isn't coming, even though it was she who bought the cut of meat, not me, and it was she who made sure it was a good one. She's never once asked to come with me on these trips. She's said instead, "I'll go if you want me to," and I love her, I love her, I love her for caring so much and doing me the kindness of pretending not to.

In the car, at the first stoplight, I take out my phone and peck out an apology that spills over into four texts, explaining why I am running late.

The reply buzzes back immediately.

A single, stoic *K.*

Fifteen minutes later, I'm parked at the base of the stairs to Callie's apartment. I text her again, press send, but she does not reply. I just hear her front door slam, a few flights above me, and then I see her slowly make her way down the stone staircase.

Callie lives on the other side of the city from me, just outside of Boston, in one of those Somerville apartments built into the side of a hill. Her building is at the very top of a steep rise, with a narrow concrete staircase set deep into the earth, clambering up to the front door. Callie lives at the very top of the building, up in the clouds, far removed. She's never invited me and Darla to her house. She's never invited our parents, either. She doesn't talk to any of us of friends or lovers, but it is a safe bet that she does not have any of either. As far as any of us know, in all the years she's lived there, Callie has never had a houseguest.

She walks down the stairs sideways, rolling each hip forward and carefully making sure each foot falls fully on the step below it. As we've grown up, she's only added to the weight she put on at the Toneybee, and so she is extra careful on the steep stairs. She has two shopping bags slung in the crooks of her arms. She keeps a third plastic bag close to her chest. She is wearing a purple felt overcoat and black baggy pants and a shiftless black wool sweater. Callie only wears black now. Her hair is threaded into a million microbraids that wisp around her full, pretty face and end abruptly in a severe bob, down around her chin.

When she's finished her slow progress down the stairs, she unceremoniously dumps all of these bags into the backseat of my car before throwing herself in the front.

While she settles in beside me, I scan her for evidence of her secret life. There is a flurry of animal hairs, fine and white and bright on the black of her sweater. I see that she has on one black sock and one pink.

Your socks don't match. I make a point of signing to her when we are together. I am hoping that if I say it with my hands, it will seem more like a gentle ribbing, not an accusation.

But it doesn't work that way. Callie waits, allows herself a bristle. Then she says very distinctly, making her voice full and round, "I didn't get to laundry this week."

She has never gotten to laundry in all the weeks she's lived alone. She hasn't signed to me since we left the Toneybee over twenty years ago.

I start the car, make it out of the city, and pull on to the turnpike. Callie turns on the radio, loud, as soon as she can. She picks the most obnoxious channel possible: a news station, with periodic updates of traffic, the advertisements too loud. "W-I-N-S,

the Winds of New England," says the an-
nouncer with a heavy Boston accent.

I take my hand off the steering wheel. *Do
we have to listen to this?*

"Yes," Callie says, simply, but she's smiling. This is rare. I always offend her. But
she has decided not to be right now, which
is a blessing, so I take it.

"Dad's good," I say, giving up on signing.
Callie only nods.

Unlike Callie, I see our father every
Sunday. When we left the Toneybee, we
moved in with him and Uncle Lyle and
Aunt Ginny in their house on Chalk Street.
A humiliating time for Callie, a terrible, sad
time for me, one we both prefer to forget
about. When my sister and I left for college,
he could finally afford to move out of Lyle's
house. Now, so many years later, he lives
with his new wife, Gloria, a woman who
looks eerily like our mother. She even sports
a version of our mother's old Jheri curl. But
Gloria is nothing like our mother when you
speak to her. She is adamantly passionless.
She has no strong likes or dislikes, she does
not abhor. If she has views on anything, she
is very careful not to mention them in front
of me or Callie or Darla. The rare times
when all of us eat out together, and she
catches me signing to Callie in passing,

Gloria lowers her eyes and blushes.

I don't talk about the Toneybee with our father. Any mention of it still makes him cry: it doesn't matter when or where. I can say something about the trees around Courtland County High and his eyes cloud over.

Callie would like to believe she is the only one who still lives at the Toneybee in her heart, who goes through the experiment every day in her mind, but she is not. Still, she won't give our father the satisfaction of sharing this grief.

He does not try to work past her reserve. He believes it is a just punishment, one that it is right he should endure. He accepts it meekly, but that does not mean he doesn't rage in his heart about it. Or rather, in his heart and to me.

"How's work?" I say, and watch Callie's shoulders rise up, realizing instantly, that I have made a grave mistake.

"Work," she says distinctly, "does not exist."

I was not expecting this answer. As far as I knew, up until this moment, Callie was a massage therapist and actually quite good at it. She goes to the houses of the rich and touches the smalls of their backs with the palms of her hands. She has done this since she dropped out of college. Callie did not much care for college: she fell in with a Bible study group for a while, then a vegan collective, and finally a bunch of unaffiliated house shares on the outskirts of the city's Blue line.

I should ask her why work does not exist, but she's trained all of us not to ask any questions about her personal life. Even the names and numbers of her cats are off limits. And she has told me, long ago, that she does not like it when I "brag about my life," as she puts it, so any conversation about myself is off limits as well.

I have nothing to brag about. My life is as odd and small and secretive as Callie's. I, too, live in a very small room at the top of a very tall house, all of it outside of my price range. I am a lab technician at an eye doctor's in downtown Boston. The difference between Callie and me is that I have Darla. Darla, who is not black but Indian; not from New England, but California; cannot sign and has never expressed the desire to learn. We met in college, and her complete otherness from me, what made me fall in love with her, has dulled, turned warm, and now I love her for what we share. She is not an animal lover, thank God. Still, it took her a while to realize I was not joking when I told her I do not want to have children because they only end up doing awful things.

When I first met Darla, when we were young, I thought nobody would ever remember the Toneybee. Darla had never heard of it, and when I told her about it, all of it, she was more sickened by the story than fascinated. Besides her, I only told it to a few of our friends and, then, in strictest confidence.

And then came the Internet and we are known again, or believed to be known.

Last year, 2010 was the twenty-year anniversary of the start of our experiment. The fan notes came then, sent to my work address; *Boston* magazine did a brief write-up, a few other places published that picture. A few months after the write-ups, I received an e-mail with two attachments, scans of documents on Toneybee letterhead. The e-mail itself read, "I have often thought of you." It read, "Inside these files, a kind of amends." It was signed "Max."

The first scan was of a very old and yellow document in a cramped script that hurt my eyes to read and was signed by Nymphadora. The second scan was of an old laser printout, a long, rambling letter from Julia Toneybee-Leroy.

I read both documents again and again, but I didn't show them to my family. Callie would have raged, I told myself, and my parents would have wept. And I don't think that's what Max wanted when he sent them.

On the turnpike, I take the correct exit, but we drive past the gates of the Toneybee. We head downtown instead. Even though it's February, Main Street is still decorated with pine garlands and oversized red velvet ribbons and between two lampposts, across a fine mesh of muddy netting, a string of glittering electric bulbs spell out COURT-LAND COUNTY CELEBRATES DIVERSITY.

I pull over on to a side street and park in front of one of the overly restored Victorians. Callie says, "I'll get Mom." She leaves me in the car, in the cold, and I turn off the static of the radio and sit quiet.

Each year that we make this trip back to Courtland County, I have the terrible premonition that I will see Adia. I feel it with a certainty that glows from the middle of my chest and warms my skin in prickling fear and anticipation. Even now, as I sit in the car, I catch a glimpse of the back of a brown bald head and I gasp, and fight the urge to dive down in my seat and hide below the window line.

But it is obvious, after I blink, that it is

merely the profile of a very skinny fifteen-year-old boy. And I remind myself that I am being silly, that it would be impossible for Adia to look the same now as she did twenty years ago, and impossible for her to walk down this street, precisely as I sit in a parked car, waiting for my mother. As much as I would like to believe I would be able to recognize Adia anywhere, that some small muscle in the back of my knee, or down around my elbow, say, would flip over in dull ache and recognition in her presence, I know, in reality, this would not be true. She could have passed me on the street or in an airport a dozen times in the last two decades, she probably in all likelihood has, and I have not known her.

Besides, it is impossible that she would be here, today, now, because she is a graphic designer in San Diego, married to a Polish man and mother of three sons. An entirely disappointing and pedestrian end for my Adia. It feels like an outrage. For all the torment she caused me, I willed her to grow up and become some sort of artistic terrorist: burning down monuments or etching scratchitti on the glass doors of expensive galleries or tearing oil portraits of our nation's forefathers to ribbons. Then, at least, our painful time together would have been worth it.

I prefer, in my heart of hearts, to imagine that for Adia, domesticity is only a bivouac of sorts, that she is amassing her powers and will burst back into the world, soon enough, beautiful and merciless and ready again to devour hearts and history. But this is unlikely. We are both past thirty and should have done all our bursting by now.

Callie comes down the wooden steps of the old Victorian. She is carrying a large pile of presents for my mother, who walks behind her, slim and sober in a Michelin man coat. My mother has the same hairstyle now as Adia once did: shaved close to her skull, the better to show off her long and only slightly wrinkly neck.

Callie gets into the back with all the presents and my mother gets into the front beside me.

"You look good," she says. "Both my girls look good."

Callie beams at her for the lie.

She teaches sign language to every new hire at the Toneybee, and she teaches it to the new chimps, the ones just born, though they don't allow her to ever be alone with them. The job was the Toneybee's final bribe. It wasn't needed, my mother would never have told what happened between

Callie and Charlie, but they gave it to her anyway, a kind of insurance. When the Toneybee published their groundbreaking full study of Charlie a few months later, they said the experiment ended successfully and that the Freeman children showed all signs of happiness and no one has ever contested it.

I make a U-turn in her street. We turn back on to the highway and we drive back to the gates of the Toneybee. In the gate-house is a new guard. She tells us Dr. Paulsen is expecting us. She waves us through with a smile. Lester Potter retired ten years ago, and in his place is a whole staff of security guards, mostly women and very young men, in nicer versions of Lester's uniform. The Toneybee Institute has recovered enough in its fortunes for that.

The trees along the drive are bare. Past them, I could see a little bit deeper into the forest, where a few newer outbuildings have gone up. When we get to the end of the drive, we pull into the main parking lot. My mother would prefer it if we entered through the employee entrance, but Dr. Paulsen is waiting for us on the steps, eager to usher us through the lobby.

She looks exactly the same. She hugs my mother very tightly. Callie, too.

Dr. Paulsen does not waste time on small talk. It makes her uneasy to have us there. When she ushers us through the halls, her tongue darts across her lips and her eyes are downcast. This, despite the fact that we are the cause of her unprecedented success. The new buildings and the plural security guards and the better uniforms are all because of Charlie and our family, the fame and interest we brought her.

Charlie gave up his life in science a few years ago. It was after his retirement that we began to make these yearly visits to him.

We pass the cafeteria, the downstairs labs. We go upstairs and pass our old apartment without comment. It's been converted into office space: a regular glass door where our front wooden one used to be. We are in the right wing of the building. Here, there are larger pens with two or three chimps in each: their hair is graying, their teeth are yellow, and a few are hunched over in arthritic discomfort. It's where the older chimps retire.

Charlie's pen is at the very back and he has it all to himself. He doesn't share because he still cannot stand to be around other apes. He infinitely prefers people. Dr. Paulsen tried to mate him about a decade ago, but all attempts were unsuccessful. He ignored the pretty girl apes she put before him. He has spent a furiously celibate life. Abstinence is not natural for an ape, but he has refused all other options. Eventually, in his frustration, he began to make passes at the female lab workers, then the male ones, too, and this was part of the reason he left his life in science early.

His pen is larger than the others, with a television suspended from the ceiling in a battered cage. It's always on, nearly always turned to a classic movie channel, in the hopes of catching a Western.

Callie is carrying most of the gifts. My mother has Callie's plastic bag. The velvet box is still secreted in my purse.

When we reach him, Charlie has his back to us. He is gazing up at the television, laughing hoarsely. My mother calls, "Charlie," but he doesn't turn. He very rarely turns for her voice. He's frozen her out: he's miffed, even twenty years later, that they no longer live together, that she no longer wakes him in the morning and soothes him to sleep at night.

When Callie calls, "Charlie, Charlie," he turns and happily pads over. She's gotten that, at least, his admiration.

A lab technician unlocks his pen and we file in, placing the pile of gifts on the floor.

Charlie paces back and forth anxiously as we arrange the boxes. He remembers the routine and he is rocking now, keen with anticipation for all his surprises. As soon as we've set the last box on the ground, he surges forward and starts tearing at wrapping paper with his yellowed, curling nails, his softened old teeth. He tears and tears until he's forced the first box open and then he dips his head inside and ruts. When he comes back up for air, the ends of his beard are a bright, fluorescent pink, frosted with sugar dust. Those boxes came from Callie. She's packed them to the brim with kids' cereal.

Callie gets him the same thing every year, because it is Charlie's favorite. She's brought six large boxes worth of Frosted Flakes and Lucky Charms and Trix, and he devours the cereal in every one while Callie laughs, while our mother takes pictures, while I try not to cry.

He plays inside Callie's large boxes until I get up the courage to take out my velvet box and set it on the floor. When he notices it, he's up in a flash, snatching it into his hands.

It's only when I see Charlie struggling with the clasp — first bashing the box on the ground, then grasping the clasp between his teeth, then, most frustrating and sadly of all, pinching his fingers, trying to get them small and agile enough to manipulate the catch — that I realize how perverse that box is, what a cruel present it makes. I realize why I was so eager to have it, why I saved it for twelve long months and made my wife pack it tight, why I took it out to stare at it for two hours this morning. Some part of me must have known he couldn't open it, must have anticipated his frustration, must have thrilled to play this trick. My own pettiness sears through me, a surprise.

Callie watches Charlie struggle and huff and eventually start banging again until the box falls open and he can scrape out the meat. She turns to me but doesn't say anything, only narrows her eyes. My pettiness doesn't surprise her at all. It's been proven again, my eagerness and capacity to hurt, and it is not shocking, only tells her what she already knows. She hasn't been fooled by me for a long time. Right now, she knows me best.

My mother is beside herself. She can't sit still, she wants to stop Charlie's frustration and open his box for him, and gently pull the meat apart and feed him slips of liver one by one. But he is in such a frenzy, she can't get ahold of him. She folds her hands and only allows herself to lilt forward, as if she can't help it, as if she is being called. When he finally bashes my gift open and laps at the contents, she leans forward even farther. She wants to hear Charlie gnashing his triumph.

He traces his finger along the surface of the liver, marbled with broken brown veins, and he licks the grease.

When he's done eating, he stalks away and turns his back to us. We are dismissed. We go back to the car. I usually treat Callie and my mother to dinner at a diner near town, but now, as I restart the car, Callie clears her throat shyly and proudly calls out from the backseat that the meal is on her.

My mother beams, "That's wonderful."

I am a little irked that such a simple, adult act draws such praise, but I nod and just sign *Thanks.* I also force myself not to ask how she will pay for it.

At the diner, after we've ordered and the waitress has left us, Callie clears her throat again.

"So," she says. "I have something to tell you."

She says she can afford this dinner because she's been saving. She's been saving for the past three years and she finally has enough

427

money and this spring she is moving to Kinshasa, to the Congo. She is going to volunteer with an ape sanctuary there.

"Oh, Callie, it's too dangerous. You can't go. There are sanctuaries in nicer places," my mother protests. "Go to Louisiana, go to Florida." But her cries are weak. She knows she doesn't really have a say.

"It's only for a year," Callie says, but something in her voice catches, her eyes skip. Callie is a terrible liar.

I watch her from across the table. I know, a few months from now, she will stand at the side of some unknown heat-broken highway. She will stand at the brink of a great wide forest. It will be night. She will hear through the brush that familiar, piercing cry, but it won't be frightening. She'll recognize it as the sound of home. Callie will not hesitate. She will step off the broken road into the brush and she will walk straight into the cool of the trees and she won't ever come back.

I see all this, sitting across from her in the diner, my forearms sticking to the stray maple syrup tacked across the tabletop. I lift my right hand.

Good-bye.

Callie smiles back.

Good-bye.

ACKNOWLEDGMENTS

Thanks to my editor, Andra Miller, and Algonquin Books. Thanks to Carrie Howland and Donadio & Olson.

Thanks to Colum McCann, Peter Carey, and the faculty and students of Hunter College's MFA program. Thanks to Bill Cheng, Tennessee Jones, Brianne Kennedy, Sunil Yapa, and Carmiel Banansky.

Thanks to the Lower Manhattan Community Council's Workspace Residency; Johnson State College, *Green Mountains Review* support, and Jacob White and Barbara Murphy; and Bread Loaf Writers' Conference and the many good friends and readers found there.

Thanks to the Weeksville Heritage Center and my co-workers there: Jennifer Scott, Jennifer Steverson, Kadrena Cunningham, Elissa Blount-Moorehead, Emily Bibb, Veronica Gallardo, Lauren Monsein-Rhodes, and Robin Cloud.

Thanks to Sarah Schulman and Alexander Chee.

Thanks to Laylah Ali.

Thanks to Deborah Reck, Arthur Unobsky, Ann Kinchla, Sheila Pundit, and the Writers' Express. Thanks to Aaron Zimmerman, Rose Gorman, and the staff and volunteers at New York Writers' Coalition.

Thanks to Molly Brown, Ilana Zimmerman, Lana Wilson, Margaret Garret and the Garret family, Ross Middleton, Michael J. Palmer, Rebecca Sills, and the many other friends who continually encouraged this project.

Thanks to Kirsten Greenidge, Kerri Greenidge, Ron Nigro, Katia Greenidge-Nigro, Hunter Greenidge-Nigro, Romi, Timo and Sophia Kielnecker, David Dance, Suzanne Dance, Kwame Dance, Tyron Dance, Eric Davis, Candace Corbie-Davis, Fidel Corbie-Davis, Che Corbie-Davis, Antoinette Cezair, Corryn Shaw, and Patricia Davis.

And finally, thanks to my mother, Ariel Greenidge.